Death and Denial
A Mabel and Violet Mystery Book 2
Joan Havelange

Also by Joan Havelange

Mabel and Violet Mysteries
Wayward Shot
Death and Denial

Dedication

Rosa, who took me on a grand Egyptian adventure
And Shelley, my travel companion and cover artist.

Autor Note:

Mabel and Violet, in this story, visit the old Egyptian Museum in Cairo.
The new Grand Egyptian Museum is now open, but I love the charm of the old one, so that is where they tour in this novel.

Published by Brown Wolf Publishing
Saskatchewan, Canada

Chapter One

Mabel Havelock felt a hot, moist breath in her ear. She woke with a start. "What the hell?"

A strange man's head rested on her shoulder. His mouth hung open, and his stale breath smelled of garlic. Mabel wiggled her shoulders; he groaned but didn't move. She wriggled again with more force. The portly man snorted, and his chubby red cheeks puffed out, blowing more foul breath into her face. Wrinkling her nose and using her fingertips, she pushed on the side of his forehead. The man snorted and turned his head. Mabel sighed as she looked around the darkened airplane. Everyone appeared to be asleep except her. She squirmed in her seat, the armrest digging into her side. She looked enviously at her best friend, Violet Ficher, sleeping in the seat by the window. How her six-foot-tall friend could sleep in the pocket-size closet the airline provided for their passengers was beyond her. Mabel, barely five feet tall, jammed in the middle seat, felt cramped.

Mabel and Violet, two retired nurses, were on an overnight flight to Frankfurt. There, they would change planes and continue their journey to Egypt. This being Mabel's first flight out of the country, she was nervous, tired, and uncomfortable. She shifted in the seat, her back ached, and her legs were numb. In her opinion, seven hours on the plane was way too long. Unless you flew first-class, and they certainly weren't. The big, burly man in the aisle seat snorted, his head slumped back onto her shoulder. She grimaced and jiggled her shoulders. The man's head slid back. He snored, sounding like a demented wild hog.

A baby's cry mingled with the man's snoring. Mabel twisted and reached for the skinny little airplane pillow. It had slipped down, wedged between her and the large man. She yanked on the pillow. It popped out, and the man turned to face her. She screwed up her nose and threw the thin airline blanket over her head.

Mabel sat under the blanket and sighed; her seat was hard, and now the darn armrest dug into her other side. The drone of the plane did nothing to drown out the snoring and coughing of her fellow passengers. Good Lord, she fumed silently. How on earth do these people sleep with all this racket? Wide awake, she threw off her blanket, deciding she needed to use the washroom. The thought of the tiny washroom with its supersonic flush made her grimace. But at least there would be no lineup. Somehow, everyone else was sleeping.

Her next obstacle was to negotiate past the big sleeping man. Half sitting and half standing, Mabel put one short leg over the man's crossed ankles. Grabbing the back of the seat in front of her, she pushed herself over the man. Her hand slipped, and she landed on his lap.

"Hey, what the hell," grunted the red-faced man.

Embarrassed, Mabel quickly regained her seat. "Oh, I'm so sorry. I didn't want to wake you," she apologized.

"Well, you did," snarled the man. He grabbed Mabel's pillow, tucking it under his head, and turned his back toward her.

"I'm on my way to the washroom," Mabel whispered as she glanced at Violet. Violet was still sleeping.

"Whatever," the man grumbled.

Mabel pulled the pillow from under the grumpy man's head. "I still want to go to the washroom.

The man's head fell back against the seat. "What the hell?"

"That's my pillow."

"Humph," he mumbled. Covering his shoulder with his blanket.

Mabel tapped on his arm.

The red-faced man snorted, sat up, and glared at Mabel. "What the hell now?"

"Sir, I said I still need to use the washroom. If you don't want me to sit on your lap again, I suggest you get up and let me by."

The man pushed himself out of his seat. "I suppose you're going to wake me up again when you come back," he complained.

Mabel pursed her lips. What a rude man. "Unless I parachute out of this tin box, I suppose I will."

She crept down the darkened aisle, guided by the tiny lights on either side of the carpet, past the sleeping passengers. Were the first-class washrooms bigger than the broom closets in the economy section? She had seen the pod-like seats in first class when they boarded. It was dark, and everyone was sleeping. She grinned to herself and turned around in the aisle. She would use the washroom in first class. What could they do, take away her birthday?

Mabel quietly approached the first-class section and poked her head through the curtain that separated first-class from the economy. Everyone appeared to be asleep. She stepped through the curtain, but her first step was her last. She stepped on a discarded paper cup and fell with a thump, sliding halfway under the curtain.

Embarrassed, Mabel lay perfectly still, then crawled crab-like back to economy. Rubbing her bruised bottom, she regained her feet, listening. Did anyone in first class see or hear her?

She heard a voice on the other side of the divider. "Did you hear that? What was that?" Mabel bit her lip. She'd been spotted.

"Don't worry, it was nothing. Something fell in economy," whispered a gravelly voice. "Anyway, I've thought about it, and you're right. Egypt is the perfect place to kill her. The Egyptian police are not as smart as we are. Our plan is perfect."

"Shut up, you idiot; someone could be listening," another voice whispered harshly.

"Everyone is asleep, don't worry."

"What about that noise? I'm sure I heard someone."

"No, it wasn't anybody. I told you something fell behind us in economy."

"You better hope that's all it was."

Mabel stood stock still. She had just overheard a murder plot. A hand grabbed her shoulder, and Mabel jumped.

The tall, thin flight attendant took Mabel by the arm and hustled her away from first class, pushing her along the aisle. In a harsh undertone, she scolded Mabel, "Madam, you cannot go into that section."

"I was on my way to the washroom," Mabel whispered. "And you won't believe me, but I—"

"You are not allowed to use the washrooms in first class," the stewardess interrupted, marching her down the aisle. "If you need the washroom, it's this way."

"I just heard the weirdest conversation," Mabel whispered to the flight attendant, who was ushering her toward the rear of the plane.

The attendant stopped. Her face inches from Mabel's. "Is there a threat to this flight?"

"No, nothing like that—"

The flight attendant's lips tightened. "I'm not interested in your gossip. You should not be eavesdropping. Give your fellow passengers their privacy. The washrooms you are to use are this way. And please do not wander up and down the aisle. You will wake people."

"I don't gossip," Mabel snapped. "And I do not make a habit of eavesdropping." Although, the last time she did, she and Violet discovered a killer. Perhaps this time, she could prevent a murder from happening.

The tall, willowy stewardess's eyes narrowed as she looked down at Mabel. "Be that as it may, you cannot go into first-class and use their washrooms. Come this way, please."

Mabel became rooted in place. "What? You think I'll contaminate their washrooms with my economy—"

"Madam, either sit down or use the washroom. I will have no more of your insolence."

Mabel fumed silently and stomped down the aisle to the back of the plane. She was being talked to as if she were a child or senile.

When she emerged from the tiny toilet, the flight attendant was waiting for her.

"I did hear—" she began.

"Please return to your seat. People are trying to sleep."

Mabel bet the attendant would take the time to listen to her if she was a young man and not a white-haired lady. Resigned, Mabel made her way down the aisle to her seat. She glanced back at the flight attendant, standing with arms crossed, watching her. Irritated, Mabel roughly prodded the sleeping man stretched over her middle seat. "I'm Back. Please, would you let me get past?"

The groggy man groaned, unwound himself, and climbed out into the aisle. He grunted and shuffled off down the aisle toward the washrooms.

Mabel sat in her seat, gathering up her little blanket and pillow. She looked over at her sleeping friend and poked her in the side. "Violet, wake up," she whispered.

Violet groaned and turned her back, pulling her blanket over her shoulder. Mabel gave her friend another poke.

Violet dropped her blanket. "Are we there?" she muttered, lifting her sleeping mask and peering blearily at her friend.

"No, I have something to tell you," Mabel whispered urgently.

Violet moaned and took out her earplugs. "What is the matter? Are you ill?"

"No, I said I have something to tell you."

"Just because you can't sleep, there is no reason to wake me up," she whispered grumpily.

"I don't know how you can sleep in this hobbit closet?"

"And I don't see how you can't. You're the size of a hobbit."

"Are you saying I look like a hobbit?"

Violet laid her head on the back of the seat and sighed. "No, I'm saying your hobbit-size."

"I am not. I'm over five feet tall, or I was until I got crammed into these seats."

"Whatever, why did you wake me? The lights are still down. We are probably still over the Atlantic."

"I don't know where we are, but there is going to be a murder."

"Really? You've been dreaming. Go back to sleep." Violet pulled her nightshades back over her eyes.

"I haven't been dreaming. Listen to me." Mabel reached over and flipped up Violet's sleeping mask.

Violet sighed wearily. "You will not let me sleep until you tell me whatever it is that you think you know. Or whatever it is that you dreamed. Are you?"

"No, and I told you I didn't dream it."

Groaning, Violet dropped her nightshades in her lap.

Mabel waited while Violet straightened her dress and tucked a long strand of her bright red hair behind her ear.

Her friend liked everything clean and tidy, not only on her person but also in her personal space. As soon as they had taken their seats on the plane, Violet wiped the tray and armrests with the disinfected wipes she carried in her hand luggage. "There are germs. Airplanes are notorious breeding grounds for germs. You don't want to get sick before our tour even begins." Violet had warned her.

"Are you wide awake?" Mabel asked in a low tone.

"What do you think? Of course, I am. You just woke me. And keep your voice down. People are sleeping."

"I was going into first-class and—"

"You can't go into first-class. Why were you going there?"

"I wanted to see their washrooms. Ours are so dinky."

"What do you think they have in their washroom? A jacuzzi?"

"No. But they must be bigger than the broom closet we have."

"Forget it, they're not. Mabel, you're the limit. You woke me up because of some silly dream and your misadventure into first class. I'm going back to sleep, and you should do likewise and stop snooping." Violet pulled her nightshade back over her eyes.

"I wasn't dreaming. Would you listen for a moment? I never got into first class. I was almost there when I heard someone planning a murder," Mabel said.

"Seriously." Violet took off her mask and looked curiously at her friend.

"Geez Louise, of course, seriously."

"Okay, what did you hear?" Violet yawned.

Mabel related the conversation she'd overheard.

"It was probably a movie someone was watching, like Casablanca."

"Casablanca is in Morocco, this voice said Egypt. I suppose it could be a movie, but I don't think so. The voices were whispering. Maybe a man or a woman, but there were two voices. One even told the other to shut up. Whoever they were, they were afraid someone would overhear them talking. And they talked about killing some woman."

"Even if some villains were really plotting a murder, no one would hear them. The passengers are all probably wearing those headsets that reduce noise. They give you those headsets if you're in the first-class section. I bet what you heard was a movie. Now go to sleep."

"We need to put on our spidey-senses, just in case I'm right," Mabel said. She was sure the murder plot was real, not a movie, despite what Violet said.

"The only thing I'm putting on is my nightshades. Wake me when breakfast is served."

Chapter Two

MABEL HAD NO TIME TO put on her spidey-sense. They disembarked at Frankfurt airport. She found the airport intimidating and complicated. It was a far cry from their airport in Regina, the capital of her home province. She wished she was home, back in her bed. Every bone in her body ached.

Mabel and Violet followed the long line of passengers, snaking down through the long rows of barriers. At the end of the line, passport control awaited. Everyone was either pulling or pushing their hand luggage and talking or texting on their smartphones. Mabel nudged a distracted passenger who was texting on his phone. He looked up, moved, and kicked his carry-on luggage forward, continuing to text on his phone.

Will this ever end? Mabel fretted silently. They had a long way to go before reaching the end of the line. Her eyes were dry, her skin felt itchy, and her mouth tasted like old boots. She hadn't brushed her teeth since leaving her little house in Glenhaven some sixteen hours ago. Mabel shuffled a few more feet, dragging her carry-on and nudging the texting man in front of her.

"Do you have your passport ready?" asked Violet.

"It's right here," Mabel replied, digging in her purse. A sudden surge of panic hit her as she fumbled in her purse. Where was it?

"Move Mabel," Violet urged, giving her a gentle nudge.

Rummaging in her purse, Mabel kicked her bag forward. She pulled out her wallet and a handful of tissues.

"Why do you have so many tissues?" Violet asked as Mabel pulled more and more tissues out of her purse.

"You can never be sure if toilets over here have bathroom tissues," Mabel said, searching in her purse. A roll of candies fell out of her hand and rolled across the floor. A man in another line picked them up and stuck them in his pocket. Mabel flashed him a disgusted look before digging back into her purse.

"Move, dear," Violet urged. "Germany isn't a third-world country; they will have toilet tissue."

"Well, Egypt might not." Mabel squatted on the floor, pulling everything out of her purse, the contents spilling onto the floor. Panic mounted.

Violet stepped to one side and knelt beside Mabel. "Don't tell me you've lost your passport. Good Lord, Mabel. Why did you do that?"

The line of passengers weaved by the two women crouched on the floor.

"Why did I do that? What a thing to ask, you're not helping Violet. Do you think I did this deliberately?" Mabel lashed out.

"Seriously, we're in a foreign country, and you have lost your passport. Where is it?" Violet seized Mabel's purse.

"If I knew where my passport was, it wouldn't be lost. That's what the word lost means." Mabel grabbed her purse back and checked one last pocket. With a sigh of relief, she held up her passport. "I've found it," she said, waving it in the air.

Violet sat back on her heels. "Thank goodness. I'm sorry that I was short with you."

"No problem, I'm just glad I didn't lose my passport."

Violet handed Mabel a handful of tissues. "Put these in the garbage. They've been on the floor."

"If I need them, it won't matter where they have been." Mabel stuffed everything back in her purse.

THE BUZZ OF MANY LANGUAGES filled the air of the Frankfurt airport. Crowded cafes and shops selling expensive looking items, lined the corridors. Passengers, pulling and carrying hand-luggage hurried by Mabel and Violet. Some were going in one direction, others going in the opposite. Everyone was in a hurry and everyone seemed to know where they were going.

"Which gate are we supposed to go to? What is our flight number?" Mabel asked, bewildered. They had travelled down a long corridor and up an escalator, then down another corridor, and now smaller corridors were jutting off in both directions.

Violet paused at the arrival and departure screens. "Follow me, and don't worry, the gates are all clearly marked."

"What about our luggage? Don't we have to collect it?"

"They will transfer the luggage to our plane. We will collect it in Cairo."

"I hope so," Mabel muttered, trudging beside her long-legged friend.

They exited to another hallway through sliding glass doors and down another long corridor. Mabel's shoulders sagged, longing for the automated walkways in Toronto. "Shouldn't we check at a desk and make sure?"

"No, stop worrying." Violet strode down the corridor, pulling her hand luggage, her long skirt billowing out. "You've got your boarding pass, don't you?"

"Of course I do," Mabel said confidently. But she opened her purse to check.

"Like you had your passport?"

"But I had my passport."

Violet grinned. "Yes, in that Mount Vesuvius of Kleenex."

Mabel triumphantly held up her passport and boarding pass. "Ha, I've got them both, no worries," she said, bumping into a passenger. Her carry-on slipped out of her hand and spun across the corridor, slamming against a wall. A small wheel broke loose and rolled away. "Wait, I've blown a wheel," she called, scrambling over to the little black bag lying on its side. The passenger Mabel bumped into gave her an impatient look and hurried past.

Violet dodged a group of laughing teenagers with backpacks and two well-dressed businessmen, who glanced at Mabel as she set the bag upright. "Here, do you want me to carry it for you?" Violet asked as more people surged past.

"No, I'm quite capable of carrying this dumb thing." Mabel struggled to pull the offending bag as it bumped and flopped about on the hard-tiled floor.

"We can take turns carrying it," Violet said, shaking her head at her stubborn friend.

"I'm fine." Mabel winced as the bag banged against her leg.

"What a way to run an airport. With all the tourists they get here, you would think they would make things easier," a lady complained in a high, whiny voice, brushing past Mabel and Violet. The tall, well-dressed woman hitched her big red purse over her shoulder. "Marvin, are you sure we're going the right way?"

"Don't worry, dear, we're going the right way," answered a short, slight-built man, who had a knapsack on his back, pulling two carry-on luggage bags.

A pretty young blonde woman, pulling her hand luggage, walked beside him. She gave the man a sympathetic smile.

A tall, thin man dressed in a smart black suit striding past the attractive blonde did an about-face. He stepped back, gave the blonde woman an appreciative look, and bumped into Mabel.

Her hand slipped off the handle of her bag, and the bag slid across the corridor, striking a big red-faced man on his shin.

"Y'all watch where the hell you're going, you moron," the big red-faced man yelled.

"Oh, I'm sorry," Mabel apologized.

"I don't mean you, ma'am," the big man drawled. "I was yelling at the idiot who slammed into you."

The man in the black suit spun on his heel and sped down the corridor.

The friendly man with the Southern accent helped Mabel stand her bag up. "Y'all know that wheel is gone."

"Yes, I do know that, thanks." Mabel tried to take the bag from the man's hand. His hands were as big as dinner plates.

"I'll carry it for you, little lady. That's the least I can do until I get to my departure lounge," he offered.

Two young men with backpacks dodged around them.

Mabel dithered, shuffling from foot to foot. "What do you think? They told us not to leave our luggage unattended."

"Ma'am, you will be right by my side," the big man drawled and grinned down at her.

"I'm sure it's fine." Violet turned to address the friendly man. "Thank you so much for helping my friend. My name is Violet Ficher, and this is my friend Mabel Havelock."

"Pleasure to meet y'all," the giant man drawled, tipping his Stetson. "I am Ronnie Bladek from the great state of Texas."

The women and the big Texan continued down the corridor past numerous departure lounges. Each time, Mabel looked hopeful at Violet.

A courtesy cart with a man and a woman and their hand luggage quietly zoomed past. The whiney woman with the red purse stepped in front of the cart. The driver zigzagged around her just in time.

"Idiot, if you had hit me, I would sue you and your crappy foreign airport," she raged at the driver.

"Elizabeth dear, please keep your voice down. We're the foreigners here, not them," the small man beside her said.

"I hope she isn't on our flight," Mabel muttered to Violet.

"Never mind her, here's our gate." Violet tugged on her arm.

"Isn't this just the dangdest thing? This is my gate. Y'all are going to Egypt too?" the big Texan asked.

"We are; this is a nice coincidence," Mabel smiled at the big man. "And thank you so much for carrying my luggage."

"No problem; I wonder if y'all would return the favour and watch mine while I hike over to that coffee place and get me a cup of java. Would y'all like a coffee too?"

Violet declined, taking her phone out of her pocket.

"Yes, thank you. Black, please," Mabel accepted. A cup of strong black coffee would be just the thing to get her through the next leg of their journey. She so wanted to get to their destination, and have a shower and find a nice soft bed. And a change of clothes. Her T-shirt had stains on it from their meal aboard the airline. And her wrinkled yellow Capri pants looked like she had slept in them, which of course she had.

She glanced over at Violet. How did Violet do it? She looked as fresh as when they arrived at their first airport in Regina, Saskatchewan.

"Black coffee coming right up, little lady." Ronnie grinned and set his hand luggage in front of the long row of chairs, then strolled down the corridor. Mabel plopped on a seat, jamming her bag with the broken wheel beside her.

"I'm going to text my family. I can text your family too. They will want to know we made it this far." Violet's long skirt flared out as she sat down.

"No, thank you." Mabel turned to look out the large windows facing the tarmac. Planes were taking off and landing on the runways.

"Why not? It's no problem. I know you didn't bring your phone."

"I told everyone before I left, I would not get in touch with them until I got back."

"You really should've brought your phone." Violet's fingers flew over the screen of her cell phone.

"I didn't want to." Mabel shifted on the plastic chair, her eyes not meeting Violet's. She had let herself be persuaded to buy a mobile phone. She knew what to do with her landline, but her smartphone was something else again. Mabel's neighbour, Wanda, who was looking after her cat Gertrude, had warned her about roaming charges. Mabel had no idea what roaming charges were, so she decided to play it safe and leave the phone at home.

Violet finished texting her family and turned to Mabel. "Are you sure you don't want me to text your family? It's no problem. I'm sure your family will be anxious to hear how your trip to Egypt is going. How about I just text them and tell them we're in Frankfurt?" She scrolled down her contact list.

"No, don't, please stop. They don't need to know."

"You told your kids where you were going, didn't you? That we were going to Egypt, right?"

"Well, no, actually, I didn't tell them it was Egypt." Mabel plucked at the stain on her T-shirt. "I said we were flying to Europe and going on a bus tour."

"Seriously." Violet frowned. "Why would you do that? That's plain silly." She opened her bag and rummaged inside.

"If I told the kids, then I would have to tell my mother. Can you imagine how that would go over?"

"I can't believe it." Violet snickered. "You're still scared of your mother. For heavens' sake, she's eighty years old." She took out an alcohol wipe and gave it to Mabel.

"Don't be silly. Of course, I'm not scared of my mother." Mabel took the wipe and rubbed the stain on her shirt. Although, if she were honest with herself, she would have to admit to being a little apprehensive. Her mother was a force to be reckoned with. "I don't want her to fret. I mentioned Egypt once in passing, and I got an earful of how dangerous it is to travel there. And Mom has decided to move into the new senior's condo complex in Glenhaven. That's a big step at her age. She doesn't need to worry about me too. Besides, she's still upset about that little incident at the golf course last summer."

"You mean the incident when we almost got ourselves killed by a psychopath? You mean that little incident?"

"We're here, aren't we?" Mabel crumpled up the wipe. There was a dark, wet mark on her T-shirt where the stain used to be.

Violet rolled her eyes. "Anyway, you're telling me that you don't trust your own kids. You think they'll blab to your mom?"

"You know my mother. She can be darn right, devious."

"The apple doesn't fall far from the tree." Violet chuckled. "Have it your way. Sooner or later, you will have to fess up. How are you going to explain the pictures of the pyramids and the Sphinx?"

Mabel squirmed in her chair. Maybe she should've told her kids about her trip to Egypt. But she hadn't lied. She had just evaded the truth. "I'll tell them when I get back home. I'm on an adventure. I'll worry what to say later," she said with more bravado than she felt.

"Oh, I so want to be around for that explanation." Violet logged back on her phone.

Mabel wrinkled her nose; almost everyone in the departure lounge was on their phones, like Violet. Mabel referred to herself as a Luddite, being dragged into the technology age by her friend. Across the aisle, she saw the couple she had seen earlier in the corridor. Mabel overheard the patient man call the whiny woman Elizabeth, and she referred to him as Marvin. Mabel decided they had to be married. No man would take that abuse unless they were husband and wife.

Marvin was a small-built man who appeared to be middle-aged, although his tousled brown hair gave him a boyish look. He lined up the hand luggage and set his backpack on top. His wife, Elizabeth was a pleasant-looking woman with short reddish-brown hair beautifully styled and feathered to frame her face. Or, Mabel thought, the woman would be attractive if she took the sour expression off her face. At the moment, the woman was complaining in a thin, shrill voice about the food onboard their flight to Frankfurt.

Mabel sighed. It looked like the couple would be on the same plane to Cairo. She so hoped they wouldn't be on the same tour.

Across from Elizabeth and Marvin sat the pretty young woman with long blonde hair and sparkling blue eyes. The blonde dumped her carry-on and started an animated conversation with the senior couple, who had been riding in the courtesy cart. The man had a French accent and did most of the talking, his hands waving in the air. The fashionably dressed couple appeared to be in their late fifties, around the same age as her and Violet.

Mabel looked like everyone's idea of a kindly grandmother, petite and chubby, with short, white hair and rosy cheeks. A pair of steel-rimmed glasses on her nose completed the picture. Her friend, Violet, on the other hand, was a tall, athletic-looking woman with long red hair twisted into a French knot. Silver filigree earrings hung from her small earlobes. Thin blue-rimmed eyeglasses set on her long, slender nose. Although Violet and Mabel were of the same age, Violet did not look like anyone's granny.

Mabel tugged on her Capri pants, which had ridden up. She admired Violet's multicoloured dress; her friend looked so comfortable. Violet packed her suitcase with long skirts and dresses. She'd read a travel advisory that long skirts and dresses were the proper way to dress for a Muslim country. Violet's decision didn't surprise Mabel. Her friend, a by-the-book person, always followed the rules. Mabel's only concession was to bring one reversible skirt. The rest of her wardrobe comprised of many pairs of Capri pants and T-shirts. Her biggest compromise to the conservative country was the T-shirts with no logos. She bought new ones as most of her shirts had witticisms about golf, her favourite sport, or logos of her favourite football team.

Violet shut off her phone and put it in her carry-on. "Ready?"

"For what?" Mabel asked wide-eyed. Her mind had taken a detour to the conversation she had overheard on the plane. She didn't think the voices were from a movie; she was sure she heard a murder plot.

"Are you ready for our Egyptian adventure?"

Chapter Three

THE SMALL PLANE DRONED the last leg of their journey. Mabel had gotten her second wind, no longer tired but excited. She peeked over Violet's shoulder and looked out the small window of their plane. There it was, the coast of Africa. The sky was darkening. Tiny lights flickered below with vast areas of darkness in between. Mabel's enthusiasm grew. She was going to tour Egypt and see the ancient wonders of the pharaohs. Violet, sound asleep in the seat next to her, snored. Mabel grinned. Her friend could sleep at the drop of a hat.

She scanned her fellow passengers. The majority appeared to be of Arab descent. She assumed the men were businessmen as they wore smart, expensive-looking suits, although some wore robes and headscarves. Violet had told her the scarves were called kaffiyeh. Across the aisle, Elizabeth, the cranky woman, was complaining in her high-pitched voice to her husband, Marvin. Mabel tightened her lips. Good lord, how did her husband stand her?

In front of Elizabeth and her husband, the French couple from the departure lounge were seated. The short, portly man in khaki shorts and a long-sleeved green and white striped shirt had his arm around his wife. The tiny birdlike woman wore a long pastel blue dress with a white shawl draped around her neck. Her head leaned on her husband's shoulder, and she smiled up at him. The man smiled back and laid his cheek on the top of her head.

Behind the couple sat her new friend, Ronnie, the Texan. He'd insisted on carrying her hand luggage onboard. The big, friendly man had a round, red face and big ears. His Stetson lay on his lap. Mabel thought he was probably afraid his hat would get crushed in the overhead bins. She pegged Ronnie as a man in his mid-fifties and wondered why he travelled alone. He appeared to be chatting up the blue-eyed blonde woman who sat next to him. She looked to be in her late twenties, dressed in white slacks and a bright pink blouse. The blonde with a perfect complexion and a trim figure opened a paperback novel. Ronnie gave up talking to her, closed his eyes, and leaned back in his seat.

A young, tall, dark-haired, handsome man dressed all in black sat across the aisle from Mabel. She gave the young man a friendly smile. The man looked blankly back at her; he did not acknowledge her. Or her smile. His blue eyes had a glacial quality about them.

Two men, Mabel mused, appeared to be travelling on their own in Egypt. Of the two, she thought the young man suspicious. But she supposed she felt kindly toward Ronnie, who had toted her hand luggage. Although looks could be deceiving, she and her friend found that out to their cost.

But she had no reason to suspect a murderer onboard this plane. As Violet said, the dire warnings she heard on the flight to Frankfurt could well have been a movie. And even if the plot was real, the likelihood that the plotters were on this plane was doubtful, to say the least. She would forget about the conversation she'd overheard. Egypt was on the horizon.

THE PLANE LANDED AT Cairo airport, and they disembarked up the ramp into the big, modern airport. Mabel thought every jet plane in Africa must have landed. There were hordes of people milling around, the majority Arabs. Everyone was hurrying in every direction. Mabel, who lived in a small town, had never seen so many people, people of every nationality. A multitude of languages filled the air.

She followed Violet and the rest of her fellow passengers down long corridors to a flight of stairs. "Where is our luggage?" Mabel clutched Violet's arm, afraid of being separated from her friend.

"How do we know our luggage is even here?" Elizabeth echoed Mabel's worries.

"It's fine, don't fret. We follow the rest of the passengers; everyone will go to the luggage carousels. Our flight number will be on a sign," assured Violet. "I'm more worried about finding our tour director."

Elizabeth sniffed. "If our luggage made the connections. I'll believe it when I see it."

At the bottom of the stairs, a tall, handsome Egyptian man held up a sign with the name of their tour written on it.

"That's our tour," Violet sang out.

Mabel kept a firm hand on her friend's arm as they hurried down the stairs, her bag bumping on every step. Ronnie lumbered down the stairs past them and hurried over to the man with the tour sign. The French-speaking couple rushed up and dashed in front of Ronnie. Mabel and Violet scurried to join them, followed by Elizabeth and Marvin. The pretty blonde woman dropped her bag and stood with Elizabeth and Marvin. Mabel glanced over her shoulder. The tall man dressed in black stood on the stairs, watching them. Then, he sauntered over to join the group. Mabel frowned. There was something sinister about the man.

The youngish Egyptian man with a small mustache, dressed in black slacks and a white shirt, was also sporting a blue woolly sweater. He smiled broadly and made a slight bow. "Welcome to Cairo. My name is Tarek Ahmadi. I am your tour director."

Mabel noted the sweater; it was Egypt. And this man wore a sweater?

Tarek laid the tour sign beside a small brown leather bag and took out a clipboard and pen. Mabel and her fellow passengers crowded around him.

"If you would, please tell me your names. I want to make sure all my lovely guests have arrived." He flashed them another broad smile.

"My name is Elizabeth Tuttle, and this is my husband, Marvin. We are from Omaha, Nebraska."

Ronnie tipped his hat and announced. "I'm Ronnie Bladek, and I hail from Marble Falls in the great state of Texas in the good old US of A—"

"And this young woman is Angie Morrison, my cousin, also from Omaha," interrupted Elizabeth Tuttle.

Ronnie put his Stetson back on his head and grinned good-naturedly. Tarek raised one eyebrow as he made little tick marks on his clipboard.

Angie rolled her eyes. "I can speak for myself, Elizabeth."

"I'm only trying to speed things along. I'm bushed. I want my bed."

"I'm Silvio Rossi, from Toronto, Ontario, Canada," said the tall, dark man in a low, gravelly voice.

The silver-haired couple from Lyon, France, were Mrs. Marie Drapeau and her husband, Jean.

Violet and Mabel introduced themselves. Then, like lost lambs, they followed Tarek down the crowded corridors to the luggage carousels.

Large crowds were gathered around each carousel. The din from multicultural languages enthralled Mabel. She excitedly glanced around the jam-packed lobby. Her adventure was about to begin.

"Please stay here and wait for your luggage," Tarek requested.

A big, swarthy man with a bushy mustache had followed the tour group to the carousel. "This handsome man is Asim. He is our bus driver for our stay here in Cairo."

The bus driver gave the group a big smile and a little bow. "Welcome to Cairo; it is my great pleasure to show you my marvellous city," Asim said in heavily accented English.

"Asim will help you with your luggage. I must leave you, dear guests. I have another group coming in." With that, Tarek disappeared into the crowd.

"Good Lord, is he coming back?" questioned Elizabeth.

"Oh yes, dear lady, soon, very soon," the bus driver assured, nodding his head, wearing a big smile on his face.

The luggage carousel wasn't moving, but the crowd closed in. Mabel became less enthralled with the crush of people as they jostled and pushed her to the back. How was she going to identify her luggage? She looked apprehensively at her friend.

Violet seemed quite at ease; she turned to the Tuttles and stretched out a hand. "I'm Violet, and this is my friend Mabel. So, you're from Omaha. I've never been there, but I'm sure it's a nice city."

"We were at the introductions. I'm well aware of who you are." Elizabeth pursed her thin lips, ignoring Violet's offered hand.

Her husband, Marvin, reached out his hand, shaking Violet's and then Mabel's. "Nice to meet you both. My wife is a little tired from the travelling," he said.

"I'm right here. Don't talk like I don't exist," his wife snapped.

"Hi, I'm Angie. It will be nice to share this trip with you. Where did you say you were from? Canada somewhere, right?" The young woman shook hands with Violet and Mabel.

"You wouldn't have heard of it. We're from Glenhaven, a small town about an hour out of Regina," Mabel supplied.

"No, I haven't heard of it, and I'm too tired to make small talk." Elizabeth turned her back to them. "What is taking so long with the luggage? I bet they've lost it."

"Don't mind my cousin. As Marvin said, she is tired."

"Would you two stop talking like I'm not here," snapped Elizabeth.

"You might be tired, but rude is rude. Besides, we're all tired. It's no excuse," Angie snapped back.

Mabel gave Violet a sidelong glance. It wasn't going to be any picnic travelling with this woman. Mabel hoped Elizabeth's sourness was from lack of sleep.

Fortunately, the luggage carousel began to turn, preventing the argument between the two women from escalating.

The crowd surged forward as the luggage dropped down the shoot and circulated. Mabel tried to push her way through the crowd, but she was short and quickly elbowed out of the way. Then, with bulldog determination, Mabel bulldozed her way close to the carousel and watched bag after bag tumble down the shoot. Nervously, she saw people pull their bags off the carousel and wheel their luggage away. Bags continued to pass in front of them, but there was no sign of her suitcase or Violet's.

"That's my bag," Elizabeth yelled. "Get it, Marvin. Don't just stand there with your hands in your pockets."

Marvin reached for the bag, but Asim beat him to it and lifted the big bag off the carousel.

"Get your grubby hands off my luggage. Good lord, Marvin, what is the matter with you? Don't let this man steal my luggage; grab it."

Asim jumped back and looked with concern at Elizabeth.

"Asim is our bus driver. He's here to help us," Angie scolded.

"Oh, sorry," Elizabeth whined, and then in a voice loud enough for all to hear, she continued, "But how was I to know he's the driver? They all look alike."

The bus driver's brown eyes flashed with derision.

Her husband and cousin's faces blushed bright red, and they ducked down their heads. "Don't look so embarrassed, Angie," Elizabeth grumbled. "We'll tip him well. That's what he's looking for."

Asim's mustache quivered as he glared at Elizabeth.

To Mabel's relief, her bag, followed by Violet's, tumbled down the chute. The driver unloaded the rest of the luggage and tagged the bags with the tour name. Tarek returned with two more people in tow. The two women from California introduced themselves as sisters Janet and Lucy Branson.

"We are still missing two of our group. They will meet us in Luxor," Tarek told them.

They waited until the latecomer's luggage showed up, and then Tarek led them out of the airport terminal to the bus. Everyone pulled their carry-on except for Mabel and Elizabeth. Mabel's new friend Ronnie carried her small black bag and pulled his own. Marvin trailed, carrying his backpack on his back and pulling both his carry-on and Elizabeth's. Asim, the bus driver, took pity on him and added both pieces of the hand luggage to the big pile on the trolley he was pushing.

They had been travelling for hours, but Mabel was excited as she took in the bright lights and heavy traffic as the bus made its way to the hotel. She had not expected such a modern city.

"I want to visit the bazaars. Where are the bazaars?" Elizabeth asked.

"Dear, it's far too late to visit bazaars," her husband answered.

"I wasn't talking to you; I was asking our guide, What's his name."

"Ma'am, my name is Tarek." He spoke in the hand-held mic from the front seat. "And yes, there are bazaars, and we will make sure everyone will have time to shop. We do have a busy schedule for the first few days. But I assure you, you will get free time to explore the bazaars. Tomorrow is the Cairo Museum, where you will see the ancient treasures of the pharaohs. And, of course, Tutankhamun's magnificent Sarcophagus. We will visit the White Mosque and the Citadel of Saladin. The following day, the Great Pyramids of Giza, the famous Sphinx, and much more. How does that sound?" Tarek asked the tour group in perfect English. They rewarded him with a round of applause.

MABEL STOOD AWESTRUCK in front of the Cairo Marriott Hotel; it looked like a golden palace. "Oh, Violet, I can't believe we are staying here, this is absolutely marvelous. I have never seen anything as majestic as this. You sure know how to show a girl a good time." Mabel beamed at her friend.

Violet, who had booked the tour, also gazed in wonder. "This is even better than I hoped. To be honest with you, I was only interested in the sights we will see. I'm so glad I chose this tour."

The hotel even appeared to impress Elizabeth, as she didn't seem to find fault with anything. That was until they stood in line, waiting to put the luggage and themselves through a scanner. "Like we haven't been scanned enough, for goodness' sake. Is all this really necessary?" she complained.

"Dear, they have to scan us before we are allowed to enter the lobby. It's for our own protection. There are people who might try to bring bombs and guns in here. Just relax, dear."

Scanners at a hotel? Mabel tugged the bag with its broken wheel and stood in line, waiting to be scanned. Was there some kind of threat? As she set her bag down, she saw Angie give Marvin a sympathetic smile.

He shrugged and gave Angie a boyish grin.

"Do we look like terrorists? This is ridiculous; they should scan their own kind," Elizabeth snapped.

"Everyone gets scanned regardless of nationality," scolded Angie. "And keep your voice down, please. You're liable to offend our hosts. We're guests here."

"Mind your own business. I didn't ask for your opinion," Elizabeth snarled.

"Well, pardon me all to hell." Angie turned away.

Mabel's luggage bumped along as she dragged it to the scanner. She glanced at the woman out of the corner of her eye. Good lord, she would be with this woman for two weeks! She made a mental note to steer clear of Elizabeth.

"I hope you will enjoy your first night in Cairo." Tarek ushered them into the massive lobby. "This hotel once belonged to a Pasha. This palace was built to resemble one he had seen in France. The Palace of Versailles."

"Ah, yes, I see some resemblance, but it looks more Arabian to me," Jean Drapeau agreed. "What do you think, Marie?"

She looked at her husband, uncomprehending. He launched into a French explanation. Marie replied in her accented English, "I am not sure, perhaps a little." She gave a Gallic shrug and then nodded enthusiastically. "But it is very grand, very beautiful."

"My wife understands English, but unfortunately, not as well as I do. But that is why she has such a good husband." Jean beamed adoringly at his wife. His wife returned his smile and squeezed his hand.

Tarek smiled at Jean's interruption and continued, "When our famous Suez Canal opened, this was where the French Empress Eugenie and her husband Napoleon III stayed for the canal's grand opening."

"I hope the service lives up to this opulence," Elizabeth's shrill voice carried across the lobby.

"It will, I promise you," Tarek said. "Please to wait here, I will go to the desk and get everyone's key and assign you to your rooms."

Mabel gazed at the lobby's grandeur, so extravagant with its marble floors and decorative embossed walls, high ornate ceilings with crystal chandeliers. Plush seating areas were scattered throughout the lobby. She left her hand luggage with Violet and wandered off to have a peek at the other equally extravagant rooms, that branched off the lobby. A grand piano and a baroque fireplace stood in the middle of one lavish room. A fireplace in Egypt, Mabel marveled. It all seemed too much.

Beaming happily, she returned to the lobby. "You have done yourself proud, Violet. This tour you booked us on is out of this world. Imagine us sleeping in a palace."

Violet grinned at the praise.

Tarek sat on a deep blue velvet chair and spread his paperwork and room keys on the mahogany coffee table. He called out their names and gave them their room keys. "Your luggage should be in your rooms, but please call down to the desk if your bags don't arrive."

The tour group each took their keys, and everyone followed Jean and Marie down a wide corridor branching off the lobby. This led to another long marble passageway; the light from the crystal chandeliers gave everything a golden glow.

"This hotel has two towers and over a thousand rooms. It has swimming pools and restaurants inside and outside, and a casino," Ronnie said, ambling down the hallway behind them.

"You've been here before?" Marvin asked, hitching his backpack on his shoulder.

"No, I just read the little old brochure," Ronnie drawled.

The group walked under marble arches to another wide corridor and ended outside in a well-lit garden. Tables and chairs with folded umbrellas ran the length of a bricked walkway. On the other side of a well-sculptured hedge stood Grecian statues. Water flowed from fountains, and music wafted up from a casino across the garden. They wandered down one long and wide gleaming hallway, past pillars, and up another marble hallway, ending back outside in the courtyard. They were lost.

"Where are you taking us? You don't have a clue, do you?" Angie complained to Jean. She pulled up her carry-on and plopped down on it.

"Did I ask you to follow me?" Jean spread his hands' palms outward. "No, I do not think I did," he defended. "*Mon Dieu,* it is not like I have lived in Versailles."

Marvin parked the two-hand luggage he was toting and growled. "So, where are we? I suppose we can backtrack the way we came. But I don't even know how we got here. Does anyone know?"

The California sisters each pulled out a chair and slumped down. "I'm too tired; I'm not wandering up and down these corridors until someone figures out where we are," Lucy moaned. She took off a shoe and rubbed her foot.

"Yeah, I'm bushed." Ronnie dumped Mabel's carry-on beside his bag and leaned up against a wall.

"Sitting here won't get us to our rooms. I'll go back to the desk and ask for assistance or a map," Violet said. "Does everyone want to wait here?"

"I'm coming with you," Mabel said. There was no way she was letting Violet out of her sight. "You'd probably have a hard time finding your way back here." Mabel, who was usually a take-charge person, was apprehensive. She hated to admit it, but it scared her to be alone in a foreign country. What if Violet got lost?

"This is terrible. They should have sent someone with us or given better directions," Elizabeth complained.

For once, Mabel agreed. "Are you coming with us or staying here?" she asked the group.

Three fashionably dressed Egyptian ladies appeared. "Are you having problems finding your way?" one of the beautiful women asked in lilting English. She wore a figure-hugging black dress with a huge gold pendant.

"Yes, please. Can you help us?" Violet asked, showing them her room number.

"It will delight us to show you the way." The woman in the black dress smiled, her dark eyes sparkling. "Come with us." The ladies giggled as they teetered away in their very high heels.

Silvio sped up, walking between two of the girls. "It's a pleasure to meet such beautiful ladies," he said, grinning from ear to ear.

The girl in the red dress, with a sparkling tiara on her head, tittered. She said something in Arabic, and the girls giggled. The woman in the black dress replied in the same language, then turned and said, "Naughty man." The girls exchanged looks and giggled again.

Silvio retreated to walk with the tour group.

The woman in black appeared to be the only one who could speak English. "This way, please." She led them around a corner and down a corridor to a big glass door. She turned and said, "This is the tower; your rooms will be found here."

"Thank you so much. It is very nice of you to take the time to help us," Violet said.

After the rest of the tour group echoed their thanks, the girls waved goodbye, giggling and whispering on their way back to the garden.

"Well," Elizabeth said. "I'm surprised. I didn't think the Arab women would be so cosmopolitan. These women dress much as they do anywhere, and they must be wealthy. Did you see the jewels they were wearing? And their dresses, haute couture."

"They are ladies of the evening," Silvio explained in his raspy voice. "High-class hookers."

"Ladies of the evening, hum." Ronnie's eyes lit up.

"You'd never afford these women," Marvin joked.

"And you better not even think about it," Elizabeth snapped at Marvin. "If I see you even look twice at those women, you'll be sorry."

Mabel sighed. Maybe when they got to the Nile, Elizabeth would fall overboard. She immediately felt guilty, remembering the conversation on the plane. Mabel looked at Marvin. Was his the voice she'd heard? And if it was, who was he plotting with? There were two voices.

Chapter Four

MABEL SQUINTED IN THE bright morning sunlight as she and the tour group filed out of their luxurious hotel to the blue and white tour bus parked at the curb. Tarek and Asim stood beside the bus. A skinny young man in an ill-fitting brown khaki uniform with a rifle slung over his shoulder stood a few steps behind them. Tarek, clipboard in hand, greeted each tour group member and checked off their names. As they trooped past, they gave the young soldier a wary look.

When everyone was seated, Asim, Tarek, and the newcomer boarded. The soldier with the rifle slung over his shoulder made his way down the aisle, grinning at each passenger. Everyone's head turned to watch as he sat on the long seat at the rear of the bus. Only eight people were in the tour group, and they all sat near the front, leaving empty seats between them and the young soldier. He flashed them a smile, unslung his rifle, and laid it across his lap. The gun looked menacing, but the boy's wide grin did not. The soldier raised a hand and did a little wave.

Tarek stood, held up his microphone, and smiled at the passengers. "Welcome aboard, dear guests. Our adventure into Egypt's ancient past is about to begin. For our stay in Cairo, we are joined by our good friend Amr. He is assigned to us by the Egyptian Army. This is because the media has carried news about threats of terrorism. Let me assure you, there is no threat. This is standard procedure. All of our tours have a soldier assigned to them. There is absolutely no need for alarm. There has been no threat of any kind." He chuckled. "Amr is on a kind of mini-vacation with us. Amr's name in English means companion, and that is what he is. So, sit back, relax, and enjoy the wonders of Cairo." Tarek sat, and the bus pulled into traffic.

Mabel nudged Violet. "What do you think? Do you think Tarek is telling us the truth?" she whispered.

"We have to have trust, Mabel. Outside of jumping off the bus and going back to the hotel, what can we do? I don't think the tour company or the government, for that matter, would want to jeopardize tourist's lives."

Mabel bit her lip. She guessed Violet was right. No one else seemed upset with the new addition to the tour.

The Marriott hotel was situated on Gezira Island, and a golf course was nearby. They drove past the tower of Cairo; the tall, free-standing concrete tower looked honeycombed in the early morning light. The bus took them over the Nile on a long bridge from the island to Cairo proper. Along the Nile, lush green palm trees swayed in the breeze. Tied up along the bank of the river, big white riverboats. Mabel smiled, she was looking forward to their river cruise that would begin in Luxor.

The city of Cairo captivated Mabel. Modern and old limestone buildings lined the busy streets. Cars and trucks, old and new, roared past in all directions, and occasionally, donkeys pulling carts mingled with the busy traffic. The pedestrians, both men and women, scurried across the streets. Women in modern dress with headscarves called hijabs. Others, however, were dressed more traditionally, as were some of the men.

They drove past a huge old building. The courtyard was full of people, some sitting on the ground and others lying in the open.

"What is going on here?" asked Janet.

"This is a free hospital for those that cannot pay for treatment," Tarek explained. "Unfortunately, there are so many people and so few to take care of them. They may wait days or weeks to see a doctor."

Mabel bit her lip. They were on holiday to see the ancient treasures of Egypt, and these poor people were seeking medical help.

Violet exchanged a look with her. "It's a country of contrast, Mabel. Tourism helps."

"Our first visit is the Egyptian Museum," Tarek informed them. "In this beautiful old building built in 1901, you will have a glimpse into Egypt's five thousand years of history. Soon, the new Grand Museum will be open. But for myself, I think this old building has a history and a charm of its own that you will enjoy. Come, dear guests, the dynasties of the pharaohs and their gods await you."

The first one off the bus was Amr. With his rifle slung over his shoulder, he lit a cigarette and chatted in Arabic with Asim. Mabel decided that Tarek was right; this was just procedure.

The old pink building glowed in the early morning light. And the sight of a colossal Sphinx greeted them as they entered the courtyard.

"This Sphinx, although impressive, is just one of many," Tarek told them. "But of course, you came to see the famous Sphinx on the Giza Plateau, and you will, I promise you. But now, dear guest, in this wonderful museum, the ancient treasures of the old kingdom await you." He gave each of the group a ticket to enter the museum and ushered them into the entrance. "A museum guide will give you a tour, and then you will be free to go about on your own. I will await you in the courtyard," he said, giving them a time to meet him.

Mabel tilted her head back and looked up at a colossal statue of a pharaoh standing at the entrance. They built the statue to dwarf all who stood before it. She didn't even come up to the statue's knee. She wondered who the pharaoh was and made a mental note to ask the guide. But she quickly forgot. The museum held so many wonders, and the guide gave them so much information. She loved the atmosphere of the old museum. The guide, a man with greying hair and beard, explained the dynasties and the golden days of Egypt's past. But most of the information was lost on Mabel. She was overwhelmed. The array of displays was breathtaking. Golden amulets, alabaster chests, and statues. Life-sized statues of Tutankhamun and Ramesses III and other pharaohs she couldn't put a name to. Effigies of pharaohs sitting on huge thrones or golden chariots. And the highlight. Tutankhamun's golden sarcophagus.

Ronnie caught up to Mabel and Violet as they stopped to view the golden funerary mask of a wife of a pharaoh from the 18th dynasty. "Tarek told me because of the media's reporting about terrorism, fewer tourists are coming to Egypt," Ronnie said, adjusting the lens on his camera, he snapped a picture. "This is sad for the tourism industry, but it sure gives us an unobstructed view of the antiquities."

Jean and Marie rushed past them, dashing from exhibit to exhibit. And the sisters from California seemed entranced as they walked through the maze of enormous statues of the pharaohs.

Everywhere Mabel looked were treasures, jewelry, ivory, and gold bracelets inlaid with precious gems. Golden amulets of a winged god. Statues of the god Horus, and a black and gold Jackal, the god Anubis. And hieroglyphics of the sun god Ra, with a falcon's head and a man's body. It was hard to take it all in.

Mabel spotted Silvio and Angie walking together through the exhibits of the furniture. The couple stopped by the golden throne, taken from King Tutankhamun's tomb. Silvio appeared to be reading aloud from a museum pamphlet. Across from them, Marvin and Elizabeth were admiring a display of tiny golden pharaohs.

Silvio leaned down and whispered into Angie's ear, she giggled. Marvin's head turned in their direction. Elizabeth tugged on his arm, telling him something that made him laugh. But Mabel noticed he turned back to watch Angie and Silvio as they stopped to look at the statue of Nefertiti.

Mabel gawked at mummies encased in glass cases. She saw others that were lying on shelves. She paused and wandered closer, reaching out a hand to feel the texture of the grey linen wrap around a mummy.

Violet slapped her hand away. "Don't touch that."

"Hey," Mabel said, startled. "Don't hit me. What do you think I'm going to do? Unwrap it?"

"Germs, Mabel, germs. I'm protecting you."

"Ladies," a deep masculine tone startled both women. "Do not touch the exhibits," the tall Egyptian guard said.

"What? I didn't do anything," Mabel defended herself.

"I told her not to touch," Violet said with a superior nod, crossing her arms.

"I didn't, I didn't touch it."

"If every tourist put their hands on these ancient artifacts, it would destroy the integrity of these treasures." The guard motioned for Mabel to back away from the shelves with the mummies.

"But I didn't touch them."

"Yes, it's okay. She didn't touch anything, and I stopped her," Violet voiced.

"Thanks a bunch, goody-two-shoes." Mabel scowled at her friend.

"Germs," Violet said. "There would be germs."

"Yes, yes," the tall man agreed. "You could have contaminated this ancient mummy."

"Me, she was worried about me."

"Yes, this is good. You would spread your germs."

"Not my germs, the germs of the..." Mabel's voice trailed off. "Oh, never mind. I'm not going to touch anything, I promise." She grabbed Violet by the arm and tugged her toward another exhibit. The guard followed closely on their heels.

"You could've gotten us thrown out of here," scolded Violet.

"MY DEAR FRIENDS, DID you enjoy the visit to our magnificent museum and the treasures of the pharaohs?" Tarek asked as they settled into their seats on the bus. "Everything was good? No problems, I hope?"

Mabel gave Violet a sidelong glance, daring her to said anything about her confrontation with the museum guard.

"It was all well and fine. But I had to pay to go to that disgusting toilet in the courtyard," Elizabeth complained.

"Someone has to keep it clean," Ronnie said.

"If it was clean, this toilet was not." Elizabeth stuffed a bag of souvenirs into the seat pocket. "And the food they sold in the courtyard was unbelievable; I couldn't eat a thing. I'm starved."

"Honestly, Elizabeth, we just saw the antiquities of the pharaohs. And all you can do is complain about toilets and food," chided Angie.

Elizabeth glared at Angie, then turned her head to stare out the bus window. Marvin shifted his gaze from his wife to Angie, then down to his hands.

"I am sorry about your unfortunate experience with the facilities, Mrs. Tuttle. But I do hope you enjoyed the museum itself."

Elizabeth pursed her lips and nodded. "Yes, very interesting," she said coldly.

"The museum was amazing," Mabel said. "Everything was fascinating, and there was so much to see. I couldn't take it all in."

"Yes, another visit back to the museum for sure," Lucy agreed.

All the tour group, except Elizabeth, gave Tarek a round of applause.

As they left the Cairo Museum, Mabel noticed an army vehicle following them. A soldier sat with a machine gun mounted in the back of a truck. Two more soldiers, also armed, rode in the cab. She nudged Violet. "Do you see them?"

"See what?" Violet was scrolling through pictures on her camera.

"The army guys with guns."

"Hard not to. Amr is sitting in the back of the bus."

"No, not him."

"Who then?"

"Look out the window."

"I have been. This is an incredible city."

"Yes, yes, incredible," Mabel said impatiently. "Don't you see who is following us? An army truck. And the men have machine guns."

"Well, if they are the army, they would, now, wouldn't they?" Violet glanced out the window. "They are probably going the same way we are." She opened her guidebook.

"You don't think a guard onboard and a convoy of the Egyptian army is not something to worry about?"

Violet sighed and closed her travel book. "Mabel, one truck does not make a convoy. And stop worrying, if you are going to worry about every little thing, you are going to spoil our holiday. Please, relax and enjoy the sights."

Mabel pressed her lips together. Every little thing? Violet was altogether too blasé about the dangers. But what could she do? No one else seemed to be alarmed. She looked back at the rear of the bus. The young soldier was waving to his comrades.

The Saladin Citadel, a domed medieval Islamic fortress built in the fourteenth century to protect Cairo from the Crusaders, stood atop a hill. At first glance, the Citadel looked like a medieval castle with massive high walls and round towers on either side of the big stone gate. But then Mabel saw the domed Ottoman roofs of the Alabaster Mosque. Tarek told the tour group the magnificent structure was now a UNESCO World Heritage Site. Mabel felt dwarfed, walking through the massive gate. And she wished she had more time to explore the walled fortress. But they had the White Alabaster Mosque to visit.

"When are we going to the Giza Plateau? I want to see the pyramids and the Sphinx. At this rate, I will be too tired to appreciate them," Elizabeth whined in a high-pitched voice to her husband.

"If you wanted to take it easy, you should have stayed at home," Angie interjected. "Guided tours are, all go, go, you know that."

Elizabeth curled her lips in a sneer. "Was I talking to you?"

Angie's eyes widened, and her lip tightened as she gave Elizabeth a mutinous look.

Silvio put his arm around Angie, and she snuggled into his embrace.

Marvin frowned at Silvio.

Mabel rolled her eyes; these people should never travel together; they were always bickering.

Tarek, the ever-patient guide, held up his hand and spoke into his microphone. "It seems some of you are not familiar with the itinerary. We will end the day after the tour of the White Mosque, which I am sure you all will enjoy. Tomorrow, we will see the great Pyramids of Giza. The Sphinx, Memphis, and the oldest pyramid, the Step Pyramid. It will be another full day. And on the following day, we fly to Luxor, the next leg of your Egyptian adventure. But first, welcome to the White Mosque."

"This beautiful alabaster mosque you see before you with the dome roof is built in the Ottoman style. The tall towers on either side of the entrance are called minarets. This is where the muezzin calls the faithful to prayer," Tarek informed them as they walked into a large arched courtyard.

"The mosque is a holy site, so please, everyone, remove your footwear before entering. Paper slippers are provided. And ladies, if you would please cover your hair," he requested. "You may take pictures if you wish."

"I've never been inside a mosque. It looks beautiful from the outside," Violet said, taking off her shoes as directed and putting a scarf loosely over her head.

Mabel removed her shoes and pulled a scarf from her Lug bag. A young girl was sitting on the ground in the courtyard, leaning up against a wall. She wore a long robe and hijab and texted on her phone. The girl's skirt had ridden up. She was wearing jeans under her robe. The modern world was encroaching.

"I'm not taking my shoes off." Elizabeth wrinkled her nose, pointing to the shoes sitting on the pavement outside the mosque. "Look at all those shoes. How do we know our shoes will still be here when we come out?"

The big Texan grinned. "No one wants your shoes, ma'am."

"Maybe not your scruffy old shoes, but mine are expensive."

Ronnie grinned good-naturedly, bending down to take off his shoes. "I heard even Queen Elizabeth took off her shoes when she visited a mosque," he teased.

"She would have someone to guard her shoes, wouldn't she?" snapped Elizabeth.

"Plastic bags are provided, Mrs. Tuttle. You can carry your shoes into the mosque. You just can't wear your shoes inside." Tarek produced small, clear blue bags. "Please use these."

The group gathered around the tour director, each taking a bag for their shoes. "I'm not taking my shoes off, and no one can make me, and that's final."

"You are perfectly right, Mrs. Tuttle. No one can make you. And you don't have to. But you will have to wait out here for the rest of us. You can't enter a holy site with your shoes on. It is considered a desecration," Tarek explained patiently.

"Fine, I'll wait outside. Marvin, put your shoes on and come here," she directed.

Marvin, holding the plastic bag containing his shoes, said, "But, dear, I want to see inside the mosque. Take your shoes off and come with me, please."

"No, I will not, and I will not wait out here alone with these people. Put your shoes on."

The tour group continued to take off their shoes, glancing over at Marvin, the henpecked husband, as he put his back on.

"Angie, are you staying outside with us?" Marvin asked. Angie looked uncertain.

Lucy, one of the California sisters, put her arm around Angie's shoulder. "Come with us," she invited.

Angie looked back at Marvin and Elizabeth and shrugged. Then, covering her hair with a scarf, she walked into the White Mosque with Lucy.

"Take pictures," Marvin shouted after her.

With a smirk on his face, Silvio followed behind.

Mabel, used to Christian churches, marvelled at the beautiful mosque with its massive chandeliers. There were no pictures or statues, but the intricate designs on the pillars and arches and the small globes of glass hanging down from the ceiling enhanced the simplistic beauty. Large red carpets with complicated gold designs lay on the marble floor, where men and boys were prostrated, praying. She didn't know where the women prayed, but it wasn't with the men. Everyone was respectfully quiet. Mabel thought it was a good thing Elizabeth didn't come. Heaven only knew what the grumpy woman would have said.

Violet leaned down and whispered in Mabel's ear, "Don't ask where the women are."

"But I do wonder, don't you?"

"I do, but don't ask. All we need now is to be thrown out of a mosque."

"Violet, honestly, do you think I would make a fuss?"

"I love you, Mabel, but you know you've never been good at keeping your thoughts to yourself."

"Huh, a lot, you know." But Mabel did have to acknowledge silence wasn't her strong suit.

Back outside the mosque, a man in a traditional long robe pressed a pamphlet entitled *'Women in the Muslim faith'* into Mabel's hand. She remembered Violet's caution, so she said nothing. She nodded to the man, stuck it in her pocket, and finished tying her shoes.

With a smirk on her face Elizabeth asked, "Thinking of converting?"

"You know, Elizabeth, silence is golden, try it sometime." Mabel strutted past her out onto a platform to enjoy the view with the rest of the tour group. The wooden platform jutted out, overlooking the city of Cairo. Off in the distance through the dusky haze of sand, the great Pyramids of Giza came into view.

"Elizabeth hurry up, come here, you got to see this," Marvin called from the far end of the balcony.

Elizabeth scowled and hurried off down the wooden walkway. "What do you see there that you can't see over here? ... Help," she screamed. "Oh my god, help, help." Elizabeth had stepped into a hole in the planks. There was nothing below her but rocks. The splintered plank trapped her foot in the hole.

Marvin ran to his wife's side. He stood looking down at her, shuffling from foot to foot. "Are you hurt, dear?"

"You, moron, get me out of here," she yelled. Elizabeth tried to boost herself up out of the hole, she slipped, and her leg slid farther down.

Amr came running up to the deck with a cigarette dangling from his lips, he looked worriedly at Elizabeth.

Tarek rushed over to look down at her. "I'm sorry, madam. There should be a barricade or a sign around this opening."

"Just get me the hell out of here," raged Elizabeth.

Marvin grabbed under her armpits and heaved. He fell backward, and Elizabeth landed beside him with a thud. She rubbed her leg and glared at him. "Idiot," she snarled.

The tour group gathered around her. Ronnie offered his hand. Elizabeth slapped it away and stood. She pulled up the leg of her slacks, checking for scratches. "Good lord, what a country. I could have been killed."

Mabel looked around at the balcony. It was old and not particularly safe by North American standards. There should have been a barrier around the hole or at least a warning sign. Sure, it was only a hole, but if the surrounding planks had given way, Elizabeth could have fallen to her death, a long drop with only jagged rocks to break her fall.

"I very much doubt that you were in any danger. It was only your foot." Angie helped her cousin brush off the dirt from her slacks.

"Thank you so much for your sympathy," Elizabeth snapped.

Violet leaned down to Mabel and whispered, "I wonder why these people even travel together. They are always sniping at each other."

"Exactly my thoughts," Mabel whispered back.

"I could have been seriously hurt. I should sue," Elizabeth threatened.

Marvin put his arm around Elizabeth, helping her walk back to the bus. "Are you okay, dear?" he asked.

"What do you think? I fell in a hole, for God's sake."

Mabel frowned. If Marvin had seen the hole, did he hope his wife would step into it? She quickly dismissed the idea. The odds of that didn't seem likely.

Amr stomped his cigarette out on the deck and took up a military stance beside the hole in the planks. He planted his rifle butt down on the deck and looked sternly at the tour group. "No, no," he said, pointing to the hole, then grinned. Tarek glanced at the boy, shook his head, and ushered everyone away from the opening.

"I wonder what happened to the warning sign that was by that hole?" Janet asked her sister as they strolled back to the bus.

"A sign?"

"There was a sign in English and Arabic," Janet said.

"I didn't see it. Are you sure you saw a sign?" asked Lucy.

"Yes, the sign in English read, 'You must be the careful one. This is abscess. Do not do the step.' The English came across as kind of funny, that's why I remember it."

Lucy raised her eyebrows. "That is weird. Do you think someone moved the sign?"

Janet shrugged and climbed onboard the bus.

"Did you hear that? I don't think this is an accident," Mabel whispered to Violet.

"What else could it be?" Violet replied.

"Janet said she saw a warning sign."

"Yes, but Lucy didn't, and I didn't either, so forget about it. I do feel sorry for Tarek. Elizabeth will not forget this anytime soon. All the same, that hole is dangerous. Any one of us could have stepped into it."

"But we didn't. Are you sure you didn't see some kind of a sign by that hole? You were there before me. I was being converted by a zealot."

"You were being converted by zealot?"

"Relax, I'm still a Christian. But Elizabeth was with me."

"They tried to convert Elizabeth?" Violet scoffed.

"No. What I mean is that we came later to the lookout. And Janet just said she saw a sign warning people about the hole."

"I told you, I didn't see it. But then I was busy looking at the view, looking out across the desert at the Pyramids of Giza. You're not thinking about that silly conversation you think you heard on the plane, are you? This is an accident. We're here to enjoy the sights of Egypt. Not to find mysteries around every corner."

Mabel sighed. There was no 'think' about it. She had heard a murder plot, but was it real or a movie? That she didn't know. She turned to look out the window. The truck with the armed soldiers still followed them. And now, an army jeep with more soldiers had joined the convoy. She turned to Violet and whispered, "What did I tell you? This is no coincidence. We have an armed guard."

"I'm sure it's just a precaution."

"I don't like it, a guard onboard and the army following us. Is this normal?"

"Even if they are here to guard us, we're here now. For god's sake, don't let it bother you. Look at Amr; he seems pretty relaxed."

Mabel glanced back down the aisle. Amr had his feet up, his cap tipped over his eyes, and he appeared to be taking a nap. "Yeah, I guess, no use worrying about it now." Mabel looked warily out the bus window at the little convoy as they wound their way through the busy streets of Cairo back to their hotel. She would get Violet to text a message to her mom and her son and daughter. The least she could do was to say goodbye.

Chapter Five

BREAKFAST HAD BEEN rushed, and then an early morning bus ride out to the Giza Plateau. But Mabel didn't mind. She was excited. They had a big day ahead of them with much to see. Sand from the Sahara Desert blew across the road, reminding her of a winter snow squall back home. An army jeep and a truck with armed soldiers accompanied them on the thirty-minute drive through the desert from Cairo to the Giza Plateau. As Tarek named the pyramids, the little convoy circled at a distance around the three massive pyramids on the plateau.

"Before you, dear guests, is the Giza Plateau, the home of the most famous pyramids of Egypt. Ahead of you on the right is the Pyramid of Khafre and the Pyramid of Menkaure. And then, of course, the most famous pyramid of all. The Great Pyramid of Khufu." Tarek stood with a microphone in one hand, the other on the back of his seat, bracing himself as the bus rocked back and forth over the sand dunes. "The smaller ones were built for queens." Tarek continued to explain the history of the ancient monuments.

He finished his narration just as the bus and their armed guards parked. He then gave them a designated time to be back at the bus and a warning to be wary of souvenir peddlers and pickpockets. "You will have lots of time to buy souvenirs, much better souvenirs," he told them. "Also, you will see men with camels offering you a ride. These men are not approved by our tour company, they may be good men, or they may not be. These men will offer to take a picture of you on their camel with the Khufu Pyramid in the background. This will sound very tempting, but you may have to pay twice. Once for the picture and once more to get off the camel. It's up to you, but you will get a camel ride later if you wait. Now enjoy your tour. Khufu awaits you."

"That man probably gets a cut from the so-called approved camel rides," Elizabeth huffed as she trudged alongside her husband.

Mabel exchanged a glance with Violet. "Do you think Elizabeth is right?"

"I don't care. I'm not riding any of those big beasts. I hear they are very bad-tempered." Violet put her camera strap around her neck.

The wind had died down, and now the sand was only drifting, not blowing. Although, when she licked her lips, Mabel could taste sand. The closer they got to the pyramids, the larger they became. They were colossal. She walked with Violet along the front of the limestone pyramid, marvelling at the construction-built thousands of years before the birth of Christ. They turned a corner, walking along the side of the massive structure. Tarek had told them that at the back of the pyramid they could see the recent discovery of the

Pharaoh Khufu ship, which was to take him to the other side in the afterlife.

Fewer people were walking along the side of the pyramid, and they almost felt they were alone until Janet and Lucy caught up and joined them on their stroll.

"How exciting," Janet gushed. "This trip has been on my bucket list for a very long time. How about you?"

"Mine too," Violet replied, stopping to take a picture.

Mabel followed suit, pointing her camera and taking a shot. She had a feeling the picture would look like a stone wall.

"Cameras, how cute." Lucy held up her phone. "I used to have a camera, but not anymore. Cellphones are so easy to use and take really good pictures. I'll have to show you."

Violet turned and took a picture of a group of men leading their camels. The large beasts had highly decorated saddles on their backs. "I prefer a camera, but I guess cellphones are the new way."

Mabel tucked her camera into her Lug bag, wishing she had her phone.

"So, is it really cold where you come from?" Lucy asked, grabbing her scarf that threatened to blow away. The wind had picked up, blowing fine sand into their faces.

"In the winter, yes, it's cold, but we do get four seasons." Violet held on to her hat. Her skirt flared out, flopping against her legs with each gust of wind.

"I wish we had four seasons, especially at Christmas. Snow must be nice, so white and fluffy," Janet said.

Mabel grinned. Hollywood had painted a pretty picture of a white Christmas. The four women continued to walk alongside the pyramid. After several minutes, they all agreed it was too far to make a complete circle of the pyramids and turned back, retracing their steps.

As Mabel walked along the Khufu Pyramid, she reached out a hand to feel the craggy, worn limestone blocks, marveling again at the ancient structure, built centuries ago.

Arab men with keffiyehs on their heads and long colourful robes stood holding the reins of their camels, calling out in heavily accented English. "Come, dear ladies, come and have a ride on our beautiful camels. We take your picture. Come, come, our camels are very nice camels, very friendly camels. You will like this souvenir of Egypt. You must have a souvenir to remember the grand Giza Plateau and great the Khufu's Pyramid."

"These men look fabulous in their long robes and scarves," Janet said, snapped a picture with her phone.

"The scarfs are called keffiyehs, and the robes, I think, are called thobe," Violet volunteered.

"Good to know," Janet replied, absently snapped more pictures.

"Please hold my bag, I'm going to get my picture taken on one of those camels." Mabel thrust her Lug bag to Violet.

"No, remember what Tarek said?"

"I bet Elizabeth is right. Tarek gets a cut from some other camel herder," exclaimed Lucy as she trotted over to the Arabs. "Come on, it's okay, they're right here. What could go wrong?"

Janet hesitated, then held up her phone and followed her sister.

Mabel turned to follow. Violet grabbed her arm and held tight. "Come on, let's go back; we should climb up on the pyramid."

Mabel looked wistfully over her shoulder at the girls climbing onto the saddles. "Okay, I guess there will be more camels. It is Egypt."

First, Violet, then Mabel, climbed up a few rows of limestone blocks and posed for a picture on the pyramid. They had to be careful where they walked. The surface was narrow and uneven, worn away by centuries of unrelenting sand blowing across the desert and tourist's feet.

As Mabel climbed down the last row to the ground, two peddlers in their long robes rushed up to her, holding up ornaments of the pyramids. "Genuine hand-carved pyramids," they called to her in broken English. The ornaments didn't look hand-carved to Mabel; they looked more like plaster painted red. Nonetheless, she felt rude ignoring the men with their ornamental pyramids; it wasn't the Canadian way. But Tarek had warned them to watch for pickpockets, and she hoped the men would move on.

Amr strode up to the men and said something in terse Arabic. The hawkers replied, grumbling in the same language and then grudgingly, they moved away.

"Thank you, Amr," Mabel said.

The young man shifted his rifle and grinned. "It is good, the men mean no harm. They need to sell to feed their families. But if you do not want what these men sell. The men must move on." Amr paused to light a cigarette, then ambled away.

Mabel sighed; she felt guilty; maybe she should have bought something.

"You can't help everyone," Violet said. "I know you feel bad, but you can't."

Mabel followed Violet a short distance from the pyramid. The peddlers, who had been trying to sell Mabel souvenirs, rushed over to a group of Japanese tourists. The men held up their wares and called out in a mixture of English, Arabic, and Japanese. The Japanese group stopped to look at the merchandise, and soon, more hawkers quickly surrounded them. Mabel hoped the men would have more luck with the new tourists.

There was a loud shriek, then a sharp cry, "Watch out."

Elizabeth's screams pierced the air. She was hanging off the side of the pyramid, clinging onto one block, clawing at another. Her feet kicked against the side of the limestone blocks as she searched for a foothold. Pieces of rock and sand fell to the surface below. Her screams vibrated off the pyramid as she scratched at another block. More stones and sand fell, showering the hawkers and the tourists who turned to look up at the woman hanging precariously off the pyramid.

Elizabeth grabbed a second block. "Help, help," she screeched.

Amr trotted up to stand by Mabel and Violet. "Oh, this is not good," he said.

"You think?" Mabel asked sarcastically, looking worriedly up at Elizabeth dangling off the side of the pyramid.

"No, not good." Amr craned his neck.

High above on a ledge, Angie was clutching Silvio's arm.

"Help me, help me," Elizabeth screamed, her fingers clawing at a limestone block.

"Hold on, honey," Marvin yelled, crouching on a block, looking down at Elizabeth.

Ronnie pushed past Marvin. He knelt on the narrow path and reached out to Elizabeth. "Grab my hand," he called.

"I can't. If I let go, I'll fall," Elizabeth whimpered.

"Do it. It's the only way. Take Ronnie's hand you won't fall," Marvin encouraged. "Let him pull you up, Elizabeth."

"Angie, stay here. I'm going to help," Silvio instructed. He climbed along the narrow blocks and knelt beside Marvin. "Hold on to me, Marvin, and I'll hold on to Ronnie."

Marvin did as Silvio requested, wrapping his arms around the man's waist. Silvio grabbed the big Texan's belt as the man leaned over the edge and reached down to Elizabeth.

Everyone went quiet, watching the scene unfold as Elizabeth's hand grasped Ronnie's. And he pulled her up to the ledge above. All the tourists and peddlers who had witnessed the heroic event clapped their hands in loud applause.

Elizabeth clung to Marvin. "Thank God you're safe," he said, wrapping his arms around her. "Thank you, Ronnie, thank you for saving my wife."

"No problem, you guys helped," Ronnie drawled. "I'm just glad the little gal is safe."

"Don't thank him," Elizabeth stormed at Marvin. "He was the one who knocked me off. You big clumsy oaf."

"No, ma'am, it wasn't me who pushed you. Everyone was climbing up, and these old blocks are pretty worn. It could have been anyone, but it sure in the hell wasn't me."

"Really, Elizabeth? Ronnie saved you. And you should look where you're going. It's no one's fault but your own," Angie scolded, taking Silvio's arm. The pair turned to make their way back along the ledge.

"Come on, let's go down, this is no place for a family quarrel," Marvin urged, tugging at Elizabeth's hand.

"My fault? This most certainly is not my fault; someone pushed me," Elizabeth railed. Ronnie took a step back, pressing himself against the pyramid as Elizabeth and Marvin crossed in front of him.

"This Ronnie is a good, brave man." Amr flipped his cigarette butt into the sand. "All is well; everyone is safe." The young soldier slung his rifle over his shoulder and sauntered away.

"Yes, thank goodness Ronnie was there to save her. He is indeed brave," agreed Mabel. Then her eyes narrowed as she recalled the conversation she'd overheard on the plane. She watched as the group carefully made their way down the side of the pyramid. If Elizabeth had fallen, it would have looked like an accident. What if it was planned? Who was near enough to give her a shove? Did Ronnie really push Elizabeth? She accused him. Or did Marvin? He was beside Elizabeth, but so were Angie and Silvio. And the French couple, they were up on the pyramid too.

"Wow, that was scary," Violet said. "Lucky Elizabeth grabbed that block. I'm glad she's safe. If she had fallen, she could have been killed."

"And lucky Ronnie was there. The rest of those people just stood by looking helpless."

"I know. Some people are just not good in a crisis." Violet took the lens cap off her camera.

Mabel watched Violet line up the pyramid and clicked the shutter. "So, what do you make of that?" she asked.

"Absolutely fabulous. Imagine they built these massive spectacular structures in 3000 BC." Violet stood, her skirt billowing out. She looked up, admiring the Pyramid of Khufu. "One of the seven wonders of the world."

"No, not that."

"What do you mean, not that? The Pyramids of Giza are."

"Are what?"

"One of the seven wonders."

"Oh, those."

"What do you mean, oh those? Good Lord, Mabel, don't you appreciate these pyramids? You're as bad as Elizabeth." Violet swung her camera, snapping pictures of the peddlers doing a booming business with the Japanese tour group.

"Of course I do. The Pyramids of Giza are remarkable. And what do you mean as bad as Elizabeth?"

"Sorry, I know you're not. But you do appreciate what you're seeing, I hope. Imagine the skill it took to build these pyramids all those centuries ago."

"I said I do appreciate these wonders. I meant Elizabeth."

"I wouldn't class her as a wonder, a disaster more like, poor woman." Violet held up her camera, backing away. "Stand there, Mabel; I need you in the picture for contrast."

"A contrast, for what?"

"The size of the pyramids," Violet said, snapping pictures, trying to get Mabel in the frame.

A group of schoolchildren in uniform marched past, their teacher talking to them in rapid Arabic. Mabel briefly wondered if there was a future Egyptologist in the group of smiling children. "Everyone knows the pyramids are big, for goodness' sake; you don't need me for a contrast. Listen about Elizabeth—"

"What is it with you and Elizabeth?" Violet asked, taking pictures of the school children running to the pyramid. "It was an accident and a scary one, but she's all right."

"Let me finish. I think someone tried to push her off the pyramid."

"Seriously." Violet turned her camera to take pictures of a small group of camels lying on the sand and their colourful handlers.

"Remember the conversation I heard on the plane?"

"Oh, please, you're not still thinking about that." Violet grabbed her hat. A gust of wind picked up, spraying them with sand.

"She might be the victim I heard them whispering about." Mabel licked her lips. Was she ingesting sand?

"Let it go. We decided it was a movie you heard on the plane."

"You decided it was a movie. I'm not so sure. I think I should warn Elizabeth just in case."

"Leave her alone. She slipped on a three-thousand-year-old block of limestone. It was an accident, and she wasn't hurt."

"That makes two accidents. A coincidence? I don't think so. And I'm surprised at you, I find your attitude a little callous. Elizabeth could have fallen to her death or at least been seriously hurt." But as Mabel watched the Japanese tour group ascend the pyramid, she conceded that Violet might be right. The girls were darting in front of each other on the narrow ledge.

"I don't mean to be callous, but you do have a tendency to find a mystery behind every event. I'm sorry Elizabeth fell, and I'm glad she wasn't hurt. But it was an accident. You and I have had enough adventures with murderers. I just want us to enjoy a holiday. The only adventure I want is a tour of the ancient monuments of Egypt."

"If Elizabeth dies on this tour and I didn't warn her—"

"Mabel." Violet stopped taking pictures, planted her hands on her hips, and looked sternly down at her. "No, you most certainly should not warn Elizabeth. What are you going to say? Are you going to tell her you heard a weird conversation in the middle of the night between two people you never saw? She'll probably think you're some kind of bizarre weirdo. I repeat, leave the woman alone."

Chapter Six

TRUDGING ALONGSIDE Violet toward the tour bus, Mabel mulled over the events. First, there was the hole on the deck at the Alabaster Mosque, now the near-fatal fall from the pyramid. "Either Elizabeth is an accident-prone woman. Or she is a target," she murmured to Violet.

"Mabel, please, let it go." Violet's lips thinned as she put the lens cap on her camera.

Amr, standing at the bus door, was shaking Ronnie's hand. "You are the hero," he said.

The big Texan blushed. "Not a hero. It was nothing. I had help." He turned and climbed aboard the bus.

Tarek greeted Mabel and Violet as they took their seats. "Excellent timing, dear ladies," he said. "Only two of our little group is tardy."

Mabel noted that Silvio and Angie were missing.

"Everyone, please wait here on the bus, do not wander around. I will go and find the missing members of our little family," Tarek said and hopped off the bus.

Asim followed the tour director off the bus and joined Amr. Accepting a cigarette, he leaned against the bus.

"Silvio and Angie should be more considerate of the rest of us. We're all here. We've seen the pyramids." Elizabeth looked at Ronnie. "Where I was pushed off!"

Ronnie yanked his Stetson off his head and vigorously wiped the band with a tissue. "I damn well did not push you off that pyramid. I pulled you up if you remember?"

"Whatever." Elizabeth leaned forward in her seat, looking out the window. "Really, what are those two doing? Once you've seen the pyramid, what else is there to do?"

Marvin patted her hand. "Don't worry about Angie and Silvio. I'm sure Tarek will find them." He leaned across the aisle. "We do want to thank you, Ronnie, for coming to Elizabeth's rescue. Don't we, dear?"

There was a round of applause from the group. Ronnie's face reddened, embarrassed.

"Yes, yes, thank you," Elizabeth said, then she muttered to Marvin. "I still think he's to blame."

Ronnie lifted his eyebrows and jammed his Stetson back on his head. Tilting the hat over his eyes, he laid back in his seat.

Janet leaned over her seat and tapped Mabel on the shoulder. "You were right not to get on those darn camels. It was like Tarek said, we paid once for the picture, then once more to get off. I was afraid we wouldn't get our phones back."

"But we got our phones, and sure, we had to pay the camel guys more. But look at the pictures we got." Lucy passed her phone to Violet.

Violet scrolled through the pictures. "Yes, they are very good pictures," she conceded, passing the phone to Mabel.

Mabel looked at the pictures on the phone. "Nice," she complimented Lucy, handing her back the phone. Mabel then turned to gaze out the bus window. Another tour bus pulled alongside and parked. It, too, had an armed guard. The authorities weren't taking any chances. Mabel didn't know if the guards made her feel more secure or less. Had Tarek been honest with them? Was there a threat of an attack? Or were the armed guards just a normal precaution like he'd said? She still hadn't gotten Violet to text her family to say goodbye.

She saw Tarek returning with Angie and Silvio in tow. Silvio appeared to be turning on the charm, his arm draped over Angie's shoulder, smiling and laughing at something Angie said. Mabel watched Marvin take a long, hard look at Silvio as the man helped Angie climb onboard the bus. Did Marvin have a thing for Angie? Or was he worried about a stranger taking an interest in his relative? Mabel had to admit Silvio didn't look like someone you would invite home to meet Mother. Asim climbed back onboard and started up the bus. Amr crushed out his cigarette and stepped inside.

Without a word to Violet, Mabel jumped up from her seat and brushed past Silvio and Angie in the aisle. She hopped off the bus, waylaying Tarek. "May I speak to you in private for a moment?" she asked.

"Dear lady, we must leave. We are already behind schedule." He looked at his watch and then back toward the bus.

Mabel wondered if he called her dear lady because he didn't remember her name. "My name is Mabel Havelock," she said, taking Tarek by the arm and leading him away from the bus.

Tarek brushed her hand away and frowned. "Yes, Mrs. Havelock, I know your name."

The bus driver stepped out of the bus, asking Tarek something in Arabic. Tarek replied in the same language and turned to Mabel. "If you would be quick, please, dear lady, we must go. Our driver, Asim, is impatient."

"It's about Elizabeth—"

Tarek looked over his shoulder, the driver was shouted in Arabic. "Please, dear lady, back to the bus. I know about poor Mrs. Tuttle, a terrible thing to be sure. But she is recovered."

Mabel put her hands on her hips and planted her feet firmly on the ground. "That's not what I mean. Well, I guess I do."

Tarek, rubbing his brow, asked, "Do what?"

"I mean, I do want to discuss what happened to Mrs. Tuttle and warn you."

"Warn me?"

"Someone is planning to kill her."

"Now, now dear lady, don't worry your—"

Mabel hated being humoured. "Stop right there. If you're going to say, don't worry, your pretty little head? I—"

"Your pretty head? My dear, Mrs. Havelock, what must you think of me? I do not flirt with women. I am a married man." Tarek recoiled in shock.

Mabel's eyes widened in puzzlement. Somehow, she was making matters worse. "That's not what I meant. Please forget what I said. What I'm trying to tell you is Elizabeth is in danger."

"I beg your pardon if I misinterpreted your meaning." He sighed in relief. "Please, you must not let your imagination get a hold of you." Tarek smiled and motioned to Mabel. "Come, dear, Mrs. Havelock, we have more ancient wonders of Egypt to show you."

Mabel tightened her lips and looked up at him over her granny glasses. "It is not my imagination. There is a plot to kill Elizabeth. I heard it."

"What? What did you hear? Are you accusing me or one of my countrymen of plotting to kill Mrs. Tuttle?" Tarek sputtered in outrage. He crossed his arms over his chest, his lip curled down.

"No, no, not you or your countrymen," Mabel assured the tour director.

Tarek looked down at her with suspicion in his eyes.

"It's someone from this tour group, I'm sure of it. Elizabeth, almost falling off the pyramid, is the second attempt on her life."

"Second attempt? The second attempt? There was no first or second attempt." Tarek pinched the bridge of his nose, paused, and offered up a smile. "Don't be foolish, please, Mrs. Havelock, get back on the bus. We must go. We have much to see today." He took a few steps toward the bus, then stopped. Mabel was not following him.

"The first attempt on Elizabeth's life was at the White Mosque. She almost fell through that hole in the balcony. You must remember that."

"Mrs. Havelock, that was her foot. Her foot fell into a hole. That is hardly an attempt on her life. Now, please, Asim has started the bus."

"If the boards had given up, she could have fallen to her death on the rocks below."

"Given up?"

"If the boards had broken around that hole."

"But no boards broke. Mrs. Tuttle had her foot stuck in a hole. You are being foolish." Tarek looked up at the sky as though searching for the right words. "You are thinking bad thoughts. You should be thinking about the ancient mysteries of Egypt. Not about this silly plot. Please, these accidents are nothing."

"It is not nothing, trust me, someone is out to kill Elizabeth. I heard them on the plane, planning it."

"On a plane." Tarek looked down at her, his eyebrows arched.

"Yes, on a plane flying from Frankfurt, no, I mean flying to Frankfurt."

"I see." The muscles in Tarek's face tightened, and his lips became a thin line. "And just who are these people you heard on this plane?"

Mabel shuffled her feet in the sand. "I don't know, it was at night, and they were in another area of the plane. It was dark; I couldn't see them."

Tarek heaved a big sigh. "How many passengers on this plane where you claim you heard this murder plot?"

Mabel's brow furrowed, she shrugged. "I don't know, maybe three hundred or more. I didn't count them."

"So, my dear lady, out of all those people on a plane. A plane going to, or coming from Frankfurt, you heard a plot?" Tarek sighed heavily. "You heard a fantastic plot from people you do not know and did not see. And you think these mysterious persons or persons is on this tour? That, my dear lady, is a fantasy. Please get back on the bus; everyone is waiting."

She was fighting a losing battle. "Okay, but if Elizabeth dies in some kind of freak accident, just remember I told you so."

Tarek rolled his eyes and shepherded Mabel back to the bus. She climbed aboard aware of the inquisitive looks from her fellow tour members. Tarek and Asim spoke rapidly in Arabic. Amr came up from the rear of the bus. The three men continued to talk in Arabic. The tour director kept looking at her and shaking his head, and Asim chuckled. Amr also chuckled, he paused to grin at Mabel on his way back to the rear of the bus. Mabel took her seat next to Violet and crossed her arms, attempting to ignore the curious stares and murmurs from the group.

"I gather you didn't take my advice and told Tarek about your theory," Violet whispered.

"You said don't talk to Elizabeth, and I didn't. I told Tarek. And it's not a theory."

"It is a theory. You don't know if someone pushed Elizabeth or if it was an accident. Anyway, my guess is it didn't go well with Tarek."

"No, it didn't. Now he thinks I'm a senile old woman." Mabel blew out a long breath. "He could be right."

"You're not senile. You just have a vivid imagination. You should write for Hollywood."

"Very funny." No one took her seriously. Not even Violet.

"Forget about Elizabeth and her misadventures."

"Misadventures. That's one way of putting it."

"Anyway, I'm going to text my daughter. The reception here is good. You sure you don't want me to text one of your family?"

"No, don't bother. I'll tell them about our trip when we get home."

Violet shrugged and began texting on her phone.

Mabel thought about her earlier plans to say goodbye to her family. It now seemed like a foolish idea. All the tour buses had an army presence. She'd been as foolish about the dangers to them as she was about the dangers to Elizabeth. Or so everybody said. Maybe they were all in denial. She hoped she was wrong and not them. Tarek kept casting her strange looks. She'd have to let the whole matter drop before everybody thought she was a loon.

"The next stop is the famous Sphinx," Tarek announced into his microphone.

The tour bus and the military convoy parked along with one other bus in the big parking lot.

"It would have been as quick to walk as it was to drive," commented Lucy as they disembarked from the bus.

"True, but we don't want to lose our little army convoy," Janet replied with a laugh. "Besides, it's too hot."

The tour group followed Tarek through a maze of peddler's tents. The men called out and rushed up to them with their wares as the group walked up a short incline to view the Sphinx. The monumental Sphinx, carved from limestone, rose out of the desert sand. Mabel could only imagine what it was like when the ancient Egyptians or their enemies came upon it. The Sphinx, with the body of a lion and the head of a pharaoh, crouched, ready to pounce. There were few tourists about, so Violet and Mabel were able to get close to the colossal monument.

"I wonder why the head of a pharaoh and the body of a lion?" Lucy asked, snapping a picture of her sister Janet with the Sphinx in the background.

Janet jumped down from her perch. "Probably depicting power, is my guess. We should ask Tarek." The girls skirted around Mabel and Violet and headed toward the souvenir stands.

Mabel and Violet made their way back down the rocky path. More and more peddlers appeared, gathering on the trail. The men rushed up to them, holding up glossy picture books of the pyramids and the Sphinx. Violet stopped to buy a book from an old man with bad teeth, who bowed and thanked her in broken English.

Violet smiled back at the man and stuffed the book in her bag. As they continued down the path, young men in long robes ran beside them, holding an array of colourful scarves on their arms. Merchants called out to them, trying to entice the visitors into their tents that displayed colourful robes and dresses and tables piled with tiny glass pyramids, Sphinxes, and scarabs.

Mabel spotted a black onyx cat and dashed over to the tent displaying an assortment of figurines. She returned, clutching her treasure and stowing the cat in her Lug bag. She grinned at Violet. "I probably paid too much, but no one leaves Egypt without a souvenir."

With his camera dangling from his hand, Ronnie hurried to the women. "Are you okay, Mabel? I saw you and our guide having quite a long discussion."

"Oh, everything is fine. I was just asking about the tour." Mabel shifted her bag on her shoulder, not meeting his eyes.

"That's good. I was afraid something had happened," he drawled, putting the lens cap on his camera.

"You mean besides Elizabeth almost falling off the pyramid? You certainly are the hero of the hour. Thank goodness you were there to save her." Violet opened her sun umbrella.

"The less said about that, the better. And I did not push that woman off that pyramid so I could be a hero." Ronnie's accent deepened with emotion.

"No, of course not." Mabel smiled up at the big Texan. But what if he had? She tried to remember if one of the voices she'd heard in the dark on the plane had spoken with an accent. But they were whispering, so she couldn't be sure.

"Isn't that Sphinx magnificent?" Violet held her umbrella to the side to prevent a peddler from coming any closer. His hands held a myriad of trinkets. Ronnie inserted his large frame between the women and the peddlers, and the men backed off. The trio continued down the path, following the sisters.

"Did Y'all know it wasn't Napoleon or his men who knocked off the nose of that little old Sphinx?" Ronnie drawled. "That's a myth. They think some old Muslim leader thought the Sphinx was idolatry and lopped off the nose. He got hung later, although probably not for the nose job." Ronnie laughed at his own joke and took Mabel's arm.

Mabel dismissed all thoughts of Ronnie as a potential killer. He was a gentle giant and wouldn't hurt a fly. She listened as Ronnie expanded on the history of the Sphinx, not caring that she'd heard it all before from Tarek. She was just glad he had stopped talking about her conversation with the tour guide. Mabel resolved to forget about murder plots and enjoy her Egyptian tour. And it was good to have a man walk with them as they navigated through the maze of souvenir seller's tents. She couldn't even glance at a display for fear an anxious vendor would dash out with an armload of colourful merchandise, trying to lure them into their storefront tents.

Ronnie switched to information about the Pyramids of Giza, all of which they already knew. By the time they got to the bus, Mabel was almost ready to tell him about her conversation with Tarek, anything to stop Ronnie's continual travel log.

Chapter Seven

Mabel and Violet strolled up the path to the plateau to view the pyramids below. This time, no vendors ran toward them with their souvenirs. The authorities only allowed them on the side of the plateau by the car park. Across the plateau, the unobstructed view of the desert and the three great pyramids beyond.

They passed Marie and Jean at a kiosk. The couple were bartering with a vendor over the price of a scarab. At another tent, Elizabeth was inspecting a set of three glass pyramids glistening in the sun. She nudged her husband, who kept casting an eye at the tourists lining up for their camel ride.

"I'm going on the camel ride down to the pyramids. Tarek told us these guys are reliable. Are you coming?" Mabel asked.

"No, and I'm surprised you are. You're scared of horses, not to mention cows. These animals are huge, and they look nasty." Violet took her camera from her bag, adjusted the lens, and snapped a picture of the camels lying on the sand.

"These camels must be docile; the owners wouldn't want a tourist to fall off of one. And I'm not going to miss out on a chance of a lifetime. When will I ever get to ride a camel again?"

"Suit yourself. I'm happy taking pictures, and I'll take pictures of you on the camel. I can't wait until you show the pictures to your mother. I so want to be there when you explain how you accidentally went to Africa instead of Europe."

Mabel made a face at her friend. "I'm happy to be your entertainment. It's nice you can get enjoyment from my predicament."

"You wouldn't be in a predicament if you told the truth." The closer they got to the camels, the slower Violet walked. She paused. "Just look at that shaggy beast watching us with its big eyes. He's baring his teeth. Eww, look at its big yellow teeth. You sure you want to ride that thing?"

"Yes, I do, and I didn't lie. I evaded the truth." Mabel, too, slowed her steps. A camel curled its lips, making a low, gurgling, rumbling sound. The sound was like a plugged drain that was about to explode.

"You would make a good politician, anyway, no worries. You know I won't tell on you. I'll back up whatever cockamamie story you cook up." A pungent aroma arose from the animals. Violet stepped back, holding her hand over her nose. "You can leave your stuff with me. If you don't have your bag to hang onto, there will be less chance of you falling off."

Mabel handed Violet her Lug bag. "Thanks for the vote of confidence."

Violet slung the bag over her shoulder. "And please don't fall off. I don't want to have to explain how you fell off a camel in the middle of the Champs-Elysees in Paris."

"Very funny," muttered Mabel, pulling down the ties from her hat and tying them under her chin. She gulped, gathered up her courage, and hurried to join the rest of the tour group, preparing for the trek down the plateau to the pyramids below.

Mabel approached the camels with caution. They did look like very unhappy beasts.

"Dear lady, this one, this one is your camel," a young Arab boy told her. The animal curled its lips, emitting a low rumbling noise.

Mabel reached for the saddle horn as instructed but couldn't get her leg over the saddle. The boy laughed and gave her a sudden boost.

"Oh, oh, oh," Mabel shrieked as she flew up on the saddle, sliding over the camel's back. She grabbed the saddle horn in time to stop herself from landing on the other side of the animal. The big, shaggy camel shifted, snorting its disgust.

The young handler yanked the reins of the camel, yelling out a command in Arabic. The camel, grunting and groaning, protested as it stretched its long neck out and lurched to its front feet. Mabel rocked backward, hanging on for dear life. Then, the camel abruptly rose on its hindquarters, sending her flying forward like a crazy carnival ride out of control. She was sure she was going to fall off.

"I just got a wonderful picture of you mounting the camel," Violet shouted. "I'll take more as you set out."

The caravan of ten tourists set off on the short dusty ride over the desert to the pyramids. Mabel plastered a smile on her face as her swaying camel loped past Angie and Silvio. Silvio looked as uncomfortable as she felt. Ronnie and the California sisters waved. They appeared to be enjoying the camel ride down the side of the plateau.

Mabel opened her mouth to yelled, 'Stop, I want to go back.' But sand flew into her mouth; she spit and clamped her lips shut. Clutching the pommel of the big bulky saddle, she slid from side to side. The saddle appeared to be made from what looked like old carpets. The Arab boy laughed as he ran alongside the camel, which didn't ease Mabel's fears. Did they have to go so fast? She squinted. Sand flew up with each of the big animal's steps, and the camel kept making disturbing moaning sounds, puffing out its cheeks. Strings of spittle flew back at her.

As soon as they arrived at the foot of the Khufu Pyramid, everyone offered their camera or phone to the guides, and the handlers took their pictures.

"See, Lucy, we should have waited," Janet said, putting her phone back in her pocket.

Lucy shrugged. "Whatever, we had an adventure."

"I don't have a camera or a phone," Mabel voiced, wishing Violet could see how brave she was. She'd ridden a camel and hadn't fallen off.

"No problem." Angie pointed to Mabel. "Take the old lady's picture with my camera," she instructed the young Arab boy.

The boy dropped the camel's reins and took Angie's camera, expertly focusing the camera's lens and snapping a picture of Mabel.

Mabel forced a smile. She didn't know if she was more upset with being called an old lady, or that the camel's reins were dangling on the ground.

The camel, free of its handler, jerked its head, lurched and bolted away from the pyramids. Mabel screamed, "Whoa, whoa." But the camel paid no heed.

The tourists who came to view the pyramids were now training their phones and cameras on Mabel. She was bouncing along, swaying from one side of the saddle to the other. Sand flew up into her face as the camel loped up a dune. The young boy ran after them, calling out in Arabic to his camel. The camel ignored him, gathering speed with each step, heading off into the desert.

Mabel took a quick, terrified glance over her shoulder as they left the pyramids behind. Maybe she should jump off, but what if the huge beast stepped on her? She squeezed her legs into the camel's side so that she wouldn't fall off. This only seemed to encourage the animal to go faster.

The pyramids and the tourists were now in the distance. The camel struck out across the desert in its newfound freedom. The sure-footed animal ran up one side of a dune and down another. Mabel continued to scream 'whoa' but to no avail.

"*Awqaf, awqaf,*" hailed an Egyptian man on a camel. Sand churned as the rider came up alongside Mabel's camel. "*Awqaf, awqaf.*" The Arab man reached down and grabbed the camel's reins. But the camel would not be stopped that easily. The man and his camel kept up with Mabel on her wayward camel. He yelled again in his language, lashing out at the camel with a switch. The beast made a horrendous growling sound, then made a surprising U-turn. Mabel slid to the side of the saddle, her cheek brushing against the dusty fur of the camel. Holding tightly to the pommel, she pulled herself back on the saddle. Then, as suddenly as the camel started, it stopped. Mabel careened forward to the camel's long neck and then was jerked abruptly backward. She took deep breaths, inhaled sand, and coughed. The camel let out another horrifying bellow as the man continued to yell, swatting the animal again.

"Oh, please don't beat this creature," Mabel screamed, panting from panic and excitement; she continued, "I'm okay, please don't hurt my camel. I'm fine." She didn't feel fine, her butt hurt, and her legs felt like she had no flesh left on them. And her heart was running a million miles an hour.

The Arab man gave the camel another swat for good measure. Then he smiled widely at Mabel. "She will be a good camel now. A good camel."

Mabel smiled weakly and nodded. If she got off now. How far was it back to the lookout plateau?

"It is good now; we go back now. You are good?" The swarthy man grinned at her.

"Yes, I'm good." Mabel decided her legs would be too weak to walk back, even if she knew how to get off the monster.

The man tugged on the reins of Mabel's camel, and the little caravan trotted back up the sand dunes. A round of applause greeted them as they reached the top of the dune by the pyramid. The boy ran up and took the reins from her saviour. He kept his head down, not looking at Mabel or the man on the camel. The man said something to the boy in Arabic and laughed. The boy looked sheepish.

"Thank you." Mabel smiled at the Egyptian man who had saved her.

The man grinned at Mabel. "She a good camel now."

As he rode off, Mabel realized she had seen him before. He was one of the men who had charged Lucy and Janet extra for pictures on the far side of the Khufu Pyramid.

The boy looked up at Mabel and smiled tentatively. "It is okay?"

Mabel forced a smile; what the heck? If she made a fuss, the boy might lose his job. She didn't want to be responsible for that. "It is okay, a nice ride. Thank you."

The boy, grinning ear to ear in relief, ducked his head.

Ronnie tapped his Stetson in a salute. "Hey, little lady. Y'all are a mighty good camel rider. Y'all will have to visit my ranch sometime and go trail riding."

Mabel gave a lopsided smile as her heartbeat slowed, closer to normal. "Oh, nothing to it for an old farm girl like me," she lied. She had never lived on a farm and felt lucky she didn't end up headfirst into a pile of sand. The boy grinned up at her. She suspected he knew she'd been frightened to death.

"Oh, Mabel, we couldn't believe it when you took off on that camel. Weren't you afraid?" Janet asked.

"Not a bit. It was a great adventure, riding on a camel in the Sahara Desert," she lied. "A story to tell my friends back home." She brightened, and it would be a wonderful story to told Coffee Row. She wondered if anyone would believe her.

The caravan began its trek back to the lookout plateau. Mabel swayed back and forth as her camel lurched from side to side, plodding back over the dunes. She hung on to the saddle pommel, too afraid to dig her heels in the camel's ribs, knowing what would happen if she did. The cantankerous animal complained as it planted each foot in the sand, making ominous sounds. She was sure the big beast blamed her for its beating. Suddenly, the camel turned its head and curled its huge lips; he was going to bite her. She lifted her leg in time to escape a big glob of slobber that dripped out of the camel's mouth. It rubbed the drool on the side of the saddle, just missing Mabel's foot by inches.

Finally, to Mabel's relief, they were back at the plateau. She clutched the saddle horn and endured the rocking and tilting back and forth as the growling camel sunk to the sand. Her legs wobbled as she slid off the saddle. She rubbed her sore bottom and spit. Mabel was sure she had sand in every orifice of her body.

The young boy grinned and bowed as Mabel gave him his tip. "Thank you, thank you," the young lad said in broken English. "You are happy?"

"I am happy," Mabel said, knowing the boy was grateful she hadn't made a complaint about her wild camel ride.

Mabel hobbled over to her friend, waiting for her. Violet opened her bag and took out a package of alcohol wipes. "Did you have fun?" she asked, handing Mabel a handful of wipes. "I got some good shots of you on your camel as you came up the embankment."

Mabel, who usually teased Violet about being a bit of a germaphobe, was only too happy to wipe her hands and scrub off her leg where the drool had sprayed. "It was great. You should have come."

Lucy ran up to Violet and Mabel. "You should have been with us. Mabel was awesome. She took a wild ride on her camel over the sand dunes, leaving the rest of us at the pyramid," she informed Violet. "You are amazing, Mabel, amazing."

Mabel scrubbed her leg with a wipe and looked up at Lucy. She forced a smile, trying to forget how terrified she'd been.

"You took a camel ride off over the desert? Are you okay?" Violet's eyes widened as she offered Mabel another wipe.

"I'm fine." Mabel grabbed the package of wipes from Violet and pulled a handful out, scrubbing her face.

"Your friend is remarkable," Janet said, joining them.

Vowing to herself that she would never again ride anything that wasn't motorized, Mabel said, "It was nothing, just a camel ride."

"You went on a wild camel ride, weren't you afraid?" asked Violet

"Not a bit," Mabel lied.

Grinning, Violet's eyes rolled skyward. "You weren't?"

"No, not at all." Mabel wadded up the wipes and stuck them into her pocket.

Violet looked at Mabel with a mixture of skepticism and admiration. "Even if you were scared just a tiny bit. I think you're very brave."

Smiling, Mabel walked with a spring in her step as she followed Violet to the bus, ready for the next leg of their tour.

Chapter Eight

The little convoy of the bus and army jeeps left the Plateau of Giza behind and drove through the desert on their way to Memphis.

"I wonder if Amr can help."

Violet drew her gaze back from the endless sea of sand that was the Sahara Desert. "Help with what?"

"Someone is going to die unless I do something about it. And the most likely victim is Elizabeth."

"Good lord, Mabel, it seems to me you need to fret over something. If it isn't a conspiracy to murder, it's a terrorist attack."

"You could be a little more supportive. I may not take you on my next trip." Mabel puckered her lips and gave Violet an annoying glance.

Violet chuckled. "Who is taking who?"

"Whatever. Why don't you take anything I say seriously? I was right last time."

"There was a dead body last time."

"Yes, and this time, the victim is still walking around, and I want to prevent another dead body."

Violet sighed. "Okay. And just what do you think our little guard can do?"

Mabel shrugged. She wasn't really upset with Violet. She just wanted Violet to side with her scheme. "I don't really know, but I would like someone to take me seriously. I want to tell Amr about my suspicions."

"He's a private in the Egyptian army. He will be of no help, even if what you suspect is true." Violet held up her hand to forestall Mabel's objections. "And I'm not saying they aren't true."

"How do you know Amr is a private?"

"One stripe."

"Oh, yeah, one stripe. Still, maybe he can report my suspicions to someone higher up."

"You really think our boy scout with a gun has any connections?"

"He might not, but it won't hurt to ask. I'm going to the back of the bus and talk to him. Are you coming?"

Violet stuck her camera in her Lug bag and followed Mabel down the aisle to the back of the bus. The bus swayed as it bounded over the rocky road, and the women grabbed hold of the seatbacks and made their unsteady walk down the aisle to Private Amr.

"Good afternoon, Amr. My name is Mabel Havelock, and this is my friend Violet Ficher." Mabel reached out her hand.

The young Egyptian man looked at Mabel and then at her offered hand. He set aside his rifle and tentatively shook her hand. He then flashed her a toothy smile. "You are Americans."

"Close, we're Canadians from Canada."

"Ah." He nodded slowly, then brightened. "Canada, very cold. Ice."

"Some parts are colder than others." Violet took a seat next to him.

He edged away. Mabel sat on Amr's other side. The young private appeared to be uncomfortable with their closeness. He seemed to shrink into himself, hunching his shoulders. Mabel noted his stiff posture and shifted away from him on the long, black bus seat. The young soldier relaxed.

"But it is cold, yes? I learn about your country in school. Polar." He paused, frowning. Then said triumphantly, "Yes, the big, white polar bears."

"There are polar bears, but not where we live. I'm wondering—"

"Yes, Canada, very cold," he intruded excitedly. "How do your poor animals live? You have snow. Do they eat the snow?"

Mabel rolled her eyes as Violet stifled a giggle.

"No one eats snow. We grow food for our animals and for us. It gets hot where we live in the summer," Violet said.

"You speak very good English. Did you learn this English in school?" the private asked.

"We speak Canadian at home and in English when we travel." Mabel threw Violet an impish grin.

"Mabel, stop that."

"And ice houses, you live in ice houses. I forget the name." Amr tapped his forehead.

"Igloos," supplied Mabel.

The young soldier nodded. "Yes, I remember. Igloos."

"Mabel, stop filling this boy's head with nonsense."

"And Canada, very cold; you are very brave to live in the ice."

"It gets hot where we live, doesn't it?" Violet looked sternly at Mabel.

"Good lord, no. If it got hot, our houses would melt, and all our English books would get wet."

"Mabel, you are not helping. We should go back to our seats."

"Yes, I guess you're right." Mabel turned to the private. "It's been nice chatting with you, Amr."

"Yes, very nice, look, we are at the Memphis. You will like very much.

MABEL UNFURLED HER umbrella; the intense heat was giving her a headache. They'd disembarked from the bus and were walking toward the enormous monument of Rameses II.

"Mabel, you should be ashamed of yourself for making up stories." Violet swept her hair from her face. The wind was blowing her hair this way and that. "Our books will get wet, honestly."

"It's not my fault he had such a poor schoolteacher. We live in igloos. What a load of hooey. Imagine what kind of education that is." The wind tugged at Mabel's umbrella.

"You could have helped educate the boy instead of feeding into the myths that the schoolteacher fed him," Violet said, taking her camera from her Lug bag.

"I'm sorry. You're right. But it's done now." A gust of wind blew sand into Mabel's face. She collapsed the umbrella and tucked it under her arm. "And you were right. Amr would be absolutely no help with my investigation."

"There is no investigation. It's all speculation on your part." Violet took the lens cap off her camera.

They stopped to take in the massive statue, the colossus of Rameses II. The monumental sculpture carved from limestone lay on its back. The legs had been damaged at some point in history. But the damage did not diminish the enormity of its size. They climbed the stairs to look down at the statue. Mabel leaned on the railing as Violet snapped pictures.

"When we go back down, I want you to stand by his head."

"By his head?" Mabel gave Violet a questioning look.

"The head of Rameses II is bigger than your body. I want a perspective."

"Always ready to be your muse."

They descended the stairs, and Mabel posed for Violet. As Mabel stood camera-ready, she noticed Silvio taking pictures of Angie. The girl arched her back and thrust out her chest, and her mouth had a come-hither pout.

Marvin and Elizabeth stood on the balcony above, looking down. Marvin appeared angry about something. She wondered what Elizabeth, the chronic complainer, was on about now. Mabel's thoughts returned to the Khufu Pyramid. Did Marvin push his wife?

"What do the Egyptians think of the way Angie is posing?" Violet asked in a low voice to Mabel.

"They most likely think we're all a little odd. We are women who don't cover our heads, and we wear slacks. I don't think anything we do surprises them."

Tarek rounded up everyone. "Come, dear guests, the next stop is the Alabaster Sphinx."

"Another sphinx," Lucy said. "Before I came to Egypt, I thought there was only one."

"Before you leave Egypt, you will see many smaller Sphinxes, but today, as I promised, you will see the oldest known pyramid. It's called the Step Pyramid. There is another I would like to show you, called the Bent Pyramid or the Red Pyramid. But I'm afraid those are for you to see next time you visit Egypt," Tarek explained. "And after we visit the Temple of Djoser and the Step Pyramid, I think you will be ready for a night of good sleep. Tomorrow, we will fly to Luxor to visit Thebes and the Valley of the Kings. Have you enjoyed your Cairo visit?" Tarck asked. He was rewarded with a round of applause.

IT WAS EARLY MORNING, and the tour bus stopped at the entrance to the Cairo airport. From here, they would take a small plane to Luxor, the next leg of their tour. This time, the young army private was not onboard, and Mabel wished she'd said goodbye. She felt guilty for feeding the poor boy a bunch of malarkey. She would have liked to have a chance to apologize for her misinformation.

A security guard holding a long pole with a mirror checked the undercarriage of the bus. Another guard led a German shepherd dog around the bus. *Is this normal?* Mabel wondered.

She pushed the thoughts of danger from her mind as she boarded the small plane, determined to enjoy the flight to Luxor and be like Violet, who didn't appear to have any concerns.

And Mabel soon forgot her worries as they flew over the desert. The view out the plane window of the Sahara Desert mesmerized her. The brilliant sun shining down on the desert highlighted the endless sand with contrasts of light and shadow. Golden sand flowed across like waves on an ocean, moving mountains of sand that rose from horizon to horizon.

Violet looked out the window over Mabel's shoulder. "The sand rippling over the dunes reminds me of snow blowing across the open prairies in the winter. It's fascinating."

"I'm looking for a caravan of camels," Mabel said. "But so far, I haven't seen any."

"The Sahara is so vast a caravan would be hard to spot. I wonder if they even have caravans?"

Ronnie leaned over the seat from behind. "Tarek told me there are caravans, but we would be lucky to see any."

Mabel grinned. It seemed Ronnie was going to be Tarek's extra voice.

The flight to Luxor was short, but the stewardesses did their best to serve everyone with a flute of champagne and orange juice. They raced up and down the aisle with the libation. Mabel didn't have time to finish her drink as the stewardesses hurried back, retrieving the glasses just before they landed in Luxor.

A new bus and driver awaited them at the airport.

The driver, Lapis, was a short, squat man with a bushy mustache. "Welcome to Thebes, the gateway to the Valley of the Kings," he greeted.

"I thought we were supposed to go to Luxor?" Lucy asked, looking puzzled.

"It is Luxor. Thebes is the old name," Janet replied.

"The hotel in Cairo was a palace, and now we are going to sail down the famous Nile," Mabel babbled excitedly to Violet. "And if the hotel is anything to go by. This boat we are going to sail on down the Nile should be nothing less than luxurious."

The bus drove down a narrow street and parked. "This is as close to the Nile as Lapis can drive us," Tarek informed them. "Across the street, there is a ramp leading to the dockside. We will use this bus tomorrow, but please take everything off the bus. We can't guarantee the safety of anything left behind," Tarek said. "And as you look out the window, you will see our welcoming committee." He laughed.

The street was filling up with vendors. The bearded men in long robes held up familiar trinkets, jostling for position. They yelled and waved scarves and cheap jewelry to get the tour groups' attention.

"We will go to bazaars later, so don't be in a rush to buy your souvenirs. These vendors are harmless, but there are a lot of them. And if you are not used to bartering, it may be best to wait until we visit the bazaars in Edfu," he advised.

"Oh, I think this could be fun. I might get a good deal, I'm good at bartering." Elizabeth rushed off the bus, hurrying to the hawkers. In seconds, they closed in around her. The men yelled their prices in a mixture of Arabic and English, pressing scarves, trinkets, and other small souvenirs into her face.

"Elizabeth, dear, wait for me." Marvin stood, grabbing his backpack off the overhead luggage rack. He turned to Angie. "Angie, please go help her. I'll bring all the carry-on."

"If she would just listen for once." Scowling, Angie sped off the bus.

As everyone climbed out of the bus, more and more merchants poured onto the street from nearby shops, swarming the group. Mabel stood beside Violet, amazed at the aggressive desperation of the sellers. She was glad the big Texan was standing by their side. The bus driver, Lapis, and

Tarek yelled at the men in Arabic. The Arab men glowered and shouted back, but they stopped their mad rush and backed slowly away. Lapis scowled at the hawkers and unloaded the luggage, piling the bags by the bus.

But a group of vendors still surrounded Elizabeth, each pressing scarves and ornaments into her face. The men pushed and shoved each other. Mabel wished young Amr was with them. She was sure he would put a stop to the mad rush of peddlers.

"My jewelry is real. It is not fake," one man in a faded blue robe yelled. "Do not buy my cousin's jewelry. I have the best price."

"No, No." Another man waved a hand full of brilliant scarves. "This is the best quality. Buy my scarves. My wife she make the beautiful scarves."

"My wife cannot buy," Marvin shouted. "She has no money."

Angie tugged Elizabeth's arm, pulling her toward the dock ramp. The peddlers followed her. Tarek intervened again, yelling at them in Arabic. The merchants stopped and turned their attention to the rest of the tour group.

Mabel felt sorry for the men. The tourists were staying away in droves, and those who relied on the tourist trade to make a living were suffering.

"We can't help them all, Mabel," Violet said. "Look straight ahead and walk with me; don't make eye contact. If you do, they will surround you. Keep walking."

Mabel knew Violet was right and walked beside her friend down the ramp to the bank of the river. Despite her regret for the peddlers, her excitement mounted as she thought about the luxury riverboat that awaited them. They were going to cruise down the famous river Nile. An adventure of a lifetime.

Chapter Nine

A flotilla of decrepit old riverboats lined the shore. "Oh, what have we gotten ourselves into?" Mabel's heart sank. She looked at Violet's shocked face. Then, back at the ramshackle boats tied up a few feet from the cement steps.

Violet stood in stunned silence with her hand over her mouth. More of their tour group joined them at the end of the rickety ramp.

Jean gasped and turned to Marie. The couple waved their hands as they talked very fast in French.

Lucy laughed. "It's a joke. Tarek is playing a joke."

Janet's eyes widened, speechless.

"Have Y'all ever seen the like?" Ronnie dropped his bag with a thump on the ramp.

"Lucy has to be right. There is no way a tour company would book us on one of these dilapidated old boats," Silvio said in his hoarse voice. He draped his arm around Angie's shoulder.

Elizabeth and Marvin looked at each other and clasped hands.

Mabel looked down the shoreline, decaying boat after boat, tied along the piers. Which of these derelict boats was theirs? Would the boat float? And for how long? An ashen Violet clasped her hand.

Tarek bounded up. "Do not worry, ladies and gentlemen, this is not our boat," he said cheerfully. "These old riverboats are rafted together. Our boat is on the river, on the other side of these boats. I know the boats look bad, but ours is not like these poor old things, I assure you."

Everyone laughed as if they knew all along the neglected old boat was not theirs.

"Now, please, follow me. We must cross through these boats to get to ours. I think only three," Tarek instructed. "And please watch your step between the boats. The gangplanks are not always level or wide, but it is safe, I assure you."

Violet and Mabel fell in line behind Elizabeth, Marvin, and Angie. "This is like a conga line." Mabel chuckled.

The first boat they entered looked like the boat from the Agatha Christie movie *Death on the Nile*. Shabby old purple velvet couches set on a faded, worn carpet. A table with only three legs lay beside the old dusty purple chair. Behind a big mahogany desk hung a large mirror tarnished with oxidation. Everything was covered in a thin layer of sand. Mabel glanced at Violet, pulling her carry-on. Her friend looked horrified. They continued, astounded at the state of the boat. A small wooden plank was placed between the next boat, and it wobbled as they walked over it.

The next riverboat they passed through wasn't much better. Mabel saw a curved staircase leading to another deck, its carpet old and faded.

"Marvin, how are you managing with our bags and Angie's? Angie can take her bag if you're having trouble over these little footbridges?"

"Angie's bag?"

"Marvin, where is my bag?" Angie asked, pausing in the middle of the old dusty lobby. The conga line stopped, and Mabel dropped her lopsided luggage.

Marvin, who had his backpack slung over his back and pulling two bags, looked apologetic. "Oh, sorry, Angie. I forgot it in the excitement when those men surrounded you and Elizabeth."

"Marvin, you, numbskull, go get it for her. Can't you do anything right?"

"All will be well, Mrs. Tuttle, please, do not worry. The porters will bring the small bag with the luggage," Tarek assured her.

"No, I don't trust them. I'm not having them handle Angie's bag. She has her valuable jewelry and her medications in that bag. Marvin, stop gaping like a dead fish. Go get her bag and do it now."

Tarek gave Marvin a sympathetic smile, then continued across the plank to the next boat.

"Would you please, Marvin?" Angie asked. "Elizabeth can take her bag, and I'll pull yours."

"Yes, yes, of course, sorry about this," apologized Marvin, handing Elizabeth and Angie the luggage; he squeezed past Mabel and Violet. "Excuse me," he said, ducking around the California sisters and returning to the dusty old boat they had just come through.

"That man is the most browbeaten man I have ever seen. His picture must be under 'henpecked' in the dictionary," Janet said to her sister.

They passed through the last dusty derelict and arrived at their boat. As Mabel stepped onboard the vessel, a steward, wearing a brilliant white uniform, offered her a hot damp towel.

Mabel and Violet eagerly accepted the towels, wiping their hands.

"Welcome aboard *The Star*," the big man in uniform said proudly. "This will be your floating palace on your journey down the Nile." He offered each member of the tour group a glass of champagne. "My name is Ahmed Hakimi, the Chief Purser. If you have any concerns, please come to me." His English was slightly accented.

Mabel looked around at the old-fashioned lobby. It was a mixture of the Victorian era and the 1920s. An old mahogany desk, high-back couches and chairs upholstered in red velvet. A black wrought iron circular staircase that led to the decks above divided the lobby. The boat looked very similar to the ones they had passed through, except this riverboat was clean. She hoped it was sea or river-worthy.

She expected Elizabeth to complain, but the woman seemed elated. She was toasting with champagne, clinking glasses with Angie. "Isn't this quaint? I love it. How else would you want to sail down the Nile but in a lovely old riverboat? It reminds me of that old movie, *Death on the Nile*." She clinked glasses with Violet and Mabel.

Mabel looked at Violet. She didn't think Violet was elated. And this was not how she pictured floating down the

Nile. But what could they do? They were here; they had to make the best of it. If Elizabeth could, they could too.

"But I'm pooped. I've had a long day," Elizabeth drained her glass and set it on a tall side table by the staircase. She hurried over to the desk. "Elizabeth and Marvin Tuttle, I'll sign in," she told the concierge, then turned to her cousin. "Sign in, Angie, and be a dear and bring Marvin's carry-on up these stairs. Marvin can bring yours when he comes."

"Pooped?" Tarek's English was impeccable, but some idioms were lost on him.

"Tired," supplied Janet.

"There is an orientation with drinks and snacks in the bar right after everyone has checked in. Perhaps you will still have enough time to nap before supper," Tarek suggested.

"Yes, fine, no problem. I'll be right as rain as soon as I freshen up. Come on, Angie, let's have a look at our cabins."

"Rain?" Tarek shrugged his shoulders and went over to confer with an official-looking man with three stars on his khaki uniform. The officer with the handlebar mustache clicked his heels and reached out his hand to shake Tarek's.

Angie pouted, then flashed a smile at Silvio. "I'll meet you for drinks in the bar." She followed Elizabeth up the winding staircase.

"I'll be waiting for you," Silvio replied in his strange, raspy voice, pulling his case over to the desk to register.

Mabel and Violet stood in line and signed in. They were each given a big brass key. Mabel grinned. "We won't lose these keys."

"Madam, we ask all of our guests to return the keys when they leave the ship for the shore excursions. This way, we know if everyone has returned." The concierge gave them a big, wide smile.

Mabel followed Violet up the stairs, her bag banged against her leg on every step. They ascended to a small landing.

"One more flight," Violet encouraged.

Mabel puffed. "I sure don't envy the porters if this is how they bring up our luggage."

"This is our deck." Violet climbed the last step and set her luggage down beside her.

The landing had the same faded settees as on the main deck, but smaller. To the right was a corridor leading to the cabins. In front of them, across an old, faded rug, was another set of stairs. Mabel assumed the stairs led up to the sundeck. To the left of them was the bar. The big glass doors stood open.

"Welcome, welcome. I have refreshments, lovely ladies, please, to come in." A portly Egyptian man made a flourish with his arm, inviting them into the bar. "My name is Rabbie, which means flame, but I promise not to burn." His small goatee bounced as he laughed.

Mabel dumped her luggage and rubbed her leg. She needed to find somewhere to buy another bag. She stepped through the door into the lounge and paused to take in the decor. A big mahogany bar stretched along the back wall of the room. Behind the bar, an equally long mirror reflected the various types and brands of liquor bottles. Leather-lined chairs with brass finishing ran the length of the bar. To the right of the bar was a small raised stage. Crescent-shaped couches in the middle of the room and around the outside walls with small mahogany tables in between. It was like stepping back in time. But as Elizabeth said, this was part of the charm, cruising down the Nile in an old riverboat. That was if it didn't sink.

Violet accepted a tall glass of champagne, tentatively taking a sip. "We're going to get drunk," she whispered to Mabel.

"Hey, we're on vacation. We won't get drunk on two glasses of champagne." Mabel collapsed on one of the plush couches. She sunk onto the soft cushions; her feet didn't touch the floor.

Violet gestured with her hand, encompassing the bar. "Have you ever seen decor like this before? I wonder how old this boat is?"

"It's okay. We are here now," Mabel said.

"I still can't believe what we've landed ourselves in?" Violet took a big drink of champagne.

"Please stop worrying. This is just fine; embrace the adventure. It's like Elizabeth said. Cruising down the Nile in a riverboat. It's perfect."

Rabbie placed paper coasters on the small table in front of them. "You like? It is the old-world charm, yes?"

Violet gave the bartender a weak smile. "Oh, yes, very old-world."

"And very charming," Mabel added.

They sipped their drink and watched the rest of their tour group enter. Rabbie greeted each group member warmly and offered them all a glass of champagne. Mabel made room for Janet and Lucy, the sisters, to sit beside them.

Lucy hefted her big, brass room key. "I won't be losing this anytime soon." She giggled. "This boat is right out of the twenties or something. I keep expecting Hercule Poirot to pop out any moment with a magnifying glass in his hand."

Janet laughed. "I think you have him mixed up with Sherlock Holmes."

Mabel was relieved when Violet giggled too.

Ronnie lifted his glass. "To our cruise down the Nile." He leaned against the bar, setting his Stetson on a barstool. "I sure do hope this old tub floats."

The group laughed, returning his salute.

Rabbie frowned at Ronnie as he offered a flute of champagne to the French couple.

Jean and Marie accepted the glasses of champagne, smiled, tasted their champagne, grimaced, and then smiled politely back at the bartender.

"I'm here. I'm finally here. I have no luggage, just this little black bag. But I'm here." A woman with a loud, husky voice announced. She dumped her bag in the doorway. Tarek and a tall, handsome man stepped around the bag.

Rabbie rushed over to the newcomers, offering them each a glass of champagne.

Tarek took center stage and made the introductions. "This lovely lady is Carrie Larush, and this gentleman is Neville Hawthorne. These wonderful people complete our little family."

The woman with a big, flowing, bright red and gold kaftan teetered on platform shoes; she blew kisses at everyone. Her big red-framed glasses made her eyes look enormous. From under her pashmina, her long red hair tumbled down her shoulders.

"Her hair is as red as yours, Violet," commented Lucy.

"It's most likely dyed," Violet replied, tucking a strand of loose hair behind her ear.

Mabel grinned. Violet's hair also had help from a bottle.

"My dear, dear, peoples," slurred Carrie in a husky southern drawl. "I've, I've, had the worsted flight, the worsted of the worsted." She breathed heavily. "The transportation was the worst." The woman wobbled slightly and regained her balance. "And y'all believe it, I have no luggage. Aba, abasolot," She giggled and tried again, "Absoolootely, not a speck of luggage. Can you imagine no luggage?" She waltzed over to the bar in a meandering line and set her empty glass down, picking up another glass of champagne off the tray.

"Is that a real accent?" Lucy asked. "She sounds nothing like Ronnie."

"That's probably because the woman is as drunk as a hooty owl." Janet took a sip of champagne.

"Or a skunk." Giggled Lucy.

"What do you think?" Mabel asked Violet.

"Hmm," Violet replied.

Mabel arched an eyebrow. Violet was looking over her glass at Neville, the newcomer chatting to Tarek.

Carrie swanned around the lounge, her colourful kaftan billowing out around her. Returning to Tarek's side, she placed a hand on his arm. "I don't want you to think I blame you, my dear man."

"Blame me?" Tarek pulled his arm from her grasp.

"I know it is not your fault, my transplantations." Carrie took a drink from her glass. "My transportation." She grinned triumphantly. "My transportation arrangements were so mixed up." Carrie turned and tried to drape her arm around Tarek's shoulder. She missed and staggered into Neville Hawthorne.

Neville backed away. "My dear lady."

"I know it'ss the fault of my incomplete travel agent." Carrie righted herself and pushed her glasses up on her nose. She giggled with a deep, husky laugh. "My incompetent travel agent, who will get a piece of my mind when I get back home. I want my luggage," she said to the room in general. "What else could go wrong, I ask you? But don't worry yourself, and I will not let these setbacks spoil my Egyptian holiday, I assure you." She brightened and held up her glass of champagne, and did another little twirl. Spinning into the tour director, who put out a hand to steady her.

She downed her champagne and handed the empty glass to Tarek. "Do you mind darling? I have had a dreadful day."

Tarek looked taken aback at her endearment.

"I'm going to my cabin. I need to freshen up," Carrie said, leaning into his face.

The tour director backed away, looking agitated. "Of course, you may, madam," he said. "But you haven't meant everyone yet."

"Oh, sweetie." Carrie held on to Tarek's arm and breathed into his face. "By the time this cruise is done, everyone will know me very well, until later, y'all." She patted his cheek and did another twirl, grabbed her black carry-on, and teetered out the door and down the corridor.

Tarek seemed to breathe a sigh of relief. He smiled gamely and said, "Mr. Hawthorne, let me introduce our little family." Each group member raised a glass as Tarek called out their names.

The newcomer wore a navy sports jacket and white pants and made a little bow. "I'm so happy to be here on this lovely quaint riverboat," Neville said, smiling. "I'm looking forward to meeting all of you individually as we cruise down the Nile, enjoying the ancient sights of Egypt." His English accent left no doubt where his homeland was. He was a tall, lean man with a narrow face and a pencil mustache. His dark brown hair had little streaks of white at his temples.

"The only thing he is missing is a silk cravat," Mabel whispered to Violet.

"I think he is very dashing," Violet replied. Her eyes sparkled as she looked across the room at Neville.

Mabel looked from Violet to Neville. The Englishman was returning Violet's smile.

Angie entered, looking flustered. "Elizabeth and the room steward disagreed. I refereed," she apologized. "Elizabeth can be a bit forceful."

Mabel exchanged a look with Violet. "A bit?"

"Shush," Violet cautioned.

With a flirtatious smile, Silvio hurried over to greet Angie, taking her a glass of champagne. They sat down on a couch by themselves; Silvio snuggled up to Angie. Looking into her eyes, he lifted his glass. "To the most beautiful woman in Egypt."

Angie giggled. "To the most handsome man." They toasted each other with their champagne glasses.

Mabel rolled her eyes.

"A shipboard romance, no less," Violet whispered.

"Get a room," Lucy teased, and Janet giggled.

Elizabeth and Marvin entered the lounge, bickering as to who made who late.

In the next hour, the tour group got to know each other better. Cairo had been so busy they hardly had time to exchange pleasantries. The California girls were friendly; Lucy was the outgoing sister, but Mabel found that Janet had a quiet wit. Jean and Marie were world travellers, soft-spoken with a lilting French accent. Elizabeth and Marvin, who had arrived late, sat on barstools and drank their champagne, neither talking to the other. Ronnie removed his hat from the nearby barstool, striking up a conversation with Neville.

Tarek took to the floor in the centre of the room and explained the riverboat. "There are four decks. The dining room is on the bottom deck below the lobby. Besides the lobby on the second deck, there are cabins. But all of our little family is quartered on this deck." He smiled at his group. "And as you already know, the lounge and bar are on this deck too. The stairs just outside of the lounge lead to the top deck, the sundeck, and the open bar and pool." He then explained the times of their meals.

"And tomorrow, my friends, we are going to start the day with a visit to the Valley of the Kings." Tarek lifted a glass of what looked like orange juice in a toast. "To your Egyptian adventure."

They all lifted their glasses just as twenty Japanese tourists entered the bar with their tour guide. The Japanese bowed politely, and Tarek's group awkwardly bowed in return.

Chapter Ten

Mabel unlocked their stateroom door and lugged her bag into the cabin. She flinched as the bag bumped against her leg. "I'm so going to buy a new bag first chance I—" Mabel stopped mid-sentence. She looked around the tiny cabin. Two twin beds covered with white chenille bedspreads occupied most of the room. A huge wooden wardrobe and a very old dresser set across from the beds, leaving just enough space to walk. Old-fashioned heavy floral curtains hung across the window. Jammed up against the wall was a small wooden chair with a padded floral seat in the same faded design as the curtains. A little lamp with a yellowed lampshade sat on the night table between the twin beds.

"Move, Mabel, it appears to be a little cramped in here," Violet urged, pushing her way through the doorway.

"You think?" Mabel edged farther into the room, yanking her bag, she stood crammed between a bed and the dresser.

Violet closed the door and stood stock-still. "Oh, my goodness."

Mabel looked over her shoulder at Violet. "This is the stateroom? Did you do any research about this boat? This is our accommodation? Really?"

Violet picked up her hand luggage and placed it on a bed. "To be honest, I was more concerned with what we would see. I'm as surprised as you," Violet said as she sunk onto the bed. "I'm sorry. I had no idea. This is dreadful. I feel just awful. It's my fault. I made all the arrangements. I looked at the cabins and the riverboat online, and everything looked marvellous."

"We're here now, and we'll make the best of it." Mabel smiled weakly and set her bag on her bed. "At least the cabin looks clean." Her voice trailed off.

Violet fingered the chenille bedspread. "I guess, and we only sleep here," she said bleakly.

Violet looked so dejected Mabel felt guilty for complaining. "Hey, cheer up, no worries. We came to see the sights. If we wanted the same kind of hotel accommodations as home, we should have stayed there. This is an adventure."

"You can't even swing a cat in here." Violet looked around the small room, her lips turned down.

"And we will have to go outside to change our minds," Mabel joked, hoping to make her friend laugh.

Violet plucked at the chenille spread on her bed. "My grandmother had bedspreads like these."

Mabel squished past the beds to inspect the bathroom. The toilet was squeezed in between the shower and the sink. She backed out of the room and gave Violet a wan smile. "It's clean," she said, crowding past her to the other side of the room and opening the curtain. Sunlight streamed in.

Violet ventured into the bathroom, she came out, dolefully shaking her head and holding a small piece of tile in her hand. She dropped it into the wastebasket. "It's from the shower," she said, discouraged.

"As long as no more fall off, we will be fine." Mabel smiled, feigning cheerfulness.

"I'm really sorry. If this is a stateroom, I hate to think what the economy is."

"Like I said, we're here, and there's nothing we can do about it. We will just have to be coordinated, that's all." Mabel sat on the bed near the window. "I'll take this bed if that's okay with you?"

"Yes, I don't care," Violet said downheartedly.

"What do you think about the newest members of the group?" Mabel asked, trying to get Violet's mind off the closet, which would be their room for the duration of the Nile cruise. "That Carrie woman is quite a character."

Violet opened her bag and took out a plastic green and white cylinder. She pulled out a disinfectant wipe and wiped down the handles on the closet.

Mabel grinned, the cabin looked clean, but it wasn't Violet clean.

"The woman is a tad dramatic. And she was also a tad drunk. But I do think her kaftan is a good thing to wear in this country. The kaftan covers your body and keeps you cool. And, of course, she dyes her hair. That red can't be real." Violet stood next to the dresser. Taking a fresh wipe from the tube, she wiped it off.

Mabel chuckled; opening her bag, she took out her toiletries. "Not just a tad. The woman was drunk. She could barely stand." Mabel skirted around Violet and took her toiletry bag to the bathroom. There was one tiny glass shelf. There wouldn't be enough room for the little bag. She debated if she should leave her toothbrush. Deciding against it, she carried the bag back to her bed, uncertain what to do with it.

"Airlines sometimes ply you with too many alcoholic beverages. We mustn't judge someone with just one meeting. We really can't talk. We were served two glasses of champagne back to back." Violet arched an eyebrow and smiled. "But Neville. Now that man is yummy." She took another new wipe and lifted the lamp on the night table, wiping the surface thoroughly.

Mabel put her toiletry bag on the dresser. "Speaking of two glasses of champagne, you've taken quite a fancy to Neville. I told you not to drink that champagne."

"No, you didn't, and you drank yours too. I just think Neville is suave. That's all I'm saying." Violet went into the bathroom.

"You said yummy, that means you're interested. I bet it's because of his English accent and that pencil mustache he's sporting. Does he remind you of that old actor David Niven?" Mabel was happy to divert her friend's attention from their dismal cabin.

"Maybe." Violet appeared, holding up another piece of bathroom tile in her hand. "Good lord, look," she said, chucking it into the garbage can. She scowled and stomped back to the bathroom.

Mabel heard the water running; she suspected Violet was washing out the sink. Trying to divert her friend from the state of the bathroom, she said, "I think he is deliberately channelling David Niven."

"Whatever," Violet called from the bathroom and shut the door.

There was a knock on their door. Mabel opened it to find the porter with their luggage. The small man struggled to fit the bags through the door. Mabel moved away, making room for the bags. The porter pushed in one bag, bumping Mabel's shin. She backed up and stood inside the open closet while the porter dragged the other bag into the room; the little man looked exhausted.

Mabel dug in her pocket for some Egyptian pounds. She leaned out of the closet, stretched her arm, and gave the man his tip. He grinned, said thank you in broken English, and quickly left, leaving the two bags inside the open door.

"Did I hear the porter delivering our luggage?" Violet called from the bathroom. "Oh, for goodness' sake, this door is stuck. Maybe you can open it from the outside."

"The door is jammed shut with the bags."

"What? Seriously?" Violet rapped on the bathroom door.

"Knocking on the door won't help." Mabel scrambled out of the closet and crawled over the bags, landing on Violet's bed. "Hold your horses. I have to move these bags." She slid off the bed and pulled both bags one by one to the foot of the beds.

Violet emerged from the bathroom, the cylinder of disinfectant wipes in her hand. She surveyed the cabin. "Even if we get our clothes into the closet. Where do we put our suitcases?"

MABEL STEPPED OUT OF the shower with a towel wrapped around her, and a piece of tile in her hand. She dropped the tile in the garbage can and trotted out into the tiny room. Violet, sitting on her bed, wore a flowing green sundress with tiny darker green flowers embroidered on the bodice. She was unfolding a white pashmina with little sequins. "You look lovely," Mabel complimented. She looked at her blue tunic and white Capris, which she had laid on the bed. "I hope I'm not underdressed."

"Nonsense, it's Africa, and it's hot, wear what you feel comfortable in. You'll look fine."

Chapter Eleven

Mabel and Violet descended the stairs to the dining room, where the 1920s decor theme continued. Low free-hanging lamps lit the dark wood-paneled dining room. Tables covered in white linen were spaced evenly down the long room, each displaying a centrepiece of red and white lotus blossoms. Brown leather booths lined two of the walls, and white net curtains covered the small portholes. Mabel wondered how old the riverboat was and if it would even stay afloat when the cruise started. Were there still crocodiles in the Nile? She had not seen a life raft.

A buffet of hot and cold food tables lined the front wall. Men dressed in white and wearing tall chef hats stood behind the tables, ready to serve.

Violet and Mabel joined the members of their group at a table set for eight. Each table had candles lit and napkins folded in the shape of swans at each place setting. Waiters dressed in black slacks with crisp white shirts and black bow ties stood with welcoming smiles on their faces. The riverboat was old, but the staff of *The Star* certainly catered to the tour group.

Mabel felt underdressed as she looked around the dining room. All the women were wearing dresses. She tugged at her blue tunic, wishing she had brought a dress to wear. But at least she packed her reversible skirt. She would wear it the following evening.

"Ah, good evening, ladies," Marvin greeted as Mabel and Violet sat down.

Mabel sat beside Ronnie. The big Texan looked smart in his white dress shirt and a black Bolo tie with a silver clasp in the design of an eagle. Also at the table were the sisters, Janet and Lucy, both wearing bright flowery sundresses. Across from them sat Elizabeth and Marvin. Elizabeth looked attractive in her long burgundy dress. Marvin wore a golf shirt and khaki slacks. Mabel thought Marvin looked younger than his wife.

In a booth opposite the table sat Silvio and Angie, with Jean and Marie. Silvio looked to be giving Angie his full attention. His gravelly voice could be heard complimenting her hair and her dress. Angie was giggling, touching his arm, tilting her head, and laughing up at him. Both were ignoring the French couple.

The Japanese tour group occupied the long tables nearest to the buffet. Mabel saw that another group of tourists had also come onboard. The newcomers spoke German. They were laughing and toasting each other with flutes of champagne. Mabel took a quick headcount: forty-five passengers on this riverboat. *The Star* was at least half empty.

At the far end of the dining room, Tarek sat in a booth with the khaki-uniformed man from the lobby. The small man had a handlebar mustache and a thick thatch of black hair combed forward. Was the uniformed man another guard?

"Who do you think the officer is, having dinner with Tarek?" asked Lucy. "He looks kind of cute with his handle-bar mustache."

"Cute? Really?" Janet raised her eyebrows and looked across the room at the officer.

"The man is a police officer. I forget what his name is. Tarek introduced him when I came down to the dining room," Ronnie supplied. "I suspect he is acting as a guard of some sort."

"He looks more like an old fashion villain in a melodrama. I can just see him twirling his mustache and demanding the rent." Elizabeth laughed.

"Or a keystone cop from the old silent movies," Marvin quipped.

"Darling, you're not old enough for silent movies." Elizabeth placed her hand on his and smiled gently at him.

"I've seen clips on TV, dear." Marvin replied as he signalled for a waiter. "Let's order a bottle of wine."

"Good evening, everyone." Neville appeared at the bottom of the stairs, dressed in a white dinner jacket, bow tie, and black slacks. He sauntered over and pulled out a chair beside Violet. "Look over at the buffet tables. I'm just in time, and it appears they are about to serve. I must say this boat is a bit of a tub. And my cabin is, hum, how shall I put it? It is quaint, to say the least. But the food looks amazing. I hope it tastes as good as it looks."

The conversation paused while they each perused the wine list, then ordered.

"We could hardly believe it when we stepped on this crate. You should see our cabin; my closet at home is bigger," Lucy said.

"And the bathroom." Janet laughed. "I don't know what yours are like. But my shower at home is bigger than the whole bathroom."

"Ah, well," Ronnie drawled. "Y'all are here now, and we all came for the sights."

"You are absolutely right, Ronnie," Elizabeth chimed in. "I think this boat is charming."

Mabel smiled. Elizabeth was softening. Perhaps this trip with her might not be such an ordeal after all.

"Neville, where is Carrie?" asked Marvin. "I heard she is a bit of a character."

"I don't know, old chap. We are not travelling together, which I am quite thankful for. I may be speaking out of turn here, but that woman was drunk when she came onboard. No wonder she lost her luggage."

"You think? She was plastered." Lucy laughed.

The conversation paused again as the waiters hovered around the table, pouring the wine.

"Carrie is quite the character. I gather she's from the south. I had a chat with her before we came down, and she told me she was feeling too tired to join us. I told you that, Marvin, if you would listen for a change." Elizabeth smiled sweetly at Neville. "Or perhaps, as Neville pointed out, the woman is just too drunk or hungover to come down."

"What, dear?" Marvin smiled absently, brushing his tousled brown hair off his forehead. He seemed preoccupied with what was going on in the booth where Silvio and Angie sat.

"Marvin, would you please pay attention to this table?" Elizabeth's eyes narrowed, and she jerked on his arm.

"Sorry, dear," he said. He picked up his wineglass. "A toast to our Egyptian adventure."

Mabel wondered again if the man had a thing for Angie.

The maître d' announced dinner was ready. Mabel suppressed a small grin as she stood in line with a plate in her hand. She didn't feel underdressed anymore. You could dress up to the nines for fancy dining. But on this cruise. You dined smorgasbord style. Her tummy rumbled as she passed along in front of the hot and cold buffet tables. Mabel couldn't put a name to the dishes displayed, but the aromas were enticing. One of the meat dishes with colourful peppers and a sauce appeared to be beef. Or maybe it was camel.

"Try it. You might like it," encouraged Violet.

Mabel did, she couldn't tell what the meat was, but it tasted delicious.

As dinner progressed, Mabel noticed her friend, Violet, hanging on to every word Neville said and laughing at all his jokes. Jokes that Mabel thought were corny.

DINNER OVER, EVERYONE trooped up to the sundeck. At the stern of the riverboat, under a large canopy, groups of small wooden tables were arranged in a semi-circle in front of the bar. Rows of tiny white lights lit the area, and music from hidden speakers played softly.

Mabel and Violet strolled along the deck. Down from the seating area, yellow lounge chairs with folded umbrellas lined both sides of the deck. The women paused to look over the railing at the glistening Nile below. The bright stars sparkled, and the moon shone down, reflecting on the river. A splash of an unseen fish disturbed the water. By mutual agreement, they continued their stroll. At the prow of the boat was a small swimming pool.

"It looked bigger in the pictures," Violet said glumly as they paused at the pool.

"It's no biggie. We didn't come here to swim. We came to explore Egypt. And think of the things we have already seen. Absolutely fantastic. And we're not done yet. So much more to see."

Violet perked up. "Yes, imagine tomorrow we will be in the Valley of the Kings."

But Mabel did agree with Violet. The boat didn't meet up to her expectations either, but she didn't want Violet to feel bad for booking the tour. They paused at the bow. Riverboats tied to each other stretched out along the shoreline. Each old boat was rocking gently with the current of the river.

Silvio and Angie walked arm and arm down the deck. They paused at the poolside and removed their shoes, dangling their feet in the water. Silvio raised his eyebrow, giving Mabel and Violet a hard look.

"I feel like a third wheel. Let's have a nightcap," Violet suggested.

"Sure, I guess moonlight is for the young and romantic." Mabel followed Violet back to the bar deck.

Violet smiled at Neville as he held out a chair for her. Mabel shrugged and sat across from them.

"May my wife and I join you?" asked Jean from a nearby table.

"Absolutely, please do." Mabel shifted her chair to make room for the couple.

"You must speak French," Jean said. "You are from Canada, and Canada is multilingual, yes?"

"Not where we live, sorry, but I can read both sides of the cereal box," Mabel joked.

"Pardon? I do not understand."

"She means there is French written on one side of the box and English on the other side of the —."

A loud argument between Marvin and Elizabeth interrupted Violet's explanation.

"One of these days, you'll go too far, Elizabeth." Marvin stomped off the deck and down the stairs.

"Finally, the man is sticking up for himself," Jean voiced in approval.

"I'll have another drink, bartender, bourbon straight up," Elizabeth said. "Lucy and Janet come and sit with me. He can just damn well go and sulk. I'm going to enjoy myself."

Jean raised an eyebrow and turned to the waiter, ordering a drink for himself, his quiet wife, and the others at their table.

Neville thanked Jean, and then he turned his attention to Violet. He proceeded to compliment her hair, her dress, and the way she laughed and smiled.

Mabel looked thoughtfully at the handsome man as he swooned over her friend. Violet did look very nice, but

Neville was laying it on a little too thick. And to her disgust, her friend seemed to be eating up the flattery. There was something fishy about this man.

The Japanese tourists came on deck, followed by the German tour group. The noise level of many languages filled the night. The Japanese tour guide ordered drinks for his group. The music level was turned up, and country-western music twanged, vibrating out onto the deck. Two of their group got up to dance, much to the amusement of their friends. Waiters sped from table to table, serving drinks.

The discussion about different cultures and languages had to be yelled across the table between Mabel and the French couple. Violet and Neville got up to stroll down the deck. Mabel arched an eyebrow. Apparently, the moonlight wasn't just for the young.

Carrie, dressed in the same red and gold kaftan, swayed at the top of the stairs. "Hello, one and all," she slurred in a husky drunken southern drawl. Ronnie, on the step below her, caught her just before she teetered backward down the steps.

"My, my, so strong and so handsome." She patted Ronnie's cheek. Swirling her scarf around her head, she teetered off to join the German tour group.

A tall, handsome blond man pulled out a chair for her. "*Guten aben.*" He grinned. "*Mochten sie ein getrank?*"

"I don't have the faintest idea what you are saying, dear man," Carrie drawled, laughing throatily. "I hope it isn't an indecent proposal." She laughed again.

"I said good evening and asked if you would like a drink," explained the blond man.

"A man of my dreams." Carrie laughed.

"Carrie, too tired to come for dinner? Tired, my ass," Ronnie snorted. "Oops, sorry, pardon my French."

"Your French? I believe you miss speak." Jean looked affronted.

"Oh, sorry, Jean, old buddy, no offence. It's something we say back home." Ronnie pulled out a chair and sat beside Mabel.

"I think Carrie has had enough to drink already," Mabel said, watching Carrie order a drink from the waiter.

"I agree with you, little lady. This new member of our family has a drinking problem. She almost fell on top of me."

Mabel decided Ronnie was probably right. But her thoughts weren't on Carrie and her drinking. She wondered about Marvin and his last words when he stormed off the deck. Was Elizabeth in danger? And if she was, would anyone believe her if she said anything? Tarek already thought she was an eccentric old lady.

Chapter Twelve

Early in the morning, Mabel and some of the tour group gathered in the riverboat lobby, waiting for Tarek to appear. Mabel shifted her Lug bag on her shoulder, impatient to be off on the next leg of their tour, the Valley of the Kings.

"Sunblock, check, hat, check, umbrella, check." Violet took inventory. "Mabel, do you have your water bottle?"

"I have my water bottle and my camera, but I forgot something. Don't let the tour leave me behind." Mabel hurried up the stairs, clutching the clunky room key in her hand. "I'm going to need my hat. Where did I leave it? Maybe on the bed," she mumbled to herself.

"Ah, Mabel, is Violet in the lobby?" Neville asked, passing her on the stairs.

"Yes, she is," Mabel replied, rushing past him. She frowned, an uneasy feeling about the English man creeping over her. But before she gave Neville any more thought, she met Janet and Lucy at the top of the stairs, wearing flowery sundresses and sandals. Mabel thought the sandals were a poor choice. They would be tramping around old ruins. The sturdy walking boots that she wore were the best way to explore. She shrugged and sped down the hallway.

Marvin came out of the room next to theirs, locking the door.

"Good morning, Marvin. Are you ready for our new adventure?" Mabel greeted, inserting her key in the lock.

Marvin ignored her and rushed past. Mabel had seen his wife downstairs in the lobby. She bet Elizabeth wouldn't be pleased with his tardiness. Unlocking their cabin door, Mabel realized her hat was on her head. Laughing at her forgetfulness, she hurried after Marvin. "On to the Valley of the Kings," she called out to him. Marvin ignored her greeting.

THE TOUR GROUP, MINUS Carrie, walked back through the dusty, derelict boats to the waiting bus.

"I regret to inform you that our newest member, Miss Carrie Larush, cannot come with us today; the poor woman is ill," Tarek told them as they settled in their bus seats. "It is a great shame she will miss the Valley of the Kings. The ancients called this valley the Gateway to the Afterlife."

As Mabel looked out the bus window, watching the lush valley of the Nile fly by, Violet checked her bag for her camera.

Tarek held the microphone and informed the group about the history of the Valley of the Kings. "There are sixty-three known tombs and maybe more to be discovered. We will visit three of the tombs this day. I cannot tell you which tombs. The authorities decide daily which ones we can explore."

"You make sure we see Tutankhamun's tomb," Elizabeth voiced.

"Madam, I am sorry. I do not make the rules," apologized Tarek.

"This is bogus. We all want to visit Tutankhamun's tomb. See to it," Elizabeth commanded.

"I must tell you, Mrs. Tuttle, there is a very good reason for these rules. Archaeologists from around the world are doing explorations, studying the hieroglyphics—"

"But this is what you are getting paid for," Elizabeth interrupted.

"I assure you, Mrs. Tuttle, that all the tombs you will see are amazing. I guarantee it."

"Tarek is right, dear; you wait and see." Marvin patted her hand. Elizabeth jerked away.

The bus parked in the near-empty parking lot. Tarek led the group to the entrance of the forbidding valley, where the burial chambers were sunk deep into the heart of the red mountains. But first, they had to walk through the valley of the souvenir sellers. Every stall was a mass of colour, scarves, dresses, and robes of every shade and every size. Others had the usual cheap jewelry and trinkets. The vendors called out for them to buy. And men ran beside them, holding out their wares, eager to make a sale.

"Wait until after the tour of the tombs before you start bartering," Tarek cautioned his tour group. "The more time you spend bartering, the less time you have to explore the tombs. And it's Egypt's ancient marvels you have come to explore. Not these modern trinkets."

They passed through the market and then stopped at a small tented building manned by two Egyptian men dressed in official-looking uniforms. "Please, if you have cameras, you must check them here," Tarek informed the group. "Cameras are not allowed in the tombs. You are not allowed to take photos."

The group reluctantly handed their cameras to the attendants and received numbered tickets.

"You could have told us this before we got off the bus," Elizabeth complained. "Now we have to trust these people with our very expensive cameras. We better get them back and undamaged, or I will sue you and your tour company."

Mabel noticed Angie snickering. The girl elbowed Silvio and opened her tote bag. He took a peek and grinned back at her.

"Don't get yourself in a lather, Elizabeth. I'm sure our cameras are safe." Marvin put his arm around his wife's shoulder.

She shook him off. "Don't use that disgusting term regarding me." She stomped off, positioning herself beside Angie and Silvio.

Tarek ignored the outburst and handed everyone a ticket. "These tickets will allow you to visit three tombs. A sign with the name of the pharaoh is posted at the entrance of each tomb. It will tell you how deep you have to go to the burial chamber. And it will tell you if it is open to the public. Then you decide which tomb you want to see. This visit will be a remarkable experience, and I'm sure you will enjoy it." They followed Tarek down the canyon. "I will not be accompanying you," he said, giving them a time and meeting place.

The group split up; Jean and Marie, and the sisters went off to explore the Tomb of Ramesses I.

Violet and Mabel decided to go down into Ramses III Tomb. Ronnie and Neville accompanied them. Followed by Elizabeth, her husband, Angie, and Silvio. They showed their ticket and proceeded down wooden steps then down a long, well-lit wooden ramp. Elaborate hieroglyphics painted on the walls and pillars told of the accomplishments of the pharaoh. Others depicted the living souls of the pharaoh's journey to the afterlife. Although some hieroglyphics were damaged, others were in brilliant colours as bright as the day the craftsmen painted them. Some were life-size and larger. Multiple chambers branched off, covered with pillars and sculptures depicting the king and their deities. The deeper they went into the bowels of the earth, the more awe-inspiring it was.

Mabel noticed even Elizabeth was quiet. And it appeared she had forgiven Marvin. She held on to his arm as they descended the winding corridor. When they entered the burial chamber, Mabel heard a click of a camera. Angie was surreptitiously snapping pictures.

"Madam, the camera, please." A tall young Egyptian man dressed in full Egyptian attire held out his hand.

"What? Oh, sorry, I forgot." Angie attempted to place the camera back in her tote bag.

"No, sorry, madam. This is not allowed," the man said in perfect English, taking the camera from her hand.

"You can't do that," Angie yelled. "You can't steal my camera."

The Japanese tourists murmured to each other in confusion. The German tour group looked with dismay as the confrontation between Angie and the young man continued.

Mabel watched with interest. Silvio looked away as if studying the hieroglyphics covering the walls. Elizabeth and Marvin stood silently by. Violet and Neville looked shocked. Ronnie ignored it all and continued to look around the elaborately decorated burial chamber.

"I am not stealing your camera. I am confiscating the memory card." The tall Egyptian man deftly opened the camera and took out the card.

"You can't do that. I have all my pictures of this trip on it. Give my camera back right now. Immediately," Angie stormed.

"Madam, here is your camera. You are lucky; I am in a good mood. I could give you a fine."

"But my pictures," Angie wailed.

The young man shrugged and walked away.

"Oh, Angie, I'm sorry. We have pictures of everything we've seen so far, and we'll share them with you." Marvin put his arm around her as they turned to walk back to the ramp.

"It's your own fault for bringing your camera," Elizabeth scolded. "We left ours just like we were told, but we'll share." She turned to her husband. "Take my arm, Marvin, this ramp is steep. And look how smooth the wood is on this ramp. Someone could fall. Why these people don't have an elevator in these tombs is beyond me?"

"Because this here is not Disneyland; this is an ancient tomb of an Egyptian pharaoh," Ronnie snapped, his usual good humour deserting him.

Elizabeth glared at Ronnie.

Marvin looked from Angie to his wife. It appeared to Mabel that he was more interested in Angie's plight than his wife's fear of falling.

"Oh, for God's sake, Marvin, get over here," commanded Elizabeth. "Angie's got pretty boy here to look out for her."

Angie scowled at her cousin, and muttering her displeasure at losing her memory card, she took Silvio's arm, who was smirking at Elizabeth.

Neville was in front, leading the group with Violet by his side. They made their way back up the ramp. Mabel noticed Marvin looking longingly over his shoulder at Angie. Angie smiled at him as she passed by with Silvio. Silvio grinned and whispered in her ear, she giggled. Marvin sighed and took his wife's arm.

"It's people like them who give tourists a bad name," Ronnie drawled, putting his hand under Mabel's elbow. They fell in line behind Elizabeth and Marvin, dawdling and admiring the ancient art on the walls.

The lights dimmed, flickered, then went out. The underground passageway went pitch black. Mabel stood stock still. It was so eerie. This would have been what it was like when the Egyptologists first explored the pharaoh's tomb. At first, there were only murmurs, and then someone screamed. People pushed and shoved, yelling in several languages. The crowd surged forward, bumping Mabel and pressing her against the wooden railing. It held firm.

A cry rang out as someone fell backward, tumbling down. Ronnie grabbed the person and stopped their fall. "Oh, my God, Marvin, where are you?" the woman screamed.

The lights came back on. Ronnie stood with Elizabeth draped in his arms. She pulled herself away from him and screamed out, "Marvin, you are worse than nothing."

Marvin elbowed his way down to her as people made a mad dash, pushing their way up the ramp. Mabel and Ronnie stepped closer to the railing, letting the crowd go past.

"Thank you, Ronnie, again you've come to my wife's rescue." Marvin put his arm around Elizabeth.

She shook off his attempt to comfort her and sneered. "Yes, thanks to Ronnie, but no thanks to you. I could've been killed."

"Oh, I doubt you would have been hurt, not with the crush of people on this ramp. But I'm glad to be of help, ma'am. We all should go. These lights might go out again." Ronnie took Mabel's arm.

The people were over their fright, and everyone continued to walk up the ramp but at a slower pace.

Mabel listened as Marvin and Elisabeth bickered all the way to the surface.

Ronnie and Neville stopped to read the plaque about Ramses III. Violet's long stride left them and the group behind.

Mabel puffed, racing up to her friend. "Violet, did you see that?"

"I did. It's a dream come true, all those beautiful hieroglyphics. We literally stepped back into ancient

Egyptian history. Now, we visit Tutankhamun's tomb, where his mummy is still in the burial chamber. Are we privileged or what?" Violet wiped her hands with an antibacterial wipe.

"I don't mean that. I mean Elizabeth."

"Elizabeth? You can't be serious. You're not going to go on about that again. We've just been down to the most wonderful—"

"Just because I'm worried about Elizabeth, that doesn't mean I don't appreciate what I saw. Let me tell you, I do. It was well worth the climb down. It is amazing."

"Okay, sorry," Violet apologized.

"And I'm overwhelmed to be in the Valley of the Kings," Mabel continued. "The most famous graveyard in the world."

"You do have a way with words."

"But it is. Don't you agree?"

"I guess you're right; I just never thought of it that way."

"So, am I allowed to talk about Elizabeth?"

Violet rolled her eyes. "Really."

Mabel debated whether she should tell Violet that she believed there was another attempt on Elizabeth's life. Of course, maybe the woman was just accident-prone.

Violet gave Mabel a sidelong glance and handed her an antibacterial wipe.

"Honestly, Violet, do you think the ancient Egyptian germs are still virulent?"

"No, but how many tourists have touched those rails? You can thank me later. It is better to be safe than sorry. Look at Carrie. She's sick and missing out on all of this."

"I doubt she's sick, hungover more like." Mabel wiped her hands. "Anyway, you didn't notice that Elizabeth fell backward when the lights went out?"

"I was almost at the top when everything went dark." Violet fished in her pocket for her ticket. They were nearing King Tut's tomb.

Mabel explained the incident as they waited for the others to catch up. Finishing with her theory, Elizabeth was pushed.

"Even if Elizabeth were pushed, she wouldn't have fallen far with all the people climbing up that ramp. You said you fell as well?"

"I didn't fall. Someone bumped me into the railing. I wasn't pushed down the steps."

"Ah-ha, so Elizabeth wasn't pushed. There goes your pet theory."

"Well, maybe, I don't know."

"You must have been very good at hopscotch and leapfrog as a girl."

"Not particularly. Why?"

"You are so good at jumping to conclusions. You have a very bad habit of looking for a mystery where none exists," scolded Violet. "Please, let's just be tourists. No detecting."

"Granted, no one caused the blackout. But someone could have taken advantage of the power outage. That's all I'm saying. And if something happens to that woman, well, I told you so." Mabel handed her ticket to the Egyptian man sitting at the entrance to Tutankhamun's tomb.

MABEL AND RONNIE WALKED up the steep ramp to Queen Hatshepsut's temple. Mabel watched as Neville attentively held the umbrella over Violet's head. It was blistering hot.

"Neville probably just wants the shade," Mabel commented to Ronnie as she opened her umbrella.

The big Texan, wearing his wide-brim Stetson, had a bandana hanging from the back of his hat, protecting his neck. "Y'all a little jealous of your friend?" he drawled.

"No, most certainly not," Mabel denied, shifting her umbrella. She looked up in time to see Violet and Neville pause to admire the statues that lined the long colonnade. Was Ronnie right? Still, something about Neville didn't ring true. And where was he when Elizabeth fell?

Her attention quickly shifted back to the colossal temple built into the side of a mountain by the female Pharaoh, Hatshepsut. It was a mortuary temple dedicated to the sun deity, Amun.

Looking up at the massive edifice, Mabel said, "It's amazing to me that while the ancient Egyptians were building these gigantic temples and pyramids, my ancestors were probably still living in mud huts."

"Yeah, and to think they had a queen, way back then. This society strikes me as kind of macho. And Tarek told us that the next pharaoh tried to obliterate her existence. Just look at the destruction of some of her statues."

Mabel ran her hand over a carved figurine. "Everything built larger than life. I supposed to overwhelm the masses."

Mabel and Ronnie continued to wander through Queen Hatshepsut's temple. Attempting to figure out why the ancient Egyptians concentrated so much on the hereafter and not on the here and now.

THE TEMPLE OF KARNAK, the next stop, was just as impressive. Mabel followed the tour group down the avenue of ram-headed Sphinxes to the temple. Tarek told them the ancient Egyptians believed Karnak to be the place for the Gods. In front of the temple stood a hundred and thirty-seven highly decorated columns, over seventy feet high; they dwarfed her and everyone else. She passed more colossal statues of Ramesses II. She was no bigger than his foot. She wandered off down between a row of columns. Craning her head, she observed the faded hieroglyphics. What did the pictures depict? What story did they tell? The bright, burning sun beat down, so she set out to find shade. Overhead, a bird of prey let out a piercing shriek. Mabel approached a gigantic obelisk and paused to view the hieroglyphics.

"What the hell are you waiting for? The sooner you do it, the better."

Mabel stopped to listen. But the hawk-like bird swooped down, shrieking, masking the voice from the other side of the wall. Mabel crept forward, her shoes crunching on the pebbles. As she sped up and rounded the corner, the flare of a red skirt flashed past a pillar. Was that Carrie? No, it couldn't be. She wasn't on the bus.

Chapter Thirteen

"I'm telling you, I heard a threat," Mabel said, pawing through the wardrobe.

Violet sat on her bed, dressed in a blue and gold dress, sorting through her costume jewelry bag. Her red hair was swept up into a chignon and held in place by faux gold combs. "Okay, you heard a voice say, '*the sooner you do it, the better.*' But really, Mabel, that doesn't sound like much of a threat to me. Those words could mean anything." She fastened a wide faux gold bracelet on her wrist.

Mabel pulled her black reversible skirt over her head and tucked her black blouse into the skirt band. Her thoughts went back to the scrap of conversation she heard at Karnak. "I think I saw Carrie," she said, tying a white and purple scarf around her neck. "As I came around the corner, I saw a splash of red disappearing behind a pillar, and the skirt looked like the kaftan she was wearing."

"Because you saw a red skirt, you think it was Carrie?"

"Yes," Mabel confessed.

"I bet you were good at the high jump in track and field too."

"Would you stop that? I know what I saw."

"Egyptian men wear robes; it could have been one of them." Violet lifted her hand, inspecting her fingernails she had painted bright red.

"They were speaking English, not Arabic."

"That doesn't mean the red skirt, robe, or whatever it was didn't belong to an Egyptian."

"I think it was a woman."

"I really wish you would stop looking for trouble. Just enjoy our holiday," Violet said, setting her costume jewelry bag on her night table. "I'm looking forward to a nice evening with our new friends. Dinner and dancing on a riverboat, cruising down the Nile. Kind of romantic, don't you think? Or it would be if you would get your mind off threats. You see threats that everyone else sees as an accident, including me."

"Ha, what if you are all in denial? And I'm right."

"Whatever, finish getting dressed. I'm going to enjoy the evening. And I suggest you do the same."

Mabel sat on her bed, fastening her sandals. Romantic? She bet Violet was thinking about Neville. Violet wore a big gold-coloured pendant and bracelet. Did Neville think Violet was a rich woman? He could be a fortune hunter, travelling by himself and preying on rich, helpless old women. Not that Violet was rich or a helpless old woman, but she did seem smitten. Mabel would watch Neville closely to protect her friend from herself. "You look really nice," she told Violet.

"Thank you, and you look very smart. A little on the sombre side, all dressed in black but very smart."

"Really? They always say to have something black in your wardrobe. Black is supposed to be sophisticated and slimming." Mabel wished she had a mirror, but the only mirror was the tarnished one in the bathroom. She ran her hands down her chubby body. "Do you think this outfit makes me look slimmer?"

Violet smiled at Mabel. "I think you look wonderful, and black makes your white hair almost silver."

"Thank you. Are you all dolled up for Neville?"

"Not really, but what if I am? He's an attractive, charming man."

"I'm suspicious of all that charm, and why is he travelling alone?"

"You were born suspicious. Neville is a nice man. He might be a bit younger than me, but who cares? We're just enjoying each other's company. Relax, we're on vacation, and this is just a little fun."

"As long as it doesn't become serious, remember the two-by-four club."

Violet, who'd been married three times, had told Mabel to hit her over the head with a two- by-four, if Violet ever said she was getting married again. Mabel, a widow, had no intention of getting involved with a man. No man could fill her husband's shoes.

"Yes, mother." Violet threw her white pashmina over her shoulders and opened the door.

Mabel rolled her eyes and closed the door behind them. She locked it with the big brass key and put the key in her pocket. The weight of the key pulled one side of her skirt down, giving her a lopsided look.

Carrie stood outside their room, holding a glass of something and peering at them through her glasses. Her eyes looked as big as an owl's. Leaning up against the wall, she issued a low, husky giggle. "Evening, ladies," she drawled, slurring her words. "I'm going to have a pick me up in the bar. Care to join me?"

"No, we're looking forward to supper. Aren't you hungry?" asked Violet.

"What did you do all day, Carrie?" Mabel eyed the woman teetering on her platform shoes.

"You'd be surprised, dearie," Carrie said in a singsong voice. "I get around." She tottered off toward the bar.

Mabel gave Violet a knowing look as they descended the stairs. "I think it was Carrie; she's wearing the same grubby red kaftan."

"She's had a few drinks. She's just talking. Besides, you know she was not on the bus."

"She could have taken a taxi."

Chapter Fourteen

Mabel and Violet, and most of the tour groups trooped down the stairs from the sundeck to the lounge bar. Everyone had been on the top deck to watch as the riverboat pulled out from the dock in Luxor.

Small fairy lights lit the stage in the lounge, and loud old rock and roll music pelted out from the speakers. All the tour groups had gathered to celebrate the first night of their cruise down the Nile.

Tarek's group took seats nearest to the bar. "This is a getting-to-know-your-fellow-passenger   night," Tarek informed his group. Then he quietly slipped away to talk to the police officer with the handlebar mustache, sitting alone at the bar.

On the opposite side of the lounge, the Japanese tour group sat with their guide, drinks in their hands, chatting and laughing.

Also enjoying drinks, the German tour group sat on soft leather couches down the middle of the room. The mixture of languages added to the din, the get-acquainted night was not going to cross any language barriers.

A waiter with a tray full of drinks followed Neville to the table where Tarek's tour group sat. Not all the group had made it to the lounge. Carrie was still missing, and Marvin had spilled soup on himself during dinner and had gone back to change. Ronnie complained of a headache and went to his cabin, and the French couple was making it an early night.

Mabel sat on the big half-moon leather couch with Violet. Beside them sat the California sisters, laughing and joking. Neville, who had bought everyone in their group a drink, squeezed in beside Violet. Mabel reluctantly scooted over to the edge of the couch. Elizabeth took her glass and sat beside Angie. Silvio gave her a sour look and moved to the other side of the sofa.

Mabel leaned back, enjoying her drink, tapping her toe to the music. They were cruising down the Nile, an adventure of a lifetime. She would do as Violet advised, enjoy the trip, and stop looking for trouble. The Temple of Edfu was their next stop. But when she looked at Elizabeth, she changed her mind. The first chance she got, she was going to warn Elizabeth, no matter what Violet said. Elizabeth wasn't her favourite person, but Mabel would never forgive herself if something happened to the woman.

"What are y'all doing here?" Carrie hailed, staggering through the doorway. She righted herself and pushed her big red-framed glasses up on her nose. "It's beautiful up top on the deck. It's a shame to waste a night on the Nile indoors." One hand was braced against the door-jam, and the other gripped a mug of beer. The beer splashed over the rim. Carrie licked the side of the glass. "Yummy." She giggled. Adjusting her pashmina on her head, she weaved her way across the floor to the group. "A toast to the next leg of our adventure." Carrie held up her mug of beer, making an unsteady round by clinking her glass with everyone. She continued on her wobbly path, ending with Elizabeth and Angie. Carrie's mug collided with Angie's glass. The mug and the glass fell onto Angie's lap, the contents spilling over her and splattering Elizabeth.

Wiping splatters from her arm, Elizabeth jumped up. "You clumsy drunk," Elizabeth shouted, backing Carrie up. "Get the hell out of here, you boozy old broad."

Carrie appeared startled at Elizabeth's rage. "It's a teensy weenie spill. I'm wet too," she slurred in her husky southern drawl.

"You didn't even get half." Angie jumped up, shaking her skirt. "My dress is saturated."

"Stop it, Angie, I don't want anymore on me," Elizabeth shrieked.

"What the hell am I supposed to do?" Angie snapped.

"Oh, for God's sake, go change, it's only alcohol."

"I'm sorry, my love," slurred Carrie. She twirled and fell onto the couch.

Elizabeth grabbed Carrie's arm. "I said leave. Can't you take the hint?" She sneered into her face. "No one wants you here."

Carrie shrank back on the couch.

"Lady, you have had too much to drink. You should leave," Silvio scolded in his gravelly voice.

"You, stupid fat old cow, you're smashed. Why you ever came on this trip is beyond me. You're a drunken lush," Angie yelled at her. "I'm going to change." She bunched up the skirt of her wet dress. "You've ruined it, you stupid old drunk."

Carrie staggered to her feet. "To hell with the lot of you." She beat a meandering path to the door.

"Don't you dare come near me, you drunken old sot," Angie snarled, storming past her out the door.

"Such a lot of fuss over one little old spilled drink," Carrie slurred, staggering out the door after Angie.

Silvio jumped up to follow Angie. Elizabeth put her hand on Silvio's arm. "Best to leave Angie alone for now. When she's angry, there is no dealing with her. Unlike me, who lets bygones be bygones."

Mabel rolled her eyes and picked up a napkin. Who did Elizabeth think she was kidding? Elizabeth, let bygones be bygones.

"Come on, let's have a drink. Angie will get over it. She'll pout a bit, then change and come back, you'll see." Elizabeth followed Silvio to the door.

Silvio brushed past Elizabeth. "When she comes back, tell her I'm on the sundeck. I'm going for a smoke."

Elizabeth stood at the door, shrugged, and returned to the couch. Violet, Lucy, and Janet joined Mabel, wiping the spilled drinks with napkins.

"No, no, dear ladies, allow me." Rabbie, the bartender, brought over a big cloth and finished cleaning up the mess.

"Rabbie, I think everyone would like another drink," Neville said. "Not everyone got to finish their drink before this unfortunate incident happened."

"I'm buying. You already bought the first round," Lucy volunteered.

"This evening has gotten off to a rotten start. Time to change that," Janet said.

"I agree; bring me something sparkly and cold, please." Violet smiled.

"Can you make a Manhattan?" Janet asked Rabbie. He smiled at Janet and nodded.

"What the heck, why not?" Mabel agreed, tossing back the last of her whiskey. "The same again, please."

"I'll have a martini and one for Angie and the same for Marvin," Elizabeth requested. "Speaking of Marvin, where the hell is that man?" She jumped to her feet. "I'm going to go and get him. How long does it take to change a shirt?" Elizabeth walked briskly to the door. "Oh, here he comes." She cupped a hand and called out. "It's about time I've ordered a drink for you. Oh and, Marvin, be a dear; I left my scarf down in the dining room; go and get it for me." Elizabeth put her hands on her hips. "Do not shake your head at me. I want that scarf. And for God's sake, do it now before they shut the doors to the dining room."

Elizabeth flounced back to join the group. "What an idiot. Honestly, if it weren't for me, that man would get lost going to the bathroom." She settled back on the couch, looking over at the door. "I sure hope that disgusting Carrie doesn't return. What a lush."

"I agree; I don't think I've seen Carrie without a drink in her hand," Lucy commented, coming back from the bar with a small waiter in tow, carrying the tray of drinks.

"Carrie was so hungover she couldn't even make the tour today," agreed Janet, taking her drink from the smiling little man.

Mabel swirled the whiskey sour in her glass. Were they right? Did Carrie really miss the tour? She was sure she had seen the skirt of Carrie's grubby red kaftan at the temple. And the woman said you'd be surprised what she had gotten up to. Something wasn't right about that woman.

Rabbie flipped a switch behind the bar, the lights lowered, and the music rose. Lucy and Janet danced their way to the dance floor, joining the other passengers. Neville offered his hand to Violet and led her out on the floor to an old-time rock-and-roll number from the 50s, Bill Haley's *Rock Around the Clock*. Mabel sipped her drink and smiled. Neville would get a surprise.

Neville's eyes widened. He had a painful smile plastered on his face as he tried to lead Violet around the dance floor.

Mabel grinned. Her tall friend Violet danced like a giraffe on stilts having a seizure. She loved her friend, but she had to acknowledge Violet's dancing looked a little weird. But Violet was having fun, and that's all that really mattered. One tune ended, and another began, Chubby Checker, told everyone to *Let's Twist Again*. Neville bravely continued to dance with Violet.

Silvio wandered in and sat down beside Mabel. "I wonder what is keeping Angie. Shouldn't she be back by now?"

"My boy, you don't know much about women, do you?" Elizabeth laughed. "It takes us women a while to change and then pick out what we want to wear. But it's Marvin who is making me a little peeved. What the hell is he doing chatting with the kitchen staff?" She took a drink from Marvin's glass. "Dance with little Mabel. I bet you would like to dance, wouldn't you, dear?" She gave Mabel a condescending smile.

Silvio looked at Mabel and smiled politely. "Would you like to dance?" he asked.

Silvio was being pressured, but she did want to dance, and unlike Violet, she was a good dancer. She might be a little on the chubby side and built close to the ground, but she was light on her feet. She would surprise this young man.

Mabel followed Silvio onto the dance floor as The Beatles belted out *Twist and Shout*.

Elizabeth sat watching the dancers and glancing impatiently at the door.

One song ended, and much to Mabel's delight, they danced the second number, this time one of her favourites. The Bee Gees *Staying Alive*. When the music stopped, Silvio led her back to the couch. Lucy and Janet applauded, Neville joined in, and Violet smiled proudly at Mabel. Only Elizabeth, who sat with her arms crossed, looked unimpressed.

Silvio smiled at Mabel. "Wow, you are a good dancer."

"Thank you." Mabel grinned. "My generation invented Rock-and-roll." She picked up her drink, downing it. Dancing had made her thirsty.

Marvin entered the bar, waving Elizabeth's scarf like a flag. "I need a drink." He flopped on the couch, picked up an empty glass and signalled to a waiter.

Elizabeth slid a drink over in his direction. "About time you came with my scarf. What were you doing with the kitchen staff? Comparing recipes?"

"You missed the excitement." Lucy picked up her drink.

"If you want to call it that, more like a calamity, Calamity Carrie." Janet fanned her face with a napkin. "Dancing is hot work." She grinned.

"What did I miss? Where's Angie?"

"That drunken broad, Carrie, spilled her drink all over Angie's dress. She's gone back to change," Elizabeth informed him.

"I'm going to see if Angie is all right." Silvio downed his drink, getting to his feet.

"I'll go with you. I have to go to our room. I bet Marvin didn't soak the shirt he spilled soup all over. Or did you?" Elizabeth stood, giving her husband a questioning look.

"Oh, no, sorry, dear."

"Of course, you didn't. Give me our room key, and I'll check on Angie on the way."

"You stay here, Silvio, I'll go with Elizabeth," Mabel volunteered. Now was her chance to warn Elizabeth.

Silvio shrugged and sat back down, signalling for another drink.

Elizabeth took the key from Marvin and flipped her scarf over her shoulder. "Well, at least you brought my scarf." She looked at Mabel and smiled. "Sure, come with me. We can help dear Angie get dressed. I'm beginning to wonder why she hasn't returned."

Mabel followed Elizabeth out of the lounge, her mind racing on how to warn her. What should she say?

Elizabeth put her arm through Mabel's. "How are you enjoying the trip?" she asked.

Mabel's eyes widened in surprise. Elizabeth's actions were uncharacteristic. How much did the woman have to drink? "I think Egypt is wonderful; I never expected to see the sights we've seen; how about you?" Elizabeth appeared to be in a good mood. Should she just flat out and say, 'Someone is trying to kill you?'

"I loved the Cairo museum. Tutankhamun's sarcophagus was amazing. All that gold." Elizabeth released Mabel's arm. "But the food, ugh, and did you use their bathrooms?" Elizabeth didn't wait for Mabel to reply. "The pyramids, now they are something. Of course, they darn near killed me."

Now, thought Mabel, now was the time to warn her.

"But the Valley of the Kings is something else entirely. Those old Egyptians were certainly morbid. All this is for dead people; I can't understand it. They were a bunch of superstitious fools. And I was disappointed in Tutankhamun's tomb. The walls are nicely decorated, but Tutankhamun, he's just a wizened-up little body."

Mabel was about to say, 'Well, his body is over three thousand years old,' but she clamped her lips shut as Elisabeth continued.

"All these pyramids and temples make me wonder how they built them. I asked Marvin how he thought those primitive people could build these magnificent structures. It makes you almost believe in aliens from outer space."

Mabel sighed; Elizabeth was not only a bad-tempered woman but a prejudiced one with weird theories. She didn't like the woman, but she would never forgive herself if something happened to Elizabeth, and she'd done nothing to prevent it.

As Elizabeth continued to critique the tour, Mabel rehearsed in her mind how to broach her suspicions to Elizabeth. *I think your husband is trying to kill you.* No, that wouldn't work. Elizabeth would believe she was a nutbar. She needed to be subtler.

"Elizabeth," Mabel said timorously. She would segue into the warning. "We sure have had a big police presence, haven't we? Have you ever felt, well, have you felt unsafe?"

"This is Angie's stateroom." Elizabeth tapped on the door. "Angie, can we come in?" There was no answer, she rapped again. "Angie, it's me, Elizabeth and Mabel. Let us in, dear." Elizabeth tried to open the door and then knocked again. "Angie, are you all right?" She rattled the door handle, looking anxiously at Mabel. "Angie has asthma. She was distraught when she left the bar. Maybe she's had an attack. You try the door. I think it's locked. I can't budge it."

Mabel turned the knob and pushed on the door. It didn't open.

"What should we do?" Elizabeth looked flustered.

"Do you want me to go and get the room steward? He'll have a key."

"Not the room steward. I had words with that man when we came aboard. You stay here and try to rouse Angie. I'll go down to the lobby and get the purser; he'll have a key."

Mabel rapped on the door. "Angie."

"I'm getting very worried about her. Something's not right. Keep trying." Elizabeth sped down the hallway.

Mabel continued to knock on the door and call out Angie's name. "You need a key?" asked a heavily accented voice at her side.

"That was quick." Mabel held out her hand. "The key, please."

"Oh, this not your room." A little man clad in white took back the offered key.

"My friend is sick, and I need to get into her room." Mabel held out her hand for the key. "Are you the room steward?"

"Oh, my yes, I am your steward," the little man said proudly. "Anything you want, you ask me. I will get for you."

"I'm asking you for the key."

The skinny little steward shook his head vigorously. "No, not the key, this is not your room. I cannot open for you."

"Didn't a lady send you here to give me the key? Please, give me the key."

"No one sent me. I forgot towels for the big Mr. Roundie." There were towels draped over one arm.

"Please, help me by opening this door. I think something may be amiss."

"Yes, a young miss is in this room, not you, madam. Would you like more towels?" The small, gap-tooth man held up the towels.

"Never mind about those bloody towels." Mabel reached for the key.

The steward jumped back. "No, no, not bloody, these are clean towels, very clean towels, see." The affronted little man stretched out a towel.

"I don't care about the towels. I need the key. I need to open this door." Mabel reached into her pocket and gave the little man an Egyptian pound. The little steward looked at the pound and looked back at her. She added two more. "Now open the door for me, please. My friend might be ill. This is a very good thing for you to do," she encouraged.

The little man's attitude changed in an instant. He bowed and grinned from ear to ear. "My name is Ali." He put the key into the lock and opened the door. "Anything you need, please to ask for the Ali." Flipping the light switch on, he turned in the doorway to make room for Mabel.

Mabel entered. Angie was lying on her bed, still wearing her stained wet dress.

Chapter Fifteen

The little steward, Ali, stood in the doorway and popped his hand over his mouth. "Oh, the poor lady, she is ill?"

Brushing past him, Mabel stumbled over a pillow and hurried to the bedside. Angie's bloodshot eyes stared back as Mabel felt for a pulse. Nothing. The body felt warm to her touch, but Angie was dead.

Ali shuffled from foot to foot. "Something is wrong?"

Mabel returned to the doorway and said to the room steward, "Something is very wrong. This lady is dead. Go and inform Tarek and the police officer."

Ali threw up his arms, and towels flapped as he raced down the corridor, chattering excitedly in Arabic.

Mabel turned back into the room, crossing her arms over her chest; she furrowed her brow. The pillow and a small bedside lamp lay on the floor. The faded green lampshade was broken and twisted. The closet door was closed, and no fresh clothes were laid out. Whatever happened to Angie happened before she had a chance to change her clothes. She brought a clenched fist to her mouth, tapping her lips gently. Carefully, she stepped back over the pillow and stood beside the bed. She looked gravely down at the dead girl lying there. "Oh, Angie, you poor girl," Mabel said softly.

The bedspread was rumpled and twisted under Angie's body, the girl's hair in disarray. But not her drink-stained dress. And her hands lie by her sides as if someone had carefully placed them there. There was no sign of a struggle from looking at the body. But the pillow and the lamp on the floor told a different story. Mabel picked up the dead girl's hand. Under Angie's fingernails, she saw fragments of filmy pieces of plastic.

Ahmed Hakimi, the purser, entered the room, followed closely by Elizabeth. The big, burly man filled the small room. "What is happened?" he asked.

Mabel turned. "I'm sorry," she said.

Elizabeth gasped and put her hand on the dresser, then fell into the big man's arms in a faint.

Ahmed let Elizabeth sag to the floor; he looked worriedly from Elizabeth to the girl on the bed and then to Mabel. "Oh my, what to do? What to do?"

"Oh, my goodness, take her out in the hallway. There's no room here," Mabel directed. She knew she should feel sympathy for Elizabeth, but all she felt was surprise. She had been so sure it was Elizabeth who was in danger. Not her cousin Angie.

"My, my, my goodness me," Ahmed echoed in his heavily accented English. He wrung his hands, looking helplessly at Mabel.

"Oh, for god's sake." Mabel grabbed Elizabeth under her armpits. Elizabeth's head swung side to side as Mabel groaned and dragged the woman to the doorway. Mabel dumped her in the hallway in front of the door. She brushed her hands together and stepped over Elizabeth back into the room.

Ahmed furrowed his brow and looked at Mabel. "The lady on the bed. She is sick?"

Mabel stepped around the big man and stood by the bed, looking with Ahmed at the dead girl. "No, I'm sorry, she is dead." It flashed through her mind she had just done the typical Canadian thing and apologized for something she had nothing to do with.

She remembered Elizabeth told her that Angie was an asthmatic. So, where is the inhaler? She looked around the room. The faded decor was the same as her and Violet's room and the same size. But because there was only one bed, the room seemed bigger. There was nothing on the bedside table. On the dresser, an open jewelry box, her room key, and a hairbrush, but no inhaler.

Ahmed muttered something in shocked Arabic, then in English, he exclaimed, "Oh, my goodness me." Backing out of the room, he narrowly missed stepping on Elizabeth.

Ali appeared in the doorway, dancing and waving his hands. "He come, he come." The little steward lapsed into Arabic, chattering excitedly to Ahmed.

Ahmed pushed the little man to the side and stepped over Elizabeth back into the room. He confronted Mabel. "You have alerted the captain?"

Ali nodded. "Yes, the captain is on his way."

"Who? The captain of the ship? We don't need a ship's captain. Get the police officer. I will stay here with Angie."

"No, no." Ali bobbed up and down. "The captain of the police, he is on his way."

"Oh, that's good. Now, Ali, you should go and find this woman's husband. She has fainted," Mabel instructed.

Ali gasped. "You said the dear lady is dead."

"Yes, the lady is dead."

"Poor dear lady." Ali clasped his hands and bowed in reverence as he looked down at Elizabeth.

Mabel took a deep breath. "No, not the lady on the floor. Elizabeth is not dead. She has fainted."

"Oh, my yes, fainted, the poor dear lady. She would like a towel, maybe?" Ali offered a towel.

"I don't think a towel will help her. Please, go find her husband. He is in the lounge. Do you know who this woman's husband is?" Mabel asked, frustrated.

"Oh my, yes, the husband of this poor woman on the floor, I know very well. It is my job." Ali flashed her a gap-tooth smile, his head bobbing up and down.

"Then, for heavens' sake, go get him," Mabel ordered.

Ali hunched his shoulders and scurried away.

Mabel pressed her lips together; she was channelling Elizabeth.

"This lady looks very unwell." Ahmed took a cautious step toward the bed.

"The lady is not unwell. She is most certainly dead."

"Perhaps the dear lady is unconscious?" Ahmed said hopefully.

"No, not unconscious." Mabel was losing patience. "Angie Morrison is dead." Mabel pressed her lips together; how many more times would she have to tell him?

"Oh, this is not good for my company." Ahmed, wringing his hands, shook his head.

Mabel looked over her glasses at the purser. "Not good for Angie either," she said.

"He is here, he is here," Ali shouted as he jumped over Elizabeth into the room.

Ahmed yelled at Ali in Arabic, and the little steward hopped back over Elizabeth. Ali turned to look down the hallway and made a sweeping bow. "He is here."

Ahmed followed Ali out of the room into the hallway, skirting around Elizabeth.

The police officer, accompanied by Tarek and Marvin, arrived at the door.

Ali said something in rapid-fire Arabic and pointed into the cabin.

The officer looked down at Elizabeth and pushed Ali out of the way. He stepped over her and paused.

Tarek glanced down at Elizabeth, paused, then followed the police officer into the room. He squeezed up behind the officer, peering over the man's shoulder. Tarek's eyes widened as his jaw dropped. He muttered something in Arabic and backed up to the bureau.

Ahmed, wringing his hands and talking in his high-pitched Arabic, crept over Elizabeth into the cabin, edging up beside Tarek.

The three men continued to converse in Arabic. Ali poked his head around the corner, his eyes darting from the bed to the police officer and Tarek, then back to the body.

Marvin stood in the doorway, looking from his wife to Angie on the bed. "What has happened?"

"It's poor Angie. She has died," Mabel said, feeling foolish for stating the obvious.

"Died?" Marvin put a hand to his mouth. "What? No, it can't be." His voice trembled.

Mabel gave him a sympathetic look. "I'm afraid it's true."

"No, not Angie." Marvin took a step over his wife into the room.

"Keep back," instructed the police officer.

"But I must go to her," Marvin insisted, his lips quivering.

"You can't help her." Mabel put a hand on his arm. "It might be best if you did as the officer asks."

"Please, Mr. Tuttle, please, stay by your wife. We will sort this out," Tarek requested.

Reluctantly, Marvin retreated to his wife's side and sank down beside her, mumbling, "Angie, I can't believe it. Angie."

The police officer took off his hat, patted the hair on his head, and tucked his hat under his arm. "What has happened here?" He moved toward the bed, stumbling on the pillow. Bending, he picked up the pillow from the floor.

Mabel gasped, "Don't do that, the pillow could be evidence."

"Evidence?" The officer raised his caterpillar eyebrows. He handed the pillow to Tarek, who gave it to Ahmed. Ahmed tossed the pillow to Ali. Marvin grabbed it from Ali and placed it under Elizabeth's head. Elizabeth groaned.

"That pillow, you, you, oh well, it's too late now." Mabel pressed her lips together in disapproval.

"Do not babble, woman," the officer commanded. "Tell me what has happened here."

"For goodness' sake, just look at the girl. You can see for yourself she is dead." Mabel gestured to Angie.

There was a gasp from someone in the doorway. Mabel didn't know if it was from Marvin or Ali. Maybe she was a little too blunt.

"What do you mean dead?" he asked, puzzled, fingering his mustache; he peered at Angie from a distance.

"I mean dead, as in no longer living, not breathing, dead," Mabel snapped. There was another collective gasp from the doorway. Her face reddened. She had consumed too many drinks in the lounge. Alcohol was not her friend. She would have to pull herself together.

The captain inched closer to the bedside. "Dead?" He picked the lamp off the floor and set it on the night table, adjusting the lampshade.

"Yes, dead." Mabel bit her lip. He was disturbing the crime scene, or as Constable Robert from back home would say, '*a suspicious death.*'

The officer took a deep breath and loomed over the body. Angie stared back at him with dead eyes. He jumped back from the bed, pushing Mabel to the side.

Mabel stepped on her lopsided skirt and stumbled. She reached for the bed, but she missed it. She grabbed Angie's foot and fell to the floor. Angie's body slid down the bed. Mabel sat on the floor, her face flushed with embarrassment. Angie's foot stuck out over the end of the bed.

Tarek put his hand up over his mouth in dismay. Ahmed gasped, his eyes widening as he muttered in Arabic. The big man returned to the door and pushed Ali out of the way. His mouth was agape as he stared back into the room at Mabel. Ali slunk down behind the purser, eyeing the dead girl with apprehension.

"Good lord." Marvin leaped to his feet. "Leave poor Angie alone. What are you thinking?" He attempted to enter the cabin.

Ahmed laid a restraining hand on his shoulder. "Please, Mr. Tuttle, stay here with your wife." Marvin scowled at Mabel as he knelt beside Elizabeth.

"Oh, I'm so sorry," Mabel apologized, reaching up and patting Angie's foot. "It's very close quarters in here." She pulled herself up and looked down at Angie. Darn, she had disturbed the crime scene too. Should she slide the dead girl's body back up on the bed? She settled, for arranging Angie's skirt down over her knees.

The police officer's caterpillar eyebrows wiggled up and down as he glowered at Mabel. He shoved her out of the way, sending her back against the closet. "Stay away from the bed," he shouted. He bent over the body, clasping his hands behind his back, he looked down at Angie. He straightened his shoulders, unclasped his hands twirled his handlebar mustache, and said. "I think she might be dead."

Mabel threw up her hands. "You think? Of course, she is dead. What do you think she's doing? Acting?"

"Who are you, woman?" the officer stormed. He puffed out his chest and glared at Mabel. "And what are you doing in this cabin?" he demanded in heavily accented English.

Tarek edged his way over to Mabel. "This is Mabel Havelock, one of our guests aboard the cruise."

"And who are you?" Mabel asked, planting her hands on her hips, looking over her granny glasses at the police officer.

"Who am I?" he bellowed.

Mabel leaned away from the officer. The man had halitosis. "Yes, that's what I asked, who are you? Do you have any experience with this sort of thing? Are you really a police officer? You don't act like one." Mabel folded her arms, looking sternly at the man whose face was becoming an unhealthy shade of red.

Ahmed's mouth fell open. He looked from Mabel to the captain. Ali's eyes widened; he took one last look at Mabel and scurried down the hallway, muttering in Arabic.

Tarek gave Mabel a horrified look. "This is Captain Burhan from the Luxor police force."

"Well, this captain from the Luxor police force has made a complete mess of this crime scene."

"I have what?" Captain Burhan yelled.

"You are like a bull in a china shop. You have destroyed evidence."

"A bull," the captain sputtered. "A crime scene, evidence, ridiculous, you are hysterical. Woman. Remove yourself now."

Mabel stood her ground. "I am most certainly not hysterical," she huffed. "And the least you can do is bag her hands." She was sure that was the proper procedure. She'd seen crime shows on TV.

"What an outrageous request. Show some respect for this poor woman." The police captain turned to Ahmed and switched to Arabic.

Ahmed replied in the same language. Mabel made out the words doctor and captain.

"What are you saying? Are you getting Angie a doctor?" Marvin stood peering into the cabin. "Please, get Angie a doctor."

"The captain has asked for a doctor. But I am sorry, there is no doctor on *The Star*," Ahmed replied.

"No worries, a doctor wouldn't be much help, anyway," Mabel said.

Elizabeth sat up. "Angie, is something the matter with Angie?"

Marvin helped his wife to her feet. "I'm so sorry, they tell me she is gone."

"Gone? You mean..."

"Yes, gone, she has, she has..." Marvin's voice trailed off.

"Oh no, please don't tell me Angie has died."

"It looks that way, dear. I think she's had an attack of some sort."

"I knew something was wrong. Angie wouldn't answer her door. Mabel and I tried to open the door, but it was locked." Elizabeth held on to Marvin and looked across at Mabel.

"Yes." Mabel's eyes darted to Angie, and she frowned. "Yes, the door was locked," she said in a puzzled voice.

"Poor, poor Angie. I can't believe it. So alive and vibrant just minutes ago." Elizabeth staggered. Marvin kept his arm around her, propping her up.

The purser stood by the door, wringing his hands.

Mabel turned to Captain Burhan. "There is something very odd. I must tell you what I saw."

"You are a silly woman. I do not care what you saw. You must stop with the poking the nose. This poor, unfortunate lady has had a heart attack. Stop with your hysterical ravings," commanded the police officer. He seized Mabel by the arm.

Ahmed's eyes widened. He moved quickly aside as the police officer pushed Mabel out the door. Elizabeth and Marvin also stepped out of the way, looking uneasily at her.

"But, but," Mabel sputtered, incensed. Instead of listening to her, this man called her silly and accused her of being hysterical. She wanted to yell at him and ask him what experience he had investigating a murder. Instead, she closed her mouth, seething. If she uttered any defiance, it would only confirm his prejudice.

"Inspector," Elizabeth sniffed, wiping her eyes with her fingertips, she shuttered. "She is my. She is my cousin."

"I am not an inspector yet." The officer smiled at Elizabeth. "I have just been promoted to my rank as captain."

Marvin handed her a tissue. Elizabeth wiped her eyes and blew her nose.

Mabel's lips twitched, newly promoted. What did that mean? They probably promoted him so they could stick him on this boat and be rid of him, she thought uncharitably.

"I am Captain Mustafa Burhan, a member of Luxor's finest police." He clicked his heels and gave a little bow. "I am sorry for your great loss."

"Angie suffers from asthma. Or rather, she suffered from asthma." Elizabeth heaved a sob. Marvin wrapped his arm around her shoulder. "I think Angie has had an asthma attack. She has...," Elizabeth sobbed.

"Dear lady, how sad. Your dear cousin has died from an asthma attack. Dreadful, dreadful. And to die here in our great country, now she will not see the monuments of Egypt's past, so sad."

Mabel wrinkled her nose. Captain Burhan was a police officer, but she doubted he was Luxor's finest. The man was a bumbler, and he was either incompetent or lazy. She shuttered when she thought of how Captain Burhan had destroyed the crime scene. Then, with no evidence to back up his statement, he declared Angie died of a heart attack. And now, with no examination, he accepted that she died of an asthma attack. How was she going to persuade this man that Angie was murdered?

Chapter Sixteen

"We opened the door, and there on the bed lay Angie. The poor girl was dead."

"How shocking and so tragic." Violet sat on her bed with her long legs crossed in her bright green pyjamas, listening to Mabel's account of finding Angie in her stateroom.

"Yes, then Elizabeth came back with the purser and fainted."

"The purser fainted? You wouldn't think a big man like the purser would faint at the sight of a dead body."

"Pay attention. The purser didn't faint. Elizabeth did. And I had to drag her to the doorway. Ahmed just stood there. I guess he was as stunned as Elizabeth. Anyway, Captain Burhan, Marvin, and Tarek arrived. And that's when that bumptious man threw me out of the room."

"Tarek threw you out of the cabin?"

"No, Tarek did not throw me out of the room. Why would you think Tarek would throw me out of the room?"

"You can be a little rambunctious, and you and Tarek had words at Giza."

"I wasn't rambunctious, and Tarek and I did not have words. He just wouldn't believe me that Elizabeth was in danger."

"And she wasn't," Violet reminded her.

"Yes, okay, let's get back to the murder room."

"The murder room, really, Mabel."

"Just hear me out. You'll know why I call it the murder room."

"Murder cabin, you mean," Violet corrected her.

"Violet, please, back to getting thrown out of the room." Mabel rolled her eyes. "Oh, pardon me, out of the cabin."

Violet uncrossed her legs. "Okay, you were thrown out of the cabin by this Captain Burhan."

"Yes, by the captain, he's a little bully." Mabel hitched up her nightgown and picked up the small wooden chair by the window.

"The captain of the boat?"

"You're not taking me seriously?" Mabel dropped the chair and gave Violet a hard look.

"I am, but you need to be factual. Who tossed you out? The boat captain or that silly little man with the handlebar mustache we saw in the dining room with Tarek?"

"The silly little man is an Egyptian police officer. One of Luxor's finest, he said. But you're right to call him silly. I don't think he's the finest of anything." Mabel picked up the chair again.

"Why did this Captain Burhan make you leave the cabin? Were you, hum, how shall I put it? Were you just a little caustic?"

"I was not, well, I might have criticized him just a little," confessed Mabel. "But that man rubs me the wrong way." Mabel inched her way past the end of her bed, struggling with the chair she held out in front of her.

"You criticized an Egyptian police officer? Oh, Mabel, that's not wise; this isn't nice, Constable Robert from back home. This attitude of yours will not help. Especially if someone murdered Angie."

"What do you mean, if? And what about my attitude? You weren't there. You didn't hear how he talked to me. He called me a hysterical female. You were busy with your new boyfriend, Neville, who, by the way, I don't trust." Mabel plunked the chair in front of the cabin door, then tipped it, bracing the chair against the door handle.

"Yes, yes, you have made it quite clear you don't like Neville. Anyway, he's not my boyfriend, we're just friends. And for goodness' sake, what are you doing? Are you afraid we'll be attacked in the night? Do you really think a crazy man is going around throttling people?"

"Who knows? There could be. Someone certainly killed Angie." Mabel trotted to her bed and turned back the bedcovers. "That door to Angie's cabin was locked."

"You're sure it's murder?"

"If you'd been with me, you'd be as sure as I am." Mabel shook off her slippers and crawled into bed.

"Don't start on Neville again."

"He's a single man travelling on his own. I find that suspicious."

"What about Silvio? He is travelling alone. And so is your buddy, Ronnie." Violet turned down the sheet on her bed.

"Ronnie isn't my buddy. He's just a nice man helping a lady."

"He's close to your age; looks can be deceiving."

"What do you mean? Do you think I look old?"

"No, of course not; all I'm saying is he's no spring chicken."

"Whatever. Let's get back to poor Angie. If you'd seen her body, you would know." Mabel sat up and punched her pillow, stuffing it behind her back.

Violet folded her bedspread at the foot of her bed and crawled into bed, spreading the sheet neatly. "I would know what?"

"You would know someone murdered Angie."

"Maybe Angie died of natural causes? People do you know, even on vacation. You said Elizabeth told you Angie was an asthmatic."

"Angie's death is not from an asthmatic attack." Mabel shifted on her pillow. She sat up and punched her pillow again.

"Okay, tell me what makes you think her death wasn't from natural causes."

"The tiny red spots, petechiae, on her face, for one thing. And her lips pushed back in a hideous grin. That doesn't look like an asthmatic attack. It's at least suspicious. And an asthmatic attack that kills is rare," Mabel said.

"It happens."

"Rarely, and I didn't see an inhaler near or around her bed."

"Hum, no inhaler. Angie would have felt an attack coming on. There should have been one near at hand." Violet leaned back on her pillow.

"There wasn't, and her eyes were wide open and bloodshot."

"So what do you think happened?" Violet sat up and fluffed her pillow, then stared at it.

"I think someone suffocated Angie."

"Smothered? What, with a pillow?"

"Probably not with a pillow, but there were signs of a struggle. The bedside lamp and her pillow lie on the floor. That was until Captain Bungle moved everything." Mabel sat up in her bed. "The broken fingernails and the little plastic under some of her nails confirmed my suspicion. I think the killer used a plastic bag of some sort to smother her."

"And Captain Burhan didn't notice anything?"

"That man couldn't find an elephant in a phone booth. First, he proclaimed Angie had a heart attack. Then Elizabeth told him she was asthmatic. And he accepted that without a question. And Luxor's finest police officer wouldn't even touch Angie's body like he was afraid to."

"Maybe because she is a woman, and this is a Muslim country. Men probably don't touch women they're not related to."

"Well, he had no problem touching me when he manhandled me out of the room," Mabel fumed. "He's a police officer, for goodness' sake; he didn't even look around at the room. And he certainly didn't preserve the crime scene. All signs of a struggle are gone because of that officious idiot. We should search Angie's room for an inhaler."

"Oh, no." Violet shot up in bed. "We're not doing anything of the kind. This isn't Canada. And the captain isn't Constable Robert. If the police caught us snooping in a crime scene, it would be an Egyptian jail. I can just imagine how awful that would be."

"Captain Burhan doesn't think it's a crime scene. So, it wouldn't be an offence."

"I don't know about that. Anyway, we just can't barge into his investigation. This is a foreign country; we need to be careful."

"Captain Burhan is not investigating. I don't think he knows how or even wants to investigate," Mabel said. She pulled her pillow from behind her back and stuck it under her head. "He thinks Angie's death is from natural causes, and I imagine he is pleased to think that. If someone murdered Angie, it would be an embarrassment for him and the cruise line."

"Angie's eyes were bloodshot, you said." Violet picked up her phone from the night table and turned it on. "I'm going to look up asphyxiation online."

"Good idea, goggle it." Mabel flipped the covers off and climbed over to Violet's bed, peering over her shoulder.

"You mean, Google it."

"Whatever, I think I'm right about the petechiae and the bloodshot eyes. I know I'm right about an asthmatic attack. There was no bluing on Angie's lips. And don't forget the broken fingernails and the plastic bits."

"I've got no bars."

"You're hungry? Forget about your cravings and goggle."

"Google. You're such a Luddite. I'm not hungry. It means there is no internet reception. I'll try again tomorrow." Violet shut off her phone.

Mabel climbed back into her bed, pulling the sheet up. "It's even too hot for this sheet, this air conditioner is more ornamental than useful," she muttered.

"If someone murdered Angie, and I'm saying if. Why would anyone want her dead?" Violet set her phone on her bedside table. Frowning, she pursed her lips, studying her pillow.

"I don't have a clue. I thought Elizabeth was in danger, not Angie." Mabel put her glasses on the night table.

"That's probably because that woman is so unlikeable. If Elizabeth was dead, I would suspect Marvin. What a whipped puppy that man is." Violet took off her glasses and put them in her glass case. She eyed her pillow and turned out the bedside lamp.

"Maybe Carrie killed Angie," Mabel said, staring into the darkened room.

"Why would Carrie kill Angie? Not over a spilled drink." Violet laid her head gently on her pillow.

"No, of course not, but there has to be more there than meets the eye."

"So, who was missing, or rather, who wasn't in the bar while Angie was dying or being murdered?" Violet questioned.

"You believe me that someone killed Angie?"

"I know you aren't an alarmist, or as Captain Burhan so diplomatically put it, hysterical."

"Don't even joke about that man. I get mad just thinking about him, Luxor's finest. What a laugh."

"But just to be on the safe side, I will still look up the symptoms of asphyxiation when I get connected to the internet. We need to be sure that Angie died of asphyxiation and not of an asthmatic attack before we voice our suspicions. This is the Egyptian police. And you and your Captain Burhan are not on the best of terms."

"I want to be sure too. So, who left the bar? Carrie left at the same time as Angie. And Marvin was gone, oh and Silvio, he went too, he said he was going for a smoke. But did he? They all have an opportunity, but do any of them have a motive?" Mabel tossed in her bed.

"And the Drapeau's told us they were having an early night. But were they?"

"Seriously, Violet? You think that little French couple snuck down the hallway and smothered Angie. Ridiculous. Do you think there are international serial killers that travel the world looking for victims?"

"Okay, not them. But your buddy, Ronnie, he wasn't in the bar." Violet turned the lamp on, got out of bed, and put on her slippers.

"Ronnie isn't my buddy, well, I guess he is, as in a friend. But not in any other way."

"Just as Neville is my friend," Violet shot over her shoulder as she went into the bathroom, returning with two bath towels. "Anyway, if we do find out someone murdered Angie, should we even get involved?"

Mabel's nostrils flared, and she looked disapprovingly at Violet. "You can't mean we let someone get away with murder?"

"No, but even if we get the evidence, we can't go barging ahead. We must show the evidence to your Captain Burhan. He's the police. He can deal with it." Violet refolded the towels and handed one to Mabel. "Remember what happened last time. We almost got ourselves killed."

"Would you stop saying, my Captain? He dislikes me. The man thinks I'm just a silly woman." Mabel took the towel and asked, "What do you want me to do? Go have a shower?"

Violet laid her bath towel over her pillow. "You don't know who's laid their heads on these pillows. Just thinking about it makes me queasy."

"You think germs don't migrate through the towels?" Mabel rolled her eyes but spread the towel over her pillow.

"It's the best I can do. Now back to you poking your nose into this murder, if it is a murder. We will inform Captain Burhan of the findings from Google and tell him our suspicions, and that's that."

Mabel sat up, rearranging the towel over her pillow. "I doubt he will take anything I say seriously, just because we goggled, I mean Googled. Inspector Clouseau wouldn't even believe me when I said Angie was dead. He's sure not going to believe me if we don't have proper evidence to back up our claims."

"Then we get the proper evidence. I just don't want you to go off half-cocked and get into trouble. This is a foreign country, and two ladies interfering won't go down well with the Egyptian officials."

"Exactly, it's perfect." Mabel laid back on her pillow.

"Perfect?"

"We can ask a lot of questions, and we can snoop around. Who would suspect two little old ladies like us doing detective work?"

"You're always miffed when someone thinks you're old, and now you want them to think you're old. You can't have it both ways."

"It's called playing the old lady card. You can get away with a lot of things if people think you're old. People don't look past the picture. I have white hair, so there for, I must be old."

"Whatever, just don't complain the next time you are taken for a pensioner." Violet pulled her sheet up to her chin.

"It's a disguise. It's like undercover work," Mabel said, warming to her idea.

"The only thing we should do is get under our covers and go to sleep." Violet shut out the lights. There was a long silence. "You're not going to let this go, are you?"

"I would, Violet, I really would, but someone has to steer Captain Pompous in the right direction." Mabel took the towel off her pillow and tossed it to the end of her bed.

"I can see it will be hard to convince him that someone killed Angie."

"You got that right, he is a self-righteous—"

"About this theory of yours. Remember the locked cabin door? You tried the door. The only way to lock or unlock any of these doors is with that great big brass key. How do you explain a murder in a locked room?"

Chapter Seventeen

Violet followed Mabel down the stairs to the dining room. The Japanese tourists were filing past the serving tables, filling their dishes. The chatter of the foreign language floated across the room.

Jean and Maria Drapeau were eating breakfast and waved at them. Violet wondered if they had heard about Angie's death. Mabel thought someone murdered Angie. But the locked cabin door. How did the killer get in and out? Of course, that little steward could have let the murderer into the cabin. And if it was murder, how were they going to convince the captain? He was already on the outs with Mabel. She wished her friend was a little more tactful.

"Look, Violet," Mabel gave her a poke. "There's Captain Officious."

Captain Burhan and Tarek strode past them, going straight to a table at the back of the dining room. Violet picked up a plate by the serving table. She examined it before deciding to select another, setting the offending plate aside. Her lips tightened in disapproval. "If you want Captain Burhan to help us, you have to change your attitude and let bygones be bygones."

Mabel pursed her lips and sighed. "I guess I have to. I promise to think positive, even though I'm positive he's a—"

"What did I just say?"

"Sorry, you're right. We will need him. I'll be good. Hey, do you think he's the ship's captain?" Mabel murmured and nodded toward the other side of the room as she followed Violet down the buffet line.

Violet glanced across the dining room. Captain Burhan's head was bent, conferring with a tall, grey-haired man in uniform. "You mean the tall man in uniform?"

"Yes, him. I'm thinking he must be the captain of our boat. The waiters are certainly making a fuss around him," Mabel said, picking up a plate.

Violet glanced back over her shoulder. "And seated at the same table with the captains are Tarek and the Japanese and European tour directors." She turned back to the serving table and scooped yogurt into a bowl.

"I bet they're trying to figure out how to solve the dilemma about poor Angie's death. A dead tourist is bad for business," Mabel said, picking up an orange-coloured fruit.

Violet topped her plain yogurt with fruits and added a croissant to her tray. "Let's sit with Jean and Marie," Violet suggested.

Mabel nodded as she scooped up scrambled eggs, adding them to her hash browns and prosciutto. A waiter followed them to the table and poured coffee.

"I think this might be the only way they know how to prepare the eggs," Jean said, looking dolefully at the scrambled eggs on his plate.

Ronnie brought his plate to their table and sat across from Mabel. "I know Muslims don't eat pork, so, is this really ham?" he asked.

"*Oui*, the prosciutto is *le jambon*." Marie stirred jam into her yogurt. Ronnie held up a piece of prosciutto on his fork, frowning.

"Pardon my wife's French." Jean's eyes sparkled. He grinned at Ronnie and added, "It is indeed the ham, serving it is not like eating it."

"Yeah, I guess," Ronnie drawled. "They don't drink alcohol, but there is no shortage of booze aboard this boat."

Mabel pushed the scrambled eggs around on her plate. "You did hear about poor Angie?"

"What about her?" Ronnie sliced the prosciutto into smaller pieces.

Mabel laid her fork by her plate and leaned forward. "Angie died last night."

"*Mon Dieu*, Angie, she is dead?" Jean asked in a shocked voice.

Mabel glanced at Violet. Violet shot her a warning look.

"I found poor Angie in her cabin," Mabel blurted out.

"What happened to her?" Jean asked.

"We don't know," interjected Violet before Mabel could get a word in. "Captain Burhan is onboard, he's with the Egyptian police, that's him over there talking to Tarek. The police will sort it out."

Mabel snorted, glaring down the room at the police captain.

"Ah, *oui,* the mustache man," Jean said.

"Yes, that's him. I'm sure he is looking into the poor girl's unfortunate demise," Violet quickly added. The dining room was filling up, and she did not want Mabel to raise any alarms about Angie's death. Spreading rumours would not help the situation.

Mabel gave Violet an annoyed look.

"Angie, the poor girl. She is so young, how tragic," Marie said sorrowfully. "Do they know what is happened?"

"Captain Burhan, as I said, is looking into her death," Violet repeated.

Mabel smirked. "Ah yes, dear Captain Burhan..."

Their conversation died as Marvin and Elizabeth entered the dining room, looking tired and sombre. They went straight to a booth by a window. Two waiters hurried over to their table. They appeared to be taking their breakfast orders. Violet surmised that because of the tragic death of their cousin, Tarek had arranged for the waiters.

"Those poor people, I can't imagine what they're going through," Violet sympathized. Silvio came down the stairs and walked past everyone, going to a booth by himself.

"Poor Silvio," Marie said. "He, how you say? He is sweet on Angie, everyone sees that, *n'ont- ils pas*? Such a shock for the poor man."

"Who's a poor man?" Lucy set her plate and a glass of orange juice on the table. "Janet," she called over her shoulder. "Bring me a croissant and some jam when you come."

"Did you not hear the sad news?" Marie dabbed her lips with her napkin.

"Oh, you mean poor Angie. Yes, we were all in the bar last night. Tarek came and told us. What a shame, and so young too. You just never know when your time is up, do you?"

Violet noticed Ronnie had not said a word since the news of Angie's death. She remembered neither Ronnie nor the Drapeau's were in the bar when she died. If Mabel was right and someone murdered Angie, Ronnie could be a prime suspect. Perhaps, Ronnie knew Angie, maybe he had a motive. She looked across the table at Jean and Marie. They were from France; she doubted either of them knew the American girl. As Mabel pointed out, the couple would be unlikely serial killers on the prowl for likely victims. And they did appear to be shocked when Mabel told them about Angie.

Violet rested her arms on the railing of the sundeck and looked across the Nile river at the lush green vegetation. She saw a small village perched on the shoreline and nearby a small patch of cultivated land. A man led a donkey laden with sugar cane, climbing a path into the trees. The riverboat sailed past small boats with sails, and men stood casting nets into the water. At the riverbank, women washed their laundry, and children splashed in the water. In the background, sand dunes rose, reminding her that they were never far from the desert.

Violet turned away from the view, brushing the fine sand particles off her arms. She took her phone from her pocket. "Did you notice how silent Ronnie became after you announced Angie's death?"

"No, but what of it?"

"Ronnie wasn't in the bar last night. He supposedly went to his room," Violet said, waiting for her phone to boot up.

"He told us he was tired or had a headache or something." Mabel turned and leaned back against the railing.

"Or something." Violet held her phone aloft.

"What do you mean or something? Do you suspect Ronnie of...?" Mabel glanced around her and sidled up close to Violet. "Do you suspect him of foul play?"

"As in murder. You're the one who suspects murder. All I'm saying is Ronnie wasn't in the bar during the time of Angie's demise. Think of the timeline. Marvin, Carrie, and Silvio were all gone from the bar during that time. If we're going to have a suspect list, everyone missing must be on it, even your Ronnie."

"Stop saying, my Ronnie."

Violet shrugged and moved down the deck toward the boat's bow, still holding her phone aloft.

Mabel followed. "I've been thinking about the locked door. Someone could have bribed Ali just like I did. That little steward could have let the murderer into the cabin."

"I've been thinking the same thing."

"But it doesn't add up. If Ali had let the murderer in, he would have had to wait while the killer did the deed. Because the door was locked, and only Ali had the key."

"Right."

"I doubt he is in cahoots with a killer. He would have no motive. And it would have to be an enormous bribe. And I met Ali. He may take little bribes. But of him being an accessory to murder, no, I don't see it." Mabel stopped talking as a group of German tourists arrived. Unfurling the umbrellas, they laid their possessions by the yellow lounge chairs.

The women strolled down the deck.

"Have you got any of your bars on that phone of yours?"

"Yes, finally." Violet perched on the side of a small poolside table.

Mabel stood behind her, peering over her shoulder. "So, this Mr. Goggle, will he tell you about the signs of asphyxiation?"

"It's not a Mr. anything. And it's called Google, a search engine." Violet looked narrowly at her friend. "Sometimes, I think you are putting me on. We had computers at work in the hospital, you can't be this ignorant about the internet."

"Don't be calling me ignorant," Mabel sputtered.

"No, sorry, I mean, you used the computers. Why are you, pardon the expression, so dense about smartphones?"

"I'm not dense, thank you very much," Mabel huffed. "The computers in the hospital were nothing like this phone of yours. They were big and plugged into something, and I never fooled around on them like some people I could name. And I used the computers for work and work alone."

"If you'd been a little more experimental, you would know what the internet is for. Like finding out the symptoms of asphyxiation." Violet tapped her request on the phone.

"I bought a smartphone, you know," Mabel defended.

"And you left it at home."

Mabel grinned. "That's why I brought you along."

Violet smiled back and continued her search. Their disagreements never lasted for long.

A group of Japanese girls smiled at them as they took up their positions around the small pool. Chatting and laughing, the girls took off their sandals, dangling their feet in the water.

Violet finished her search and put her phone back in her pocket. Then she looped her arm through Mabel's. They slowly strolled back down the sundeck to the bar. "I checked three sites to be sure of my findings. And yes, Mabel, you were right. The symptoms you described fits with smothering. Angie's death is not natural. Someone murdered her."

"I knew it, I knew it. Angie was murdered. Finally, you believe me."

"I just wanted to be sure, that's all," defended Violet.

"I knew it as soon as Ali turned on the light in the cabin, and I saw Angie lying on that bed."

"You never told me that."

"I did. I described Angie lying on the bed in her soiled dress. Her eyes open, and her lips peeled back in a hideous grin." Mabel shivered.

"I mean the lights."

"The lights?"

"You said Ali, turned on the lights."

Mabel gasped. "You're right. Angie wouldn't have turned out the lights and then laid down on the bed to die."

"No, she wouldn't," agreed Violet.

"And something else I remember, her hands by her sides as if someone placed them there."

"The cold-blooded killer, you mean."

"But who? Who wanted Angie dead?"

Chapter Eighteen

Mabel stepped up onto the bar deck. The Drapeaus, Neville, and Ronnie clustered around a deck table under the striped awning. Janet and Lucy lay nearby on the lounge chairs, enjoying the sun. She pulled up a chair beside Ronnie. Violet smiled at Neville and took the chair he offered.

Shrill shrieks and laughter could be heard from the Japanese girls who paddled their feet at the pool. Members from the German tour group were running laps around the deck.

Ronnie shifted his chair and drawled, "I can't get over it. Angie died; she was so young, and for her to die so unexpectedly in a foreign country. It will not be easy getting her body back stateside." He picked up his chair, moving it farther under the canopy. "Does anyone know what she died from?"

Mabel felt abandoned. Ronnie's big bulk had been shading her. She wished she had sat on the other side of the table, away from the harsh Egyptian sun beating down on her head.

"Not a clue, old boy." Neville draped his arm on the back of Violet's chair. "She's very young to have a heart attack, but you never know what is just around the bend for you."

"Word is that Angie had an asthmatic attack," Janet said sadly, spreading lotion on her legs.

As Mabel edged her chair under the awning, she saw Neville giving Janet the once-over.

"Where did you hear that?" asked Ronnie.

"May I?" Lucy asked, reaching for the bottle.

"I overheard the police officer telling Silvio," Janet said, handing her sister the bottle of sunscreen.

A gossiping police officer. Mabel curled her lip.

"I didn't know asthma could kill you. Poor Angie, it's so sad." Lucy shook the bottle, opened it, and rubbed sunscreen on her arm.

"I didn't either. Wow, you just never know." Janet stretched out her long-tanned legs.

"An asthmatic attack can be deadly. But it's rare anyone dies." Mabel silently added that's why they have inhalers. Where the heck was Angie's?

Ronnie shifted his deck chair.

Neville gave Mabel a skeptical look. "Pardon me, but how do you know?"

"Mabel is a retired nurse," Violet answered, moving closer to Marie to make room for Ronnie and his chair.

"Oh, sorry, no offence, Mabel," Neville apologized. He smiled across the table at her and moved his chair, following Violet.

Mabel arched one eyebrow and smiled back. She didn't trust the man cozying up to Violet. She'd witnessed his wandering eye.

Ronnie squinted in the sun and shifted his chair again.

Jean and Marie moved closer together, accommodating Ronnie's big bulk. "We may not know how the poor girl died, but it is very sad," Jean said.

"No, kidding. One moment, Angie was having a laugh and flirting with Silvio; the next, she's dead." Lucy capped the lotion bottle.

"Poor Silvio, he's sitting at that table by himself and looks heartbroken," Janet said.

They looked over at the brooding man. He had a cigarette in one hand and a drink in the other.

"We should ask him to join us," Violet suggested.

"Oh, I did, but he said no. He preferred to be alone." Neville's fingers lingered on the back of Violet's neck, she smiled at him.

Mabel pinched her lips. If Violet wasn't careful, she was going to make a fool of herself over this man.

"He had a great admiration for the young woman," Jean said. Marie nodded, looking sadly over at Silvio.

"Did anyone notice Marvin? He was always watching those two. I kind of thought he had a thing for Angie." Lucy gave the lotion bottle back to her sister.

"I thought so too. Did anyone else notice?" Janet asked, setting the bottle by her chair.

"The man has a wandering eye. No wonder his wife treats him like crap." Ronnie shifted his chair. "This blame sun, even in Texas, it's not this hot. I should have worn my hat."

"Marvin and Elizabeth are so very sad at the breakfast. They have, how do you say? A relationship to her," Marie added in her lilting French accent.

Ronnie continued to move his chair in an attempt to escape the hot Egyptian sun. His maneuvering had crowded everyone to one side of the deck table except Janet and Lucy, who stretched out, soaking up the sun rays.

Violet shifted her chair. "Yes, Elizabeth and Angie were cousins."

"Are you quite finished doing musical chairs, old chap?" Neville asked with annoyance.

"Yep," Ronnie answered good-naturedly, patting Neville on the shoulder.

Neville drew away.

"Has anyone seen Carrie?" Mabel asked. "I didn't see her at breakfast."

"No, but she's still probably in bed with a hangover. She was tanked last night." Ronnie settled in his chair and signalled to a waiter.

"She certainly was inebriated," agreed Neville, running his hand lightly over Violet's shoulder.

"I bet Carrie feels awful. She made such a scene, spilling her drink all over poor Angie," Janet remarked.

Neville slipped his arm around Violet's shoulder.

Mabel narrowed her eyes. Neville had an arm around her friend's shoulders; at the same time, he was ogling the California girls.

"I feel kind of sorry for Carrie," Lucy said, laying back in her lounge chair, stretching her legs. "Imagine no clothes.

She's been wearing that tatty kaftan the whole trip. Her luggage has never shown up. I would be steamed."

"If the airline or the tour company lost my luggage, I'd make sure they compensated me." Janet tugged down her tank top, which had ridden up.

Mabel wanted to shake Violet. Neville was watching Janet's every move.

Ahmed hurried over to their table. "Excuse me, wonderful guests." The big man gave them a toothy smile. "Have any of you seen Miss Carrie Larush?"

There was a chorus of no's and shaking of heads.

Wringing his hands, Ahmed smiled. "Oh, my gracious, no worries, dear guests, we shall find her."

"Carrie is missing?" Mabel asked.

"No, no, not missing," he denied. "We will find Miss Larush, do not worry. We look after all our guests." Ahmed signalled to the bartender. "Have the waiters bring drinks for all our special guests," he said, indicating everyone on the sundeck. "There will be no charge, dear guests; this is with compliments from our captain; please enjoy." With that, the purser turned and hurried back down the stairs.

"A death and now a disappearance. This is unreal. I only wanted ancient mysteries on this cruise, not real-life ones." Lucy looked around at her fellow passengers. "What next?"

"Oh, look, it's them," Janet said.

Elizabeth and Marvin appeared at the top of the stairs. Elizabeth looked drawn, and Marvin's eyes had a haunted look to them.

Ronnie jumped up from his chair. His long strides took him over to Marvin and Elizabeth, awkwardly standing by the steps. "We all are so sorry for your loss," he said, giving Marvin a bear hug. Marvin patted the big man on the back half heartily. Ronnie turned to embrace Elizabeth. She put up her hand, but Ronnie wrapped his arms around her, hugging her.

"Thank you. Marvin and I are devastated," Elizabeth said, awkwardly disentangling herself from Ronnie's grip.

Lucy and Janet rushed over, each giving them a hug. Elizabeth wiped her face, looking at the sunscreen lotion on her hand. She grimaced and wiped her hand on her skirt. Marvin and Elizabeth followed the girls to the table. Everyone stood. Marie and Jean gave them a quick French peck on each cheek. Marvin reddened in embarrassment. Neville clasped their hands in sympathy, as did Violet. Mabel hugged both Elizabeth and Marvin; they stood rigid in her embrace; it felt like she was hugging wooden posts.

Silvio stood, paused, and walked slowly to the grieving couple. "I'm sorry for your loss," he echoed Ronnie's words. He stood awkwardly, ignored by Marvin.

"Thank you," Elizabeth's voice was flat.

Marvin turned his back to Silvio and addressed the rest of the group. "Elizabeth and I appreciate your condolences."

Mabel's brow furrowed. Why were they ignoring Silvio?

Elizabeth cleared her throat. "Yes, we do. We've become like family these last few days. It helps to have you here with us now at this terrible time of loss." She took a tissue from her pocket and wiped her eyes.

More like a dysfunctional family, Mabel thought. Elizabeth had been such a shrew. She immediately felt guilty for her uncharitable thoughts. The poor woman had just lost her cousin.

"Have you heard Carrie, the drunk, is missing?" Marvin put his arm around his wife's shoulder.

"Yes, Ahmed just told us they were looking for her. Please take a chair." Offered Neville.

Elizabeth sat in Neville's vacant chair, and Marvin took Ronnie's. Ronnie took a chair from a nearby table. He sat beside Mabel in the sun. Neville stood behind Violet with his hand on the back of her chair.

Mabel watched as Elizabeth reached out her hand to her husband. He grasped it, giving her fingers a gentle squeeze. She may treat her husband like a servant, Mabel thought, but he seemed devoted to her in her hour of need.

Everyone sat around the table except Silvio, who, ignored by Elizabeth and Marvin, returned to his table. He picked up his glass and gulped the contents down.

"I blame that drunken lush for poor Angie's death." Elizabeth withdrew her hand from her husband and dabbed at her eyes again with a tissue.

Ah, thought Mabel, a motive. "I'm sorry?" she asked. "Why do you blame Carrie?"

"If you don't mind us asking?" Violet voiced hurriedly.

"Carrie, that souse spilled drinks all over poor Angie. Angie was really upset. Obviously, it brought on her asthma. Carrie caused Angie's death," Elizabeth said bluntly.

"Whoa, you can't know that for sure; that is a tad harsh," disputed Mabel.

Violet gave Mabel a sidelong look and shook her head. The rest of the tour group looked uneasily at each other.

"I believe it is her fault. Why else is this woman hiding? She's feeling guilty, that's why."

"Dear, maybe she isn't hiding. She was drunk. Maybe she fell overboard," Marvin posed.

"That's a bit of a leap," Violet said.

"No, Marvin said fell, not leap," Elizabeth corrected.

"What I mean is, we can't surmise she fell. No one saw her go over the side."

"She's probably just sleeping it off. She was pretty hammered last night." Ronnie squinted in the direct sunlight.

"Whatever, I blame Carrie, and that's that."

Ronnie shaded his eyes with his hand. "Should we help with the search?"

"I expect the crew knows where to look more than we do," Neville replied.

"I hope they find that lush, Carrie. I want to give her a piece of my mind. She is responsible." Elizabeth's voice broke as she sniffed into her tissue.

Chapter Nineteen

Mabel pushed her chair back, rose, then walked down the deck into the sunshine. She leaned on the rail, looking out over the Nile, thinking back to what Elizabeth had said. Carrie could be responsible for Angie's death, only not in the way Elizabeth meant. She frowned, where is Carrie? Did she fall overboard like Marvin said? Or is she hiding until they reach Edfu? Why would Carrie be hiding? Mabel tightened her lips into a sly smile. There was only one reason. Carrie killed Angie.

On the shoreline, young boys led an ox into the water, washing the beast. Mabel's attention turned back to the table. A waiter was circulating with a tray, taking orders. Elizabeth and Marvin had moved to a table for two.

"It's beautiful cruising down the Nile," Violet said, joining her at the rail. Then she quietly added. "Well, it would be if there wasn't a murder."

"I know, we have a murderer aboard this boat." Mabel led the way down the deck toward the bow, absently running her hand down the railing as they walked. She felt fine dust; the crew was always cleaning. It was a never-ending task; the desert was always on the horizon. "I really want to be wrong."

Violet strolled by her side. "I want you to be wrong too. I don't like us trapped on this boat with a killer. And I don't like us crossing paths with the Egyptian police."

"I don't like it either, but we can't let a murderer escape. Remember what I heard on the plane? What if Carrie was on that plane? And if she was, she has an accomplice, but who?"

"What you heard on that plane has to be a coincidence. Carrie didn't tour with us in Cairo or fly with us to Luxor," Violet reminded her.

"It doesn't mean she wasn't on the plane."

"You can't think she was holed up somewhere drinking herself silly while we were touring in Cairo."

"I don't know, but I don't believe in a coincidence. Anyway, Carrie is missing, and I think she killed Angie."

"What's her motive?"

"I don't know that either, but she must have one. We just don't know what it is. She's hiding for a reason."

"But, is she hiding? No one suspects foul play."

"Especially not that dense police captain," muttered Mabel.

"You can't really blame him."

"Well, I can. He just assumed Angie had either a heart attack or an asthmatic attack."

"The locked door."

"Ah yes, the locked door. Bribery. It was easy enough for me to get inside the cabin. Carrie could've just bribed that little steward. We need to have a chat with Ali."

"But you said he couldn't have been an accessory."

"Yes, Ali looks like a harmless little guy. Looks can be deceiving. I bet he knows something but is afraid to tell anyone, let alone Captain Pompous."

"Would you stop calling that man names? Please say Captain Burhan from now on," Violet said sternly. "If we're to get cooperation from the police, you need to change your attitude."

"He is a pompous ass. He dismissed me like I was an addled-brained child." Mabel looked sourly over the river. "But I will try, I promise you."

A riverboat cruising in the opposite direction downstream to Luxor past them. The passengers waved, and everyone onboard *The Star* waved back. Mabel and Violet made room for the Japanese girls, who rushed to the railing to snap pictures of the riverboat on their phones. Mabel and Violet continued their stroll to the bow of the boat.

"Back to Carrie, why would she kill Angie? It sure can't be because of spilled drinks and a little name-calling. Unless she is a crazy loon." Violet leaned on the railing; a breeze billowed her skirt.

"She could be a crazy nut bar; she certainly is bizarre," Mabel agreed.

"And being drunk all the time doesn't help." Violet brushed her hands together. "I brought wipes up here with me. I left my bag over there, by Neville."

"You'll be fine; it's only sand. Let's think about these two women, Carrie and Angie. We know nothing about them. What are their backgrounds? Did they know each other before this trip? It didn't appear so, but we don't know."

"We should talk to Elizabeth and Marvin. They would know of any connection," Violet suggested.

"Right, and we better do it quickly before we dock at Edfu. We'll be there by this evening. They will leave the cruise to take Angie back to the States," Mabel said, glancing back at their tour group. The waiter was still delivering the drinks Ahmed had ordered.

"On second thought, maybe we need to put the breaks on. As I've said before, we are in a foreign country. You suspect murder and..." Violet held up her hand to forestall Mabel's protest. "And I agree with you it is a suspicious death. But you said yourself, this Captain Burhan does not credit you with any observational powers."

"Or a brain," Mabel said sourly. "Violet, please don't get cold feet. We can do this, all we need is proof. And we will find it. We can't let a murderer get away just because we are not on home territory."

Violet looked skyward and shook her head. "You're going to do this no matter what I say, aren't you?"

"Murder is murder. And no, I am not letting this go. Are you going to help me?"

"Yes, of course. But we need to be careful like I said, we are trapped on a boat floating down the Nile with a murderer."

"We will. Don't worry. I would use my charm on dear Captain Burhan." Mabel sighed. "But unfortunately, I don't have any." She brightened. "But you do. If we run into trouble, I'll rely on you to charm him."

"I seriously think you have overestimated my charm. I'm just a little more diplomatic than you. Anyway, what's our plan?"

"Find Ali and ask him if he let someone in Angie's room." Mabel was glad she had Violet onboard. With Violet's help, she was sure they could solve the murder of Angie Morrison. But time was short. It was almost lunchtime, and the boat would dock at Edfu by evening. They skirted the pool where the German sunbathers had gathered. The Japanese tourists had finished taking their pictures and were now lying on the deck chairs, scanning the images on their phones.

Violet tugged on her arm. "What about Silvio? Look at him, sitting all by himself. He could use some company."

"Good thinking. Silvio and Angie got on very well, always together. Maybe he knows something."

"Or maybe he is the killer, we need to be careful," Violet cautioned.

As Mabel made a beeline across the deck to Silvio's table, she wondered briefly how many of the Japanese tourists understood English. She and Violet had been talking freely.

"Silvio, how are you doing?" Violet sat on a chair opposite him, lightly patting the man on his arm.

"How do you think? Angie is dead," Silvio answered in his raspy voice. He stubbed out a cigarette and swirled the liquid in his glass. The half-melted ice cubes clinked together. "She was such a sweet girl, not like her aunt."

"Aunt?" asked Mabel. "I seem to remember Elizabeth introducing Angie as a cousin." She took a chair beside the tall, handsome man.

Silvio gulped the remains of his drink and set his glass down on the table. He leaned forward and said, "Angie told me Elizabeth thought aunt made her seem old. So, she referred to Angie as a cousin."

"Would you like another drink, Silvio?" Mabel asked. "I'll order us all one. It's on me." She signalled a waiter. It was too early for her to indulge in an alcoholic drink, but if consuming alcohol would keep Silvio talking, she would.

Silvio ordered a whiskey on the rocks, Violet a cola with ice, and Mabel ordered the same as her friend. "Bring our friend here a double; he's in shock." Mabel had no idea if he drank double whiskey's neat. But Silvio seemed happy with her order. They passed the time talking about the history of Egypt and the fascinating sights they'd seen.

Mabel waited until Silvio had a drink. "You and Angie seem to have struck a great friendship, maybe even a little more than just friendship?"

"Yes, we did hit it off. I don't usually like the ladies, but I really did like Angie."

"You don't like women?" Mabel asked.

"Shush, Mabel, this is Egypt."

"What? Why?" Mabel was puzzled.

Violet took Mabel's arm and leaned over the table and whispered into Mabel's ear. "This is Egypt."

"Of course, I know it's Egypt," Mabel snorted. Silvio appeared amused.

Violet's eyes widened; she quickly leaned over to Mabel and whispered into her ear, "Do not say Silvio is gay. This is Egypt, and I think it might be against the law here."

"Really? Oh, sorry, Silvio, I don't think anyone heard me say you were gay."

"Mabel," warned Violet.

Silvio grinned.

"In fact, if you recall, I didn't say Silvio was gay."

"Mabel," Violet stormed. "Stop using that word."

Mabel tilted her chin. "If you recall, I just said he didn't like women. That's all I said."

"Whatever, just leave it alone. Stop talking about, well, you know, stop talking."

"I can hardly stop talking, for goodness' sake, really, Violet."

"You know what I mean." Violet's eyes narrowed.

"I'm not gay if that's what you're wondering." Silvio smiled, and the corners of his eyes crinkled. He seemed to find them amusing. Mabel wondered how many drinks he had before they sat down with him.

"I am what is quaintly called a lady's man." He arched an eyebrow waiting.

"But you said you don't always like the ladies," Violet reminded him quietly.

"Ah, but the ladies like me." His lips twitched.

"Do you make a practice of picking up ladies on holiday?" Mabel asked.

"Not that it's any of our business, goodness me. We're just curious if you show these... ah show these ladies a good time...," Violet's voice trailed off. She glanced at Mabel out the corner of her eye.

Mabel shrugged. If they didn't ask, how would they find out? "Showing lonely ladies a good time, is this some kind of job? Not a very good occupation, I wouldn't think."

Violet took a big gulp from her cold drink, coughing, she wiped her mouth with a paper napkin.

Silvio grinned. "I think I've shocked you, poor ladies; I'm sorry."

"No, well, maybe a little. We know, of course, this sort of thing goes on; we just never meant a...," again Violet trailed off.

"I believe the term you're looking for is gigolo." He grinned, showing his even white teeth.

"Do women pay you?" Mabel had to admit if she were twenty years younger, she would find this man attractive. But there was no way she would ever pay a man to show her a good time, as he called it.

"No, not always; they just like looking after me." He winked and said, "I can be a very charming companion."

Mabel pursed her lips. What a way to earn a living.

"So, tell me, how do you choose your ladies?" Violet asked.

Mabel smiled. They made a good team.

"I'm a watcher," he said.

"A watcher?" Mabel turned her glass on the table, making little rings.

"An observer of people, and I'm a good listener." Silvio grinned. "If you look and watch, you can easily tell who needs." His grin widened. "Who needs company. And who is worth my time."

Violet took a napkin and cleaned the table, wiping off the rings Mabel's glass made. "You say you're a watcher and a listener. How does that work?" She wadded up the damp napkin and stuffed it into her empty glass.

"Angie's luggage was expensive, as were her clothes, and when we arrived at the hotel in Cairo, she wasn't blown away with its opulence. Oh, and I found out they flew first class all the way. And the jewelry she wore, I can tell you was not fake." He sat back in his chair, looking smug.

Mabel wrinkled her nose. Silvio looked less and less charming, the man turned his charm on and off like a spigot. "Did she say anything about Carrie? Like did she know this woman before meeting her here on the boat?"

"Not that I can remember. Angie didn't like Carrie, but who does, that woman is such a lush." He drained his drink, setting the empty glass on the table.

Mabel pasted a smile on her face. Kettle, pot, black, she thought.

"Did you know Carrie before this trip?" Violet asked.

"Good God, no. I don't care if she has a fortune stashed away somewhere. That's one woman I would steer clear of."

"Mabel, I think I want to change into something cooler. Do you want to come with me?"

Mabel agreed. Silvio had said he knew nothing about Carrie, but if he was her accomplice, he would be lying. It didn't pay to make him suspicious.

They left the deck, descending to the stateroom lobby. Mabel and Violet stopped at the foot of the stairs. Four burly porters held a mummy over the balcony to the main lobby below.

Chapter Twenty

Mabel and Violet stood beside Rabbie, the bartender, watching as the porters tipped the white linen-wrapped mummy over the balcony of the spiral staircase. The body wrapped in white bedsheets the men wrestled with was Angie. Miraculously, they got her body down two flights of stairs without dropping her.

"Where are they taking her?" Mabel asked Rabbie.

He looked both ways and then leaned down between Violet and Mabel and whispered in their ears. "They are putting the poor woman in the freezer. Captain's orders."

Mabel had to agree with the captain. The freezer would be the best place for Angie until they reached Edfu because the air-conditioning on the boat was sadly lacking. But she wondered what the other passengers would say if they knew a corpse was stored with their food. No wonder the chief purser ordered drinks for all of the tour groups. His attempt to keep everyone up on the sundeck. They wanted no one to witness the transfer of Angie's body or where they stored it. But if it was to be a secret, she didn't think it would be a secret for long. She thought Rabbie was a talker.

"Violet, should we have a cold drink before we go to our room?"

"What about—"

"A cold drink first," Mabel said forcefully.

Violet shrugged, following Mabel into the empty bar lounge.

Mabel climbed up on a stool at the bar. "Two ice-cold colas, please," she requested as Violet took a barstool beside her. "Ahmed told us Carrie is missing," she added.

"Yes, this morning, Ali went to her stateroom to clean and make up the bed." Rabbie opened his fridge and took out the ice. "And her bed not slept in. Ali became worried and alerted our purser, Ahmed. But do not worry. Our crew is searching for this lady."

"When was the last time you saw Carrie?" Mabel asked.

"Last night, when she spilled her drink on the unfortunate Miss Morrison, the lady who sadly died." Rabbie dropped the ice cubes into the tall glasses.

"And none of the staff have seen her?"

"No one, not even the staff in the dining room, she did not come to the dining room for breakfast. It is a mystery for sure; there is no place to get off the boat; we are in the middle of the Nile." The bartender's little goatee bounced as he chuckled. He poured the cola into the tall glasses and passed one to Violet and then to Mabel.

"What floor is her room?" Mabel didn't know how much more liquid she could drink, but she took a sip.

"This floor, Ali is the steward for this deck."

"You must have seen a lot of Carrie." Violet swirled the cola in her glass and looked at the bartender.

Rabbie set clean glasses on a rack at the back of the bar. "No," he said, turning to face them. "No, Miss Carrie, she go out on tours to see our wonderful monuments like all our lovely guests." Rabbie gave them a big, wide grin. "I only see her when she is with her friends."

"Her friends?"

"Yes, with you and your fellow tour members, your friends."

"She was three sheets to the wind last night. I thought she must've spent the day in here drinking." Mabel poked at the ice in her drink with her finger.

"Sheets blowing in the wind? She is doing laundry?" Rabbie frowned. "We have people to do our guest's laundry."

"No, not laundry, although I suppose she could have done laundry. I don't think her luggage has caught up to her yet," Violet said.

Mabel shook her head. "No, what we mean is Carrie was drunk last night. Didn't you notice?"

"What our wonderful guests choose to do is no business of mine. I do not put my nose there."

"But you did see Carrie, didn't you? She was very drunk." Violet gave him a winning smile. "You're a very perceptive man. A very smart man, you see much more than most people."

Rabbie nodded and grinned. "Yes, you are right. I am a wise man, and I not to talk about my guests and their peculiar behaviour."

Mabel gulped her drink, she would get no more information out of him.

VIOLET PUT HER HAND on Mabel's arm as they left the bar. "Carrie didn't spend the afternoon drinking in Rabbie's bar. But she could have been on the sundeck drinking. Let's go ask the bartender up there."

"I am not downing another glass of anything to get more information. Let's go find Ali."

"You go, I'm going back up to the sundeck. I'll ask the bartender. Don't worry, I'll be subtle. And you be subtle when you talk to Ali."

"You sure it's the bartender and not Neville you're going to see?" Mabel asked.

"Maybe both." Violet smiled, batted her eyelashes, and waltzed back down the hallway, her skirt swaying as she walked.

Mabel watched her friend sashay away. "I suppose everyone is entitled to a little romance," she said aloud.

"Pardon me, my dear lady, you are looking for romance?" Captain Burhan stroked his mustache. His eyebrows wiggled up and down.

Mabel's face flushed hot. She half expected him to click his heels and say at your service. "No, I am not looking for romance. And certainly not from you. What kind of woman do you think I am?" Mabel stormed.

The captain puffed out his chest. His lips drew back in a scowl. "Madam."

Immediately, Mabel regretted her response. He was probably just being friendly. Maybe she should flirt with him? She shifted from foot to foot, uncertain of what to do.

She needed to get on his good side. If they found out who killed Angie, they would need his cooperation. She took a deep breath, deciding to flirt. How hard could it be? Looping her arm in the captain's, Mabel tried a simpering smile. Looking up at him, she batted her eyelashes at the surprised man. "Sorry, I didn't mean for you to hear me...I mean, I didn't mean not with you. I mean, I didn't want romance with you. No, what I mean is that I ah... Have you been a captain long?" Mabel finished lamely.

"Is there something wrong with your eyes? And why do you ask me this question?" He jerked his arm from her grasp.

"My eyes? No, my eyes are fine. I was just wondering how long you've been a captain. How many unexplained deaths have you investigated?" she asked, and gave the man what she hoped was a charming smile.

"Do you doubt my abilities?"

"Oh, my dear captain, that's not what I meant." Mabel batted her eyelashes again.

The captain's brow furrowed. "You have a problem with your eyes?"

"No, my eyes are fine. I was asking if you have investigated many murders."

"Murders? This is not a proper conversation." He gave Mabel a wary look and sidestepped away from her.

"Proper? I'm just asking if you have investigated many murders. I mean, deaths." Mabel moved to retake his arm.

He jerked away. "Murder? What murder?"

She turned to face the man and ran her fingers along his arm, giving her best flirtatious smile.

Captain Burhan's eyebrows raised, and he brushed her hand from his arm. "Why do you ask questions about murders?" he huffed.

Mabel looked up at the man, puzzled. Why wasn't her charm working on him? She was flattering him. *Always appear interested in what a man does for a living,* was her mother's advice. And she was following her advice to a tee.

Ali, the steward, with a load of fresh towels piled high, hurried down the hallway toward them. Mabel zig to the side, but unfortunately, Ali zig the same way. Towels flew out of his arms, and one flew up, and then dropped over the captain's head.

Ali screeched something in Arabic and reached for the towel. The captain slapped Ali's hand away and tore the offending towel off his head. His cap came off with the towel, revealing the man's comb-over.

Mabel giggled, then quickly put her hand over her mouth. Too late, the captain heard. Captain Burhan shrieked in Arabic, his face red with fury. Mabel thought he was cursing as Ali cowered behind a towel he held up in front of his face and scurried behind her.

The little steward peeked over Mabel's shoulder at the captain. Captain Burhan yelled again in Arabic and reached for his hat at the same time as Mabel. They bumped heads.

Embarrassed, Mabel giggled again and reached out a hand to brush his black, stringy hair off his forehead.

The captain slapped at her hand and jumped back, tumbling into Ali, then tumbling to the floor and landing on his backside. Ali knelt over him with his hands clasped as if in prayer.

"Hey, don't be slapping me," Mabel snapped, ready to reprimand him further. But then relented. He looked so helpless sitting on the floor with his hair hanging over his forehead, surrounded by towels. She reached a hand down to help the man up.

The outraged man pushed her away and regained his stance. He brushed at his hair and yelled in Arabic. Scowling at Mabel and Ali, he grabbed his hat and jammed it on his head, storming off down the hallway to the stairs. His hair hung down his forehead like very long bangs.

"So much for charming Captain Burhan." Mabel grinned as she stooped to help Ali pick up the towels.

"No, dear lady, please, I will do this." Ali looked fearfully at the captain's back.

"Nonsense, let me help you." Mabel bent, picking up towels.

Ali snatched them out of her hands. "No, no, you are a guest. My job."

Violet came down the hall. "What happened here?" she asked, kneeling to pick up a towel.

Ali pushed her hand away. "No," he shouted. "My job, my job, this is not proper."

Violet threw up her hands and stood. She turned to Mabel. "What did you do to Captain Burhan? He came storming past me. He seemed to be in a huff. Did you argue with the man again? By the way, that man has very weird hair."

"No, I didn't argue with him. I tried to charm him, but it didn't work out. I'm not sure why. He must have been in a bad mood even before the towel incident."

"You mean this towel incident?" Violet grinned.

"I'll tell you later, it actually is quite funny, well, not for the dear captain."

"No, not funny," Ali muttered. He picked the last towel off the floor and sped down the hallway.

Mabel and Violet trailed after the little steward. Ali had towels draped around his shoulders and arms; he stopped at his trolley adjacent to a cabin. The door to the cabin was wide open. Ali dumped the towels on the cart and started folding them haphazardly.

Violet's eyes narrowed. "You're not using those towels, are you? You're not putting them in the rooms? Those towels have been on the floor."

Ali looked out the corner of his eye at Violet and gave her a gap-tooth grin. He shook a towel. "See, dear lady, all dirt has fallen away." Folding the towel, he added the towel to the pile.

Glowering, Violet's lips turned down. "We use these towels," she mumbled to Mabel. "How do we know our towels haven't been dropped on this dirty carpet?"

Mabel ignored her and peeked in the open doorway of the tiny stateroom. "Whose room is this, Ali?"

Ali continued to fold the towels at a furious pace. He glanced at the open door. "The Mr. and Mrs. Tuttle. Very messy people," he said. His pronunciation sounded like Turtle.

Mabel wandered in and gazed around the room. "You're doing a great job, Ali. It looks very neat."

Violet looked over Mabel's shoulder, her brows knitted in a disapproving frown.

Mabel winked at her friend. It was not Violet clean, but it was Ali clean. It was apparent that Ali was not responsible for tidying up. Or perhaps he didn't want to touch women's clothing. The bed was made, but clothes were piled in an open suitcase jammed in the corner. Scattered across the desk was Elizabeth's makeup. And a blouse and a pair of pantie hose hung over the back of a chair. She followed Violet out of the cabin. "A lot of work for you, Ali. Are you responsible for this whole floor?"

"Oh, my yes," he said proudly. "I clean the floor."

"Ah, that's good, but what I mean is, do you look after all these rooms on this deck?"

"I am fast worker." He took two large folded bath towels into the Tuttle's bathroom. He scooted back, grinning, adding two hand towels and face cloths to his load, balancing a roll of toilet tissue on top.

Mabel traipsed after Ali into the room and stood in the doorway. Violet stayed by Ali's trolley, folding towels. "I hope ours aren't the ones from the floor." She muttered. "Do you think he gave us clean towels?"

Mabel furrowed her brow and hurried back to Violet's side. "Forget the towels. This is Marvin and Elizabeth's room."

"I know, that's what Ali told us." Violet brought her voice down to a whisper, "And Ali just runs off, leaving the door open. Anyone could go in. Well, we did." She folded the last towel, giving Ali's trolley a hard look.

"Never mind the door. Remember yesterday when we were going off on our tour, and I thought I'd forgotten my sun hat?"

"Yes, your hat was on your head." Violet began taking toilet tissue rolls off the bottom shelf of Ali's trolley. "Hold out your hands," she instructed Mabel.

Puzzled, Mabel did as she asked. Violet piled the toilet tissue onto Mabel's arms. Then she scooped up small packages of soap and piled them on top of the toilet tissue.

Mabel peeked over the top of her burden. "Stop this; we have more important things to do than reorganize Ali's cart."

"Never mind, I'm almost done." Violet took the bath towels from the top shelf and set them beside the hand towels and facecloths that were on the bottom shelf. Taking the small packets of soap, she placed them on the second shelf with the facial tissues.

"Then, for goodness' sake, hurry up; my arms are getting tired holding this toilet tissue."

"You need to exercise." Violet unloaded Mabel, piling the rolls of toilet tissue on the top shelf.

"There," she said with a satisfied smile. "Isn't that better? And it didn't take that long now, did it?"

Mabel glanced at the cabin door. "I'm not sure Ali will like it."

"What's not to like?" Violet beamed at her handiwork. "Anyway, you had your hat on your head and went to look for said hat." She chuckled. "Next trip, I may have to put a name tag on you."

"Yes, a big laugh; you forget things, too. Anyway, I came back to our cabin to get my hat, and I realized I was wearing it." Mabel kept glancing at the open doorway to the Tuttle's cabin.

Violet straightened the row of toilet tissue. She curled her lip at the bucket of water hanging off the side of the cart. "Have you seen this water? It's disgustingly dirty. I'm wiping our room down again with my wipes."

"Would you please listen to me for a moment? When I went back to our cabin to fetch my hat."

"Which was on your head. We just went through that. Get on with it."

"I would if you let me finish. I was standing at our door, and guess who I saw coming out of the next cabin to ours?"

Violet leaned down, lining up the little bars of soap. "Who?"

"I saw Marvin." Mabel waited for a response.

"Marvin? But this is his cabin. So he was visiting someone in the next cabin to ours. Who is in the cabin next to ours?" Violet stood, giving Mabel her full attention.

"I don't know, but I have my suspicions. Right now, it would just be a wild guess."

"Like that would be a first."

Mabel threw Violet an impatient look.

Ali reappeared from the room. "I make the nice swan towel sculpture for the Mr. and Mrs. Turtle." He locked the door and turned. His mouth fell open as he stared at his trolley. "What, what has happened here." Ali's eyes narrowed as he looked at the women. "What have you done?" The little man threw his hands up in the air.

"It wasn't me," Mabel said quickly.

Violet smiled proudly. "I've reorganized it for you. Once you're used to it, you'll love it. If everything is in its proper place and stays in that place, you'll find life is much more—"

"Why do you touch my things? Do not touch my things; it is very wrong of you," Ali sputtered, tossing the toilet tissue off the cart onto the floor, some rolled down the hallway. Mabel chased after them, kicking them back to the cart. Violet bent to pick up a roll.

"No, no, do not touch," Ali shooed her away, pulling towels from the cart and then flinging them back on top in a jumble.

"Violet likes to organize, she does this to me, too, Ali. Please don't take offence; she can't help it," Mabel soothed, kicking more rolls of tissue back toward the cart.

Ali grabbed the rolls off the floor, stuffing them back on the bottom shelf of his cart.

"What do you mean, I can't help it? It's not a disease, for goodness' sake. I'm trying to help people." Violet crossed her arms, her lips set in a hard line.

Ali's eyes darted from one woman to the other. He jammed the rest of the toilet rolls into the bottom of his cart. "Guests must not touch with my things. You must not touch my cart again." He stuck out his chin, straightened his shoulders, and pushed his trolley away from Violet down the hallway. The little cart bumped, a wheel caught on a frayed seam on the carpet, and jolted to a stop.

"My friend is very sorry, aren't you, Violet?" She gave Violet a pleading look. Violet tapped a tattoo on the carpet with her toe and glared back at Mabel.

Ali lifted the cart over the rip in the carpet. Water sloshed out of the bucket, splattering Violet, who yelped and danced back.

"Say you're sorry, Violet," Mabel urged. This time, she was the one who was turning on the charm. "Come on, Violet, you know you're sorry."

Violet brushed at the splatters on her skirt, grimaced, and finally said, "I'm sorry I moved your things, Ali. I don't like my stuff touched either. I'm very sorry."

Ali looked up from his cart, and with his chin held high, he turned. "It is good you have learned your lesson. Perhaps where you come from, this is allowed. But not in Egypt, dear lady," he said, nodding regally.

Mabel smiled. Thank goodness Violet apologized. They needed information from the little steward. "And Ali, my friend, you are a very organized man. I bet you know where everyone's stateroom is on this floor."

"You want to bet?" Ali asked, confused. "You want to gamble? I do not gamble." He parked his cart beside the next cabin.

"No, I don't, I don't want to gamble. What I'm saying is you're so clever. You know what cabin people are staying in."

Ali preened at the praise. "Oh, my yes, it is my job. I am good at my job."

Violet rolled her eyes.

Mabel continued, "For instance, you know where Violet and I are staying, right, Ali?"

Casting Violet a cautious look, Ali refolded the towels on his cart. "Oh, my yes, I know this very well."

"And who has the room to the right of us in cabin number nine?" Mabel asked.

"The Mr. and Mrs. Drapeau, very neat people; they speak the French. They speak the English too. Not as good as mine, I don't think," he said proudly. Mabel thought his pronunciation of Drapeau was bang on. But since her French was limited to the back of a cereal box, she wasn't sure.

Ali continued to reorganize his cart.

"All my good work is undone," Violet murmured.

Mabel put out a hand to shush her. "And to the left of us in cabin number eleven, who has that stateroom?"

"The Miss. Carrie Lush, she is very neat." Ali stuffed the last towel in with the soap and tissue. He turned, looking very serious. "But the nice lady is gone. Today, I go to her room, and she is gone. I tell the purser the lady is gone, and now everyone looks for the lost lady, Miss Lush."

Mabel grinned. Ali said Lush instead of Larush. She thought it was an apt description. But the main thing was she got the information she wanted. Cabin number eleven was the cabin she had seen Marvin coming from on the day of the tour to the Valley of the Kings.

Chapter Twenty-One

Mabel led the way back down the corridor, feeling pleased. "We have new information. Although I'm not sure what to do about it."

"Do you suppose Marvin and Carrie are having an affair?" Violet asked, shaking the skirt off her dress.

"I saw him come out of her cabin. What other explanation?"

"Carrie and Marvin? Not a likely pair; she's no prize."

Mabel shrugged. "There is no accounting for taste. I've seen enough unlikely couples to know that."

"What are you saying? Are you talking about Neville and me? Not that we're a couple," defended Violet.

"No, are you having second thoughts about Romeo?"

"Don't call him Romeo and leave Neville and me out of this?"

"I didn't bring Neville up; you did."

"Okay, okay, what were we talking about?" Violet asked.

Mabel heaved a sigh. "Carrie and Marvin."

"Oh, right. Yes, those two are an odd couple. Carrie has no class whatsoever, and she's a drunk." Violet brushed at the skirt of her dress. "Can you see any splatters from that dirty water bucket on me?" she asked.

Mabel looked at Violet's dress as she turned in a circle. "No, you're fine. But back to Marvin. Elizabeth treats that man like dirt. He might look for comfort from another woman. Any port in a storm, as they say."

Violet shook out her skirt and took another look down the front of her dress. "Even if they are attracted to each other, it would have to be love at first sight. Carrie didn't join us until Luxor."

"That doesn't mean Marvin didn't know Carrie from before. She could've come later to divert suspicion about their affair," Mabel said.

"Okay, saying that is true." Violet paused and waited until a group of German tourists passed them down the hallway. "If those two were having a thing, it would be Elizabeth that Carrie would want to get rid of, not Angie," Violet continued in a hushed voice.

Mabel waited until another German couple passed them. They nodded a polite hello. "Carrie has to know Elizabeth treats Marvin like a dogsbody. Elizabeth isn't a threat to her. If she saw Marvin ogling Angie, she would suspect Marvin had a thing for Angie. Angie is, or rather, she was, young and beautiful. Carrie could have killed Angie in a fit of jealousy. Perhaps that spilled drink was no accident. Maybe she wanted to get Angie alone."

"I guess Carrie is a possibility." Violet frowned. "But don't forget Silvio, that slimy gigolo, left the bar. What if he followed Angie and made unwanted advances, she rejected him, and things got out of hand, and then he killed her? Maybe his drinking himself silly is guilt eating him up."

Mabel nodded and resumed walking down the corridor. "Yes, if Angie reported him, he would spend a long time in an Egyptian jail. That would certainly be a good motive for Silvio to kill her."

"But Marvin, he wasn't in the bar either. He could have killed Angie." Violet tugged on her arm.

Mabel stopped. "But what motive would Marvin have to kill Angie? Everyone, including us, thought he had a thing for her."

"What we said about Silvio could apply to Marvin; he presses Angie, and she rejects him. Maybe she threatened to tell Elizabeth. And don't forget your friend Ronnie."

"Are you doing this because I tease you about Neville?"

"Doing what?"

"You always say, your friend Ronnie."

"Well, he is, isn't he?" Violet gave Mabel an innocent smile.

"Whatever."

"Ronnie, who is everyone's friend." Violet grinned.

"All right, all right, what is the point you're trying to make?"

"He should be on our suspect list. Ronnie had an opportunity. He said he was in his cabin with a headache. But was he?"

"But what's Ronnie's motive?" Mabel asked.

"The same motive as Silvio and Marvin. An advance that went wrong. Angie was a beautiful girl. Attractive enough to stir the ardour of any of these men."

"I guess one never knows, but Ronnie just doesn't seem the type."

"Don't forget the locked door. The key was inside," Violet added.

"Oh, darn it, I forgot to ask Ali if he let anyone else besides me into Angie's cabin."

"And where the heck is Carrie? Have they found her? Or did she fall overboard like Marvin said?"

"Or was she helped overboard? Maybe she was a witness." Mabel lowered her voice as a troop of white-clad waiters mounted the stairs from the deck below.

Violet paused at the stairs leading to the sundeck. "Speaking of Carrie, I had a chat with the bartender, Fahim. He's a very nice man with a wife and four children."

"Madam, please make room." A man wearing a tall chef hat waved them away from the stairs. Mabel and Violet quickly scooted back from the stairwell. The army of waiters carrying platters, salvers, and chafing dishes clambered up the steps to the sundeck. The uncovered dishes were piled high with delicious-looking food.

Mabel marvelled; not a dish teetered, and nothing fell off as the men sped up the small staircase. Her stomach growled as she waited. "It's Carrie we're interested in, not good old Fahim and his wives."

"He doesn't have a harem. I said he has one wife."

"Right, okay, one wife. And Carrie? What did he say about her?"

"Nothing."

"Violet, you were up top for a great length of time, and you found out nothing? Who was taking up your time, I wonder?" Mabel teased.

"You're beginning to sound like a broken record."

"Sorry, but you found out nothing?"

"When I said nothing, I meant Carrie didn't spend the afternoon up there drinking while we went to the Valley of the Kings and the temple. So, you could've seen her at Karnak. She might have taken a taxi."

"Aha, I was right," Mabel said. "I'm betting after Carrie snuck to Karnak, she came back aboard and hit the bottle. Because she sure was weaving her way down the hallway when we met her on our way to supper. And she was a total mess by the time we all met in the bar."

"Then Carrie is a closet drinker because she didn't frequent either bar."

"I'd sure like a look in her room." Mabel followed Violet up the stairs leading to the sundeck.

"So, where is she now?" Violet asked. "Maybe she witnessed something. And she is lying dead somewhere below deck?"

"I think she's hiding. I think she killed Angie." Mabel was puffing as they climbed to the top of the stairs. The staff had set large buffet tables on the sundeck in front of the bar. The food looked and smelled incredible.

"This boat is antiquated, and our so-called staterooms are tiny. And Ali might not be the best steward," Violet said as they looked across the deck at the food-laden tables. "But the food is fabulous, and the sights of Egypt make up for the lack of amenities."

Neville waved them over to his table and pulled out a chair for Violet.

"Have you been up here all morning?" Mabel pulled out a chair from the table and sat.

"Yes, I've been enjoying the vista. What were you two doing below deck? You're missing all this." He waved his hand, gesturing toward the lush shoreline. They were passing by a small village, and children stood on the riverbank, waving.

"Oh, you know, lady stuff." Mabel smiled. The mention of lady stuff scared men skinny.

Neville's face flushed. "Marvin and Elizabeth stayed up top too. I'm glad they aren't holed up in their room."

"Shall we eat?" Violet asked. "A line is forming at the buffet tables."

Mabel spied Marvin and Elizabeth at a small table across the deck. She turned to Violet. "I'm going over to the Tuttle's table."

"Good idea, they look kind of lost," Neville agreed

Violet stood. "I'll join you."

"What about lunch? You said you were hungry." Neville frowned.

"We won't be long. It's only proper to offer more condolences," Violet said and followed Mabel.

Marvin and Elizabeth stopped talking as they approached. Mabel wondered if they were arguing again. They both seemed tense. But then she supposed they would be. It would take a lot of red tape to get Angie's body back stateside.

"We're so sorry for your loss," Violet said.

"You've already said that," Elizabeth said sullenly, bringing a tissue to her nose and sniffing.

Violet's eyes widened. She tightened her lip and paused, then sat in a chair beside Marvin.

Mabel sat beside Elizabeth, grasped one of Elizabeth's hands, and patted it. "What a terrible shock for you."

"And on holiday too." Elizabeth gave them a sad smile.

"And we're so far from home," Marvin added. "But what can you do? These things happen."

"You have a very good attitude about it all." Mabel wondered how she would cope if anything happened to Violet. Elizabeth was a lot stronger than she had first thought, but of course, Elizabeth didn't know someone murdered Angie.

"I knew Angie was asthmatic, you know. I wish I had gone back with her when she went to change." Elizabeth's voice quivered, "Maybe I could have saved her life."

"Where was her inhaler? I didn't see the inhaler, did you?" Mabel asked Elizabeth.

"I didn't look. I was much too upset to look for her inhaler." Elizabeth shuttered and withdrew her hand.

"Did Angie know Carrie before this trip?" Mabel asked.

Marvin shrugged. "I don't know?" He glanced at his wife.

Mabel thought Marvin looked uncomfortable. Was he hiding something? An affair? Her suspicions that he knew Carrie before the trip might well be right.

Elizabeth rose from her chair. "No, I don't know either. But I do know she is a dreadful woman, a drunk. I hold her responsible for poor Angie's death. She put dear Angie in such a state. She had an asthmatic attack," she said, repeating her earlier accusations.

"I agree with Elizabeth. Carrie may not have taken Angie's life. But she is responsible. No wonder she is hiding." Marvin stood, pushing the chair back to the table. "Elizabeth, I think we should go to the buffet before the food runs out."

At the buffet table, the Japanese and German tour groups lined up. Behind them, the California sisters, followed by the rest of their tour group, except Silvio, who sat alone at a table looking downcast.

Elizabeth and Marvin fell in behind Marie and Jean. Neville made way for Violet to stand in front of him in line. Mabel was famished; she was torn between continuing her investigation and eating. Her tummy won out, and she followed Neville and Violet.

After filling her plate, Mabel carried it to Silvio's table. "Do you mind if I sit here, dear?" she asked.

Silvio motioned for her to sit down.

Mabel unfolded her cutlery from her napkin. "Not hungry?"

"I will eat when the horde is done," he said morosely.

Mabel dug into the food on her plate, wondering what more she could learn from Silvio. He and Angie must have exchanged information as a matter of course. But he was a philanderer, and he might be the killer. She needed to be careful about how she asked her questions. Smiling innocently at the man, she asked, "I admit, I'm rather naïve. But I'm curious about your occupation. How did you get into this line of work?"

Silvio gave her a big, wide smile. "You don't want to know my life story." He lit a cigarette, coughed, and continued in a hoarse voice. "I'm afraid it's a little too sordid for your delicate ears."

Mabel tried another tact. "These women you're attracted to. You said you could spot them by how they dressed and so on. But people have credit cards. How do you find out if they have money? For instance, was Angie wealthy? And how did you know for sure?"

"I ask questions. But mostly, I listen. It's easy; people like to talk, and they like to brag. I found out Angie had money. Her dad had invested in an offshore drilling company. He left her a bundle. She and Elizabeth travelled a lot, and Angie always paid for all the expenses. Then Elizabeth married Marvin, and Angie felt left out. So, when she got to Egypt, she was up for a little romance." He flashed Mabel a smug smile.

Mabel placed her fork on her plate and leaned her elbows on the table. "You said Angie had the money, and she and her cousin, or rather her aunt, travelled a great deal."

"Yes, Angie said they had a great time."

"Did she say when Elizabeth and Marvin married?"

"No, and I didn't ask. It didn't interest me." He looked over at the buffet table and stubbed out his cigarette. "The line is gone, I'm going for something to eat."

Mabel finished eating while waiting for Silvio's return. She noticed Violet at the nearby table, deep in conversation with Neville. Was Neville in the same profession as Silvio?

Silvio plunked his plate down on the table. "I should have gone earlier; it's all picked over," he lamented.

When Silvio finished his meal, Mabel asked, "Forgive me for asking, I am just a silly old woman who is curious about the ways of the world." She hoped she wasn't laying the old lady bit on too thick; she smiled and continued, "But from what you've said, I think Angie paid for both Elizabeth and Marvin's trip to Egypt. Did she say?"

"Yeah, Angie bragged that she paid the whole shot for her aunt and her husband." Silvio wiped his mouth with a napkin and signalled to a waiter. He ordered another whiskey on the rocks.

Mabel took a drink of her water and peered over the glass at Silvio. "It must have been hard for Angie travelling with an aunt who is so demanding."

"I did ask Angie how she could stand that woman? She said Elizabeth wasn't always such a crank. It started just as they got to Egypt. She didn't really know what got into her aunt. She thought maybe Marvin had an affair before they left, and Elizabeth found out."

Carrie. Mabel's eyebrows rose. She congratulated herself, Carrie and Marvin were having an affair.

"She treats Marvin like a dog," Silvio snorted. "The man has no self-respect and deserves what he gets."

"Does he know?"

"Does he know what?"

"Does he know Angie is the one with money and not his wife?"

"Search me, but I guess it won't matter much now. I expect Elizabeth will inherit all Angie's loot." Silvio looked across the sundeck at the Tuttle table. He had a sly smile on his face.

Mabel's spidey-senses picked up, money and sex. If Elizabeth suspected Marvin of carrying on with someone, her temperament would change, making life miserable for Marvin. And if he discovered Angie, not Elizabeth, had all the money. That was a motive for murder. Carrie might be Marvin's accomplice. Now, she had her first solid motive. And Angie might be only the beginning. Would Elizabeth be next? She would inherit Angie's money. Mabel looked across the sundeck; Marvin was sitting with his arm around Elizabeth's shoulder. A chill ran up her spine.

But as she eyed Silvio, she remembered he had left the bar during the time Angie was murdered. She couldn't rule him out. He said Angie was up for romance, but maybe she wasn't up to what he was after.

Chapter Twenty-Two

Mabel realized she had no proof, and she might be jumping to conclusions. She needed Violet's take on her new suspicions. Violet was the level-headed one. But her friend was deep in conversation with Neville. What the heck did she see in that smarmy man?

Tarek, circulating, was stopping at each table to talk to each member of his tour group. He paused at their table. "Did you enjoy the buffet?" he asked.

"Not much left by the time I ate, but okay, I guess," Silvio replied.

"Everything was delicious; Silvio was a little late, is all." Mabel smiled up at her tour director.

Silvio gave her a sour look.

"Have they found Carrie?" Mabel asked. "I hope nothing has happened to her."

"Do not worry, I am sure the crew searchers will find her," Tarek replied.

Mabel thought he looked worried.

"She's probably holed up somewhere, sleeping one off." Smirked Silvio.

Tarek arched his eyebrows. "I am sorry. I am afraid I do not understand. Hold up? Asleep off?"

"Silvio means Carrie drank too much and is asleep somewhere," Mabel explained.

"Ah, I see." Tarek smiled uncertainly and moved on to the next table.

"Do you go on a lot of trips looking for rich women?" She didn't expect a straight answer.

"Sometimes I luck out, and I find one, but sometimes it's just the thrill of the chase."

What a sleazy operator, Mabel thought as she got to her feet. She hoped he would get his comeuppance. "What are you going to do now?" she asked, pushing her chair back to the table.

"Maybe I'll romance Elizabeth; she most likely will inherit Angie's money. She has no respect for her husband. It shouldn't be too hard." Silvio knocked back his drink.

Mabel's lips curled down. "She just lost her niece; show some respect. And you know what they say. Karma sometimes comes back to bite you in the butt."

"You're going to tell Elizabeth, aren't you?" he accused, his eyes narrowed.

"And what would I be telling her?" Mabel leaned on the back of her chair, giving him a steely look.

"What I do for a living. That I take advantage of rich women and get them to take care of me," Silvio sneered.

"Your words, not mine. You know what kind of man you are. It might not be too late for you to change. At least, I hope not."

"You have no idea what kind of a man I am." Silvio's naturally raspy voice had an icy quality about it.

Mabel shivered. Was that a warning? She felt his eyes follow her as she walked away. Trying to look unconcerned, she touched Violet on the arm. "I'm going to take a stroll around the deck. Would you like to join me?" she asked.

Violet got to her feet. "Sure, I need to burn off some calories; that was a great lunch."

"I would join you lovely ladies, but I will just relax here if you don't mind," Neville said. Mabel wanted to say no one asked you, but smiled instead.

Violet measured her long stride to Mabel's shorter one. "Did you find out anything more from Silvio?" she asked.

Mabel related the information she'd gleaned.

"So Angie was loaded, and Elizabeth and Marvin have marriage problems. If Marvin is having an affair that explains why Elizabeth has been such a cow," Violet said as they passed the pool where some Japanese tourists were splashing each other. She sidestepped to the rail and just missed getting wet.

"It's hard to believe, I know. But Marvin might, and I stress might, be having an affair with Carrie."

The girls splashed each other again, cool water sprayed onto Mabel's feet. It felt good. The Japanese girl yelled out in heavily accented English, "Sorry."

Mabel shrugged and smiled back.

"Marvin is a handsome man, and Carrie is not what you call attractive. Elizabeth is pretty. That is when she doesn't have a sour look on her face. Why would he cheat on

Elizabeth with a lush like Carrie?" Violet asked, stepping carefully on the wet deck.

"But what if Elizabeth was a shrew before this Egyptian trip? Angie might not know the whole story in that marriage. If Elizabeth was treating Marvin like dirt for a lot longer, he looked for love and found it with Carrie. And if he found out Elizabeth had no money, that would give him the motive to kill Angie. Marvin and Carrie could be in it together. First, they knock off Angie. Then my guess is they kill Elizabeth next. Remember all those close calls Elizabeth had."

"Those incidents might well have been just accidents. And Marvin in love with Carrie? Really?" Violet ran her hand down the railing.

"Okay, maybe the love is one-sided. Carrie loves Marvin, and she kills Angie for him."

"I think Marvin had a thing for Angie. He doesn't look like a killer, and a lush like Carrie would be the worst kind of accomplice. I think you are way off the mark." Violet wrinkled her nose as she looked at her hands.

"Who looks like a murderer? Looks can be deceiving, and you know that."

"True, but Carrie? I can't see her as a murderer. And the locked door. Don't forget that. All this is you speculating, and speculating is not proof. Your Captain Burhan will want proof." Brushing off her hands, Violet continued to stroll by Mabel's side.

"Of course, he'll want proof. And stop saying, my captain."

"Okay, but it's proof we need, and it's proof we don't have."

"I know we only have theories. Meanwhile, poor Angie lays in cold storage, waiting for justice."

Violet gave her a sidelong glance. "Geez, you do have a way with words."

"Really, Violet, have you just met me? Anyway, our theories are not going to convince Luxor's finest to investigate."

They stopped and leaned on the railing. Four old sailboats passed; they waved at the men in the boats, and the men waved back.

"It all comes back to Carrie." Mabel continued, "Why is she hiding? As you said, Carrie would make a terrible accomplice. So, what if after she killed Angie, Marvin kills Carrie and throws her overboard? I asked Tarek if they had found her, and they hadn't. And by now, the crew should've found her. This boat isn't that big."

"Do you really think Marvin threw Carrie overboard?"

"Who knows, maybe? Or, the murder has nothing to do with Marvin. Did Carrie know Angie before this cruise? I don't agree with you when you say she couldn't kill anyone. How do we know? We know nothing about that woman. And we won't until they find her. If they find her?"

"Right. The crew will have searched every inch of this boat. It's very strange." Violet rested her arms on the railing and looked across the Nile.

"Darn Silvio and his black heart, he brought all these thoughts to my attention."

"Maybe it's a smokescreen, and Silvio killed her. So, what now?"

"I don't know. If you would spend less time with that David Niven look alike, you might have a plan. Why do I always have to have a plan?" Mabel skirted around a group of German tourists with towels draped around their necks on the way to the pool. She seriously doubted they all could get into the pool at the same time.

"Mabel, Mabel, such little faith you have in me, tisk, tisk. I was investigating." Violet stepped aside as a big man wearing a yellow Speedo loped toward her.

Mabel glanced at the large man and then quickly down at her feet. Why any man thought they looked good in a Speedo was beyond her. "Sorry, Violet, I wasn't listening; you said you were investigating? Who at that table was able to shed light on our suspects?"

"Neville, the poor man you have been disparaging, that's who," Violet said triumphantly.

Mabel paused at a yellow plastic lounge chair, beckoning Violet to do the same. Violet unfolded two large white pool towels and laid them on the lounge chairs. "If you remember, Neville and Carrie were the last ones to join our tour group in Luxor."

Mabel struggled to open the big umbrella. Ronnie trotted over and grinned. "Men's work," he said, unfurling the umbrella.

"Thank you, Ronnie. You are a true gentleman." Mabel gave him a grateful smile.

"No problem, ma'am; I'm always ready to help a lady." He adjusted the umbrella. "It's a terrible thing, poor Angie dying. I'm a little embarrassed to say this, but I am enjoying this cruise down the Nile. And I'm looking forward to exploring the temples at Edfu. Marvin told me they are really something. The temple is dedicated to the ancient Egyptian god Horus. And did you know the temple fell into disuse as a religious monument during the time of—"

"That is fascinating," interrupted Mabel. "We're looking forward to seeing the temple."

Ronnie nodded. "Oh, sorry, I don't want to spoil it for you, but it is fascinating—"

"Wow, this sun is scorching," Mabel interrupted again; she looked at Violet for help. Ronnie was liable to run on and on about temples if they didn't stop him.

"It looks like you were playing cards," Violet said, adjusting the pool towel on the lounge chair.

Under the canopy at a table, Jean Drapeau and his wife Marie sat with Neville. Neville held up his hand and waved. Violet waved back. "A nice way to enjoy the afternoon," she said.

"Yeah, we're passing the time until we dock. Poor Elizabeth and Marvin will leave us then. It's such a shame; they're nice people. Well, Marvin is a little henpecked, and Elizabeth is, well, she is who she is..." Ronnie's voice trailed off.

Mabel thought he might be trying to think of something nice to say about Elizabeth. He had saved her twice and was rebuked for it each time.

"But, whatever." He smiled. "We'll miss them, but at least they got to visit the Valley of the Kings and Karnak and the Great Pyramids on the Giza plateau." Ronnie tilted the umbrella so that the shade rested on the two deck chairs.

Mabel looked over at the sundeck. Marvin and Elizabeth were sitting by themselves. At another table, the California sisters were chatting to Silvio. "Who's winning?" she asked, looking at the card players. She wished Ronnie would leave. He was a nice man and meant well, but she had a murder to solve.

"Me, I guess. I better give them a chance to win some of their money back." He laughed heartily.

As if on cue, Neville called out, "Ronnie, we're waiting. It's your turn."

"I've got to go," Ronnie said, chuckling. "Neville is panting at the bit to give me more money." He grinned and trotted back to the table under the awning.

"Ronnie is such a thoughtful man, a real Texas gentleman, and I think he's sweet on you," Violet teased.

"Nonsense," Mabel huffed, embarrassed and swung her legs up onto the chair.

Violet grinned. She laid back on her deck chair and waited until a group of giggling Japanese girls ran past on their way to the pool. "Do you want to hear what I learned?"

"Yes, I do. What did Neville tell you?" Mabel sat up.

Violet waited while another group of German men and women made their way to the pool. "I asked Neville if he met Carrie in Cairo. He said no, he didn't. His plane arrived late, so he went straight off one plane and onto another."

"And?" Mabel looked behind her at the pool. Loud voices rose from both groups. This did not bode well for affable relations between nations.

Violet glanced over at the pool and continued, "Carrie was not on the plane from Cairo to Luxor. Nor was she on the same transport to the boat. Neville never clapped eyes on her until he was on our boat, *The Star*."

"So she didn't fly to Luxor on the same plane and didn't take the same transport?"

"Right, he never saw her. He'd met her the same time we did?"

"Interesting. Perhaps it's another flight, and I guess she came by taxi."

"Okay, maybe she did come by taxi. But another thing. If the airline lost your luggage, would you not be making a fuss? We were docked at Luxor for two days. Carrie is not a wallflower. She wears that hideous red kaftan. And I never heard her once make a complaint about no clothes."

"I thought you liked Carrie's kaftan?"

"I did, but can you imagine how gross it is to wear that dress day after day in this heat?" Violet shuttered. "And I never heard her complain. Don't you find that odd?"

"Oh, you're right, why doesn't she? But maybe she did; let's go ask the purser." Mabel jumped off the lounge chair and hurried down the stairs. She left Violet on deck, apologizing to the waiters as she dodged between two men carrying platters and serving trays down the narrow steps. Above on the sundeck, Mabel heard an escalating row going on in three distinct languages. But she paid little attention, her mind was on the mystery of Carrie.

Chapter Twenty-Three

"Sorry," Mabel apologized, pushing her way through the line of waiters carrying the dirty dishes down the stairs. Her arm bumped a waiter holding a tray of dishes over his head as he tried to negotiate a step. The tray slipped from the waiter's hands, landing on Mabel's head. A collective gasp erupted from the waiters. Fortunately for Mabel, it landed right side up. She paused in her flight to remove the tray from her head. Three food-laden dishes from the tray teetered, then slid off, crashing on the stairs. The parade of waiters halted.

"Sorry," Mabel apologized again. As she bent to pick up a shard from the broken plate, the tray she held in her hand teetered again, and the rest of the dirty dishes toppled off. Food dropped on the stairs, and the plates slid down the steps. Mabel's face reddened as she handed the empty tray back to the tall, skinny man, whose mouth hung open. "At least these dishes didn't break," she said, picking up a chicken bone and some dirty paper napkins. Where to put the rubbish? She looked at the waiter, who stood, holding the empty tray. "Here you go," she said cheerfully, setting the greasy bone and napkins on the tray.

Waiters stood with stunned looks on their faces as the man glowered at her and muttered in Arabic. He leaned down, picked up the food, and motioned for her to go.

"Sorry," Mabel said again, wiping her greasy fingers on her Capri pants.

Another waiter knelt and, picking up broken dishes, yelled, "Go, go."

"So sorry, but I'm in a hurry, ladies' issues," Mabel said, stepping over the plates and bowls scattered on the steps. She wasn't sure if the men understood, but they crowded to the wall, glaring at her. She slipped on a dirty plate, slid down a few steps, regained her balance, and made her way carefully down the remaining stairs to the main deck.

Once on the deck, she scurried over to the desk and smiled at the purser, Ahmed Hakimi. "Good afternoon," Mabel said.

Ahmed looked briefly at her, then returned to writing, his pen making big flourishes on an official-looking form. Waiting for him to finish, she watched the troop of waiters trod past on their way to the dining room below, each giving her angry glares. She shrugged her shoulders and smiled weakly. "Sorry," she said again.

Ahmed finished his paperwork and gave her a big, wide smile. "What can I do for you, dear lady?"

Were all the staff expected to call the women onboard, dear lady? Mabel returned his smile, resisting the urge to say, 'Dear man.'

"That was really rude," Violet said, joining Mabel at the desk. "Those poor guys are still cleaning up the mess you made. You should have waited."

"I know, but I said I was sorry."

"You would like something, dear lady? Is all to your liking? We are all so sorry. It is the terrible discovery of your poor dead friend. Terrible, terrible." Ahmed tisked. "You are fine?"

"Yes, I'm fine, thank you for asking." Mabel smiled up at the big man, deciding not to resist. She asked, "Dear man, we were just wondering if Carrie Larush's luggage ever showed up?"

If Ahmed was surprised by her question, he hid it well. "No, alas, nothing arrived. Perhaps when we reach Edfu."

"Has she been nagging you about her lost luggage?" asked Violet.

"Nagging? No, no one is nagging; everyone is very nice. There is much laughter, and everyone is happy. Well, except for the unexpected death of your dear friend."

"You mean Carrie hasn't been down here complaining about her lost luggage?" Mabel asked.

Ahmed's nostrils flared. "No, but this lost luggage is not my fault. We are sorry Miss Larush does not have her luggage. But this is the fault of the airline."

"We know it is not your fault, and we didn't mean that. We just want to know if she inquired about her luggage."

Ahmed shuffled papers around on the desk. "No, Miss Larush does not inquire. She does not complain. Why? Do you want to issue a complaint?"

"Good gracious, no, absolutely not. Although some of the tiles in our bathroom are falling off ..." Violet let the sentence hang.

Ahmed stuck out his chin and crossed his arms. "My dear ladies, you must talk to your stateroom steward if you have a problem with your bathroom."

"Is Ali a plumber?" Violet asked.

"No, Ali is your room steward."

"Yes, we know, but the tiles in the bathroom—"

"Violet, it doesn't matter."

"Of course, it matters; the tiles are falling off every time we take a shower; at this rate, we'll end up in the Nile." Violet's calm, charming manner had deserted her.

"What? No, dear lady, you will not end up in the Nile; this is a good boat," asserted Ahmed huffily.

"Yes, of course, a very good boat; come along, Violet. Sorry to bother you."

Violet pressed her lips in a firm line, folding her arms. "We should deal with this matter."

"Yes, but not now." Mabel grabbed Violet by the arm, tugging her away from the desk. Ahmed gave the women an unhappy look.

The waiters trooped back up the stairs, the men giving Mabel disgruntled looks. Mabel wondered how many times she would have to say sorry. She hoped she wouldn't get a bowl of soup in her lap at supper. They followed the waiters to their deck and paused.

"Ahmed is right," Mabel said.

"About asking Ali to re-tile our bathroom? Ahmed was no help at all; I'm a little miffed. This boat is hardly a luxury liner. But tiles coming off every time we shower is a bit much."

"Would you forget about those darn tiles for a moment? We decided the condition of this boat would not ruin our Egyptian holiday."

"But this murder is."

"Yes, it is, but if we solve it, we can get back to our holiday," Mabel pleaded with her friend.

"Okay, you're right. We're here, and we'll make the best of it."

"Good now, back to Ahmed."

"Must we?"

"Violet," warned Mabel.

"Right. Back to the purser. What about him?"

"It's not his fault the luggage is missing."

"Oh, for god's sake, I know it isn't his fault. That isn't my issue with the man."

"Violet, please, would you get back onboard with why we went to talk to the purser? We wanted to know if Carrie has been asking about her lost luggage. She hasn't, and that is who I would've asked about my missing luggage. Wouldn't you?"

"Yes," Violet agreed.

The army of waiters reappeared carrying trays of dirty dishes from the sundeck. Mabel stepped well back, out of their way.

"Or Tarek. Maybe Carrie complained to him. After all, he is the tour director." Violet walked down the hallway toward their room.

Mabel hurried to her side. "I remember Carrie saying she didn't blame Tarek, so it would be Ahmed she would complain to about the lost bags."

"Maybe she got her luggage." Violet slowed her stride. "But if she did, why does she keep wearing that ghastly kaftan?"

"We should find out. Do you have some Egyptian pounds on you?"

"I do, but why do we need the pounds?"

"First, we scout out Ali and find out who else he let into Angie's cabin. Then we bribe him. I'm sure he'll let us into Carrie's room."

"What do you hope to find?"

"I want to find out if she got her luggage. And I would also like to examine Angie's cabin."

"Why?"

"Captain know-it-all threw me out of the room. I never got a chance to search for that inhaler. Elizabeth told us she was asthmatic. So, where is the inhaler? Maybe I missed it, but if I didn't, did the killer take it? And if so, why?" Mabel sped past Violet, looking down the hallway for Ali's cleaning trolley.

"Why are you in such a big hurry?"

Mabel paused and asked, "Have you forgotten that we will dock soon? Time is running out. They will remove Angie's body to a morgue or a funeral home. Or whatever the equivalent is here in Egypt. The evidence of the broken nails and the tiny pieces of plastic under them will be lost. If we don't find out now who murdered Angie, no one will be held responsible. And I feel responsible. I knew there would be a murder, and I wasn't able to stop it. So I want to catch whoever killed Angie."

Violet hugged Mabel. "It's not your fault. How could you have prevented it? You couldn't." They linked arms and continued down the corridor. Violet added, "And you did have the wrong victim in mind."

Mabel sighed. "I know."

"And we have an uphill battle ahead of us, even if we find evidence. You've struck the wrong note with Captain Burhan." Violet reminded her.

"That's where you come in. Look, there is Ali's cart. I'll ask him who else he let into Angie's room. When we find that out, we will solve the case, that is, if you can persuade our dear captain to listen to us."

"You want me to persuade the captain?"

"Yes, you. I said that's where you come in, with your charm and persuasive manner."

"I think you overestimate my powers of persuasion."

Violet followed Mabel down the hallway to Ali's cart. She paused, eyeing the messy cart, her lips turned down.

Mabel yanked on her arm. "Forget about that darn cart."

Violet wrinkled her nose and trailed after Mabel to stand in the open doorway of the cabin.

Mabel watched as Ali finished creating a swan out of towels on the bed. "Hello, Ali, busy at work, I see."

Violet raised her eyebrows, making little tisk sounds. She leaned into Mabel and muttered, "It would be a lot better if he spent more time cleaning instead of messing about with the towels."

Ali turned and smiled proudly. "Do you like? I am the artist with the towels."

"Very creative, Ali. Whose room is this?" she asked,

"Mr. Roundie, he is a good tipper." Ali stood back, admiring his handy work.

Mabel grinned. Ali called Ronnie, Roundie. But Ali's English was way better than her Egyptian, which was nil. "You said Ronnie was a good tipper. Who tipped you to open the door to Angie Morrison's room?"

Ali walked past the women to his cart. He looked at his cart, then at Violet, his eyes narrowed with suspicion.

"I'm not touching your cart, Ali," Violet said, holding up both hands.

Ali eyed Violet again, then retrieved a roll of toilet tissue. And returned to the cabin, placed the toilet tissue on the roller, and folded the tissue ends into a neat V.

"Ali, you never answered my question. Who tipped you to open the door to Angie's cabin?"

"You did." He smiled.

"Yes. I know I tipped you, but who besides me?"

"Oh my, yes, you are beside me." Ali shut the cabin door, took the keys out of his pocket, and locked the door.

"No, not beside you, besides me."

"Mabel means, did you open the door to Angie's room, the room of the dead woman, for anyone else?" Violet asked, intervening.

Ali smiled. "No, I only open the door for you, Miss Marple."

Out of the corner of her eye, she saw Violet grin at the mispronunciation of her name. "Hum, I see. Would you like to make some more tip money?" Mabel asked.

"I would like a tip, yes indeed, dear lady. What can I do for you? A nice elephant? I can make you a swan like I did for Mr. Roundie. You have seen the swan, and now you want one. Oh my, yes, I will do this for you."

"No, not an elephant or a swan. I would like to have another look in the dead woman's room."

Ali's eyes darted first to Violet, then Mabel, he took a step back. "You want to look at the dead woman."

"No, she is gone. I mean, the captain has had her body removed from the cabin. The cabin is empty."

Shaking his head violently, Ali pushed his cart down the hallway, "No, no, I cannot do this for you. This is not a good thing you ask me."

"Ali, you opened the door for me last night. Why not now? I will give you a very generous tip of five pounds."

Ali paused, looking tempted, then he said, "No, I am sorry, dear lady, I must not do this thing. It is not good. Even for money, I must not. I am sorry."

Mabel put her foot out to stop the cart. "Please, Ali, I will give you more money than last time, ten pounds."

Ali tilted his head, paused, then said sadly. "It is not right, I cannot."

Violet stepped up beside her friend. "We understand it is a lot to ask of you. And we don't want you to get into any trouble. The room is empty; it will be okay."

Ali looked uncertain.

"And of course, we will reward you for helping us. Fifteen pounds."

Ali smiled and held out his hand. "Please, to follow me, we must be quick before anyone comes." He scampered down the hallway.

"We've been had." Mabel grinned at Violet as they followed the little man down the hallway. "He pumped up his price. He's good."

Ali opened the door slowly, stepped back, and bowed. "I go back to my cleaning now. You will come to find me, and I will lock the door."

"Yes, of course, thank you, Ali." Mabel was relieved he wasn't going to stand and watch. It would have been hard to search the room with him there. She quickly closed the door. The bed was stripped. The closet door was ajar, and Angie's clothes were still hanging in the closet.

"I'll look for the missing inhaler in the closet. You look in the drawers," suggested Violet. "We need to be quick. Elizabeth or someone will be coming to pack her things."

"Anything?" asked Mabel as she closed the last drawer. They had been hunting in silence.

"A lot of exquisite, expensive clothes but no inhaler," Violet said, closing the closet door.

"I didn't find one either. I think Elizabeth lied."

"Why would she lie?"

"Murder?"

"But she was in the bar when Angie was killed."

"I know it's weird. And what would be the point of Elizabeth lying?"

"And don't forget, the door was locked. You tried the door and had to get Ali to open it. How did the killer get in here? Ali said he didn't let anyone in, but that man is easily bribed."

"Let's go find the little rat." Mabel picked up the key off of the dresser. "I'll use Angie's key to lock up. Then we confront him, no more Mrs. Nice. If Ali doesn't confess, we'll tell him we'll go to the police."

Mabel tried to lock the door. Violet and Mabel exchanged a puzzled look. The key didn't fit; the door didn't lock.

Chapter Twenty-Four

Mabel held up the brass key, turning it in her hand. "This isn't the right key. The cabin number on this key doesn't match this room. This has to be the key to the killer's cabin. The murderer has Angie's key. That's how they got into the room."

"Why didn't the killer come back and exchange keys?"

"Because if the killer came back to get their key, how would they lock Angie's door? They couldn't. And they couldn't leave the door unlocked. That would create suspicion."

Violet nodded.

Mabel smiled triumphantly. "This key is the murderer's key. It belongs to someone who hasn't been able to get back inside their cabin."

Violet returned her smile. "Carrie. The number on this key is eleven. That's the cabin Ali told us is Carrie's."

Mabel beamed. "This key is a huge clue. Because of the locked door, everyone thought Angie died of natural causes."

"Except you." Violet grinned at her friend. "The perfect crime, murder in a locked room. A brilliant plan, except now, Carrie can't get back into her cabin."

"That is if we're right. And there's only one way to find out."

Mabel and Violet hurried down the corridor to Carrie's cabin. Mabel looked both ways, then inserted the key and opened the door. The room was empty. "She's not here, which is no surprise. And there's Ali's towel creation on the bed. Carrie definitely didn't sleep here last night, but she left the bathroom light on."

Violet stepped to the dresser and opened the drawers. "There is nothing stashed in the drawers." She opened the closet door. "The closet is empty, no clothes," she said. "But since Carrie lost her luggage, there wouldn't be, and I don't see her carry-on."

"Carrie was pulling her little black bag when she came to the lounge. Where is her carry-on?"

"She must have taken it to wherever she is hiding."

"She can't have. She couldn't get back in her room without her key."

"Then she must have planned to hide before she killed Angie. That's why she left the room key."

"I guess." Mabel poked her head into the bathroom. "Violet, come here and tell me what you see," she said excitedly, backing out of the small bathroom to make way for Violet.

Violet entered the small room. "We need to ask Ali a few questions."

"I agree." Mabel opened the door to the hallway and looked down the corridor. "Wait here, I'll fetch him." She closed the door, then quickly opened it, and stepped back into the cabin. "Promise me you won't clean anything in this bathroom."

Violet held up her hands, palms outward. "Really, Mabel. I'm not compulsive."

"Sorry, I just wanted to be sure," Mabel said contritely.

Violet made an impatient motion with her hand. "Never mind, go get Ali."

Mabel complied, speeding down the hallway in search of the little room steward. She found him making another towel creation.

"You like?" he asked Mabel. The creation was a turtle.

"Very nice, Ali, very nice. I wonder if you can spare a few minutes."

"Your cabin, I have not cleaned your cabin. Do you want me to clean now?"

"No, but if you would come with me. There is something we wish to ask you."

"I cannot clean the dear dead lady's room. No one tells me to clean the dear dead lady's cabin."

"No, it's not Angie's cabin we want you to see. Please, come with me," Mabel requested. Ali hunched his shoulders and followed Mabel to Carrie's cabin. She opened the door.

Ali's eyes widened. "How do you have the key?"

"Never mind, it's okay to come in." Mabel beckoned.

Ali stepped cautiously into the room, his eyes darted about, looking nervously at the two women. "There is something wrong? I did nothing. I'm a good man, an honest man, a good steward."

"Yes, yes, of course, you are." Mabel thought the little steward was bribable but honest.

"Ali, when you saw the bed was not slept in, did you clean the room?"

"No, there was nothing to clean. Oh, oh, I see, the bathroom. I forgot the bathroom, please do not tell. I will clean the bathroom, I am sorry." He sprang for the door.

"No, don't do that." Mabel grabbed Ali's arm, preventing him from sprinting out the door. "We're fine with the room the way it is. In fact, we think you should leave the room exactly this way until Captain Burhan tells you otherwise."

Ali shuffled from foot to foot, his eyes darted from one woman to the other. "Captain Burhan, he is a very wise man. Oh my, yes, wise indeed."

"Oh yes, very wise, indeed." Mabel avoided looking at Violet. "So, you will not change anything in here until the wise captain tells you to. Do you promise?"

"Yes, oh, my yes." Ali nodded his head vigorously.

"Good. Now we have just a few questions, and you can get on with your room cleaning." Mabel was proud of how official she sounded, just like dear Constable Robert back home. "Ali, you said the lady, Carrie, who has this room, was very neat, yes?"

"Very neat lady, no trouble at all." Ali's head bobbed up and down.

"You found no liquor bottles, no dirty glasses?"

"No, she is a very neat and clean lady."

"No empty bottles?" Mabel asked again.

"No, I tell you, she is the neat lady."

Mabel nodded. "In the bathroom, did you have to change many towels? I mean, did you have to bring Carrie clean towels?"

"The small one, yes, I change the small one. I'm sorry, I did not change the small one this morning."

"No, that's fine."

Violet held up a dirty hand towel with makeup smeared on it. The sink had soap scum and one long red hair. On the vanity, there was a tube of lipstick and a liquid makeup bottle with the top off.

"You changed the small towels. But did you ever have to change the large towels?" she asked. "Did you ever have to make the bed?"

"The big towels are not dirty, not need to change if not dirty. Yesterday, I make the bed, and I make the funny swan with the big towels. The towels were not dirty, so I make my swan."

"Did you ever change the big towels?" Mabel asked again.

"I told you, I change the little towel. She is a neat lady, but she does not shower."

The bathroom was small, and Violet stood in the shower and asked, "Did you ever bring Carrie toilet tissue?" She pointed to the toilet tissue roll with the V-pointed end.

"No, just nose tissue; Miss Lush uses lots of nose tissues." He pointed to the wastebasket filled with used tissues covered in lipstick and makeup.

Mabel exchanged a self-satisfied look with Violet.

"I am sorry, but I cannot let you stay in this cabin, we must leave." Ali opened the cabin door and peeked out into the hallway. He scurried out. Mabel and Violet followed him out into the corridor. "I must go and make sure you locked the dear dead lady's door. I would not like the good and wise Captain Burhan to know I let you into the dear dead woman's cabin."

"Yes, by all means, lock the door, but please, Ali, wait one moment.

Ali paused, dancing from foot to foot, looking up and down the corridor.

Violet closed the door to the cabin, locked it, and slipped the key into her pocket. "What do we do now? Do you have a plan?"

"I think we do an Agatha Christie."

Violet's eyebrows rose. "An Agatha Christie?"

"We gather all the tour group in the lounge bar. Yes, I think the lounge is the perfect place. And I have a huge favour to ask of you, Violet." Then Mabel turned to the steward. "But first, Ali, you and I have another business deal. And if you do everything I tell you, I will pay you handsomely."

"I am handsome, you want to pay me because I am handsome. Dear lady, I am married, I have six children." Ali backed up with his hands in front of his body as if holding Mabel off.

"Oh, good Lord, not that," sputtered Mabel, her face heated.

Violet giggled.

Mabel crossed her arms and made a face at Violet. "Ali, not that. My goodness me. Handsomely in English means I will pay you well to do me a favour. This favour will help the wise Captain Burhan and will make him very famous. Maybe you, too."

"Oh, my yes, the dear captain. I would like to help the dear captain," Ali said, relieved. "And money too? You said handsomely money."

"Yes, handsome money. You go and lock Angie's door and keep doing your job. Violet will come and get you when the time is right. And she will tell you what to do."

Ali frowned and slowly nodded.

"I promise you it will be easy, this thing we will ask you to do. And I will give you money, I promise you."

Ali's eyes lit up; he bowed, then scampered away down the hallway.

Violet planted her hands on her hips. "And you will fill me in on this grand scheme?" she asked.

"Trust me, Violet, this is the best idea I've had yet."

Violet sighed and rolled her eyes.

Chapter Twenty-Five

At the top of the stairs, Violet grabbed the brim of her sunhat. A warm wind had sprung up; the sand was blowing off the dunes in the distance. Already, a fine layer of sand salted the sundeck. She waved to Neville, who was still playing cards with Ronnie, Jean, and Marie. Neville waved back. She hoped he didn't come over to talk. That would spoil the plan. She made her way over to the table where Captain Burhan and Tarek were drinking tea.

"May I join you?" Violet asked, brushing sand off the chair at their table. She sat down before they could answer, straightened her sun hat, rubbed together her palms, and smiled.

Tarek smiled politely back. "Tea? May we get you some tea?"

"No, thank you, not right now. But you both could be of great service in solving a big mystery aboard this boat." Violet smiled warmly at the captain.

"How may I be of assistance, dear lady?" Captain Burhan set his teacup to one side and stroked his mustache with his thumb and forefinger.

"It is my friend and I who can be of assistance to you."

"You said we could be of great service to you. I don't understand." Tarek frowned.

"I assure all will be explained, but first, I must tell you. I have good news."

"And what is this good news, dear lady?" The captain's bushy eyebrows rose up and down, and he smiled.

Violet thought the man had winked at her, and she could detect a condescending tone in his voice. She was glad it was not Mabel breaking this news. She pasted a smile on her face. "Mabel, my friend, and I have found out what happened to Miss Carrie Larush, your missing passenger."

"You have found Miss Larush. This is wonderful." Tarek pushed his teacup aside and leaned across the table. "You have no idea what I have been going through, a member of my tour group disappearing. And I am being held responsible. You have found our missing lady. I am forever grateful to you for finding her. Is she hurt?"

"She is not hurt, I assure you."

"Where has she been? The crew looked everywhere for her."

"So where is this lady?" the captain asked.

"I'm not at liberty to say, but all will be revealed if we do as she asks," Violet said.

"What she asks?" Captain Burhan huffed, his bushy eyebrows rose up and down. "What she asks? I am of the police. She must come here and present herself. Immediately."

"I'm afraid not, captain. There is the matter of her request."

"Her request? She has a request?"

"I will tell you what she wants, and if you do what she asks. You will solve the great mystery of the missing passenger and the death of Angie Morrison."

The captain's body stiffened, and his eyes hardened as he glared at her. "Miss Morrison's death?"

"I can tell you this much, Captain Burhan, when this mystery is resolved; I think you may well be given a promotion or a medal. Carrie's disappearance has to do with the mysterious death of Angie Morrison."

"There is no mysterious death. We have resolved Miss Morrison's unfortunate death," stormed the captain.

Violet shrugged. "You know it would be a shame if the police officers in Edfu found out something you missed." She paused, letting the accusation hang in the air.

The captain drummed his fingers on the table.

"It would look bad for you if they found out Angie Morrison was murdered. And you let the murderer slip through your fingers. But I'm sure you're right." Violet hoped she didn't overstate her request. Mabel was relying on her. If the captain got his back up, what would they do? They didn't have a Plan B.

"I have not missed anything."

"Are You sure?"

"I am positive. It is obvious the poor woman died from an attack of some kind," the captain sputtered angrily.

"Yes, an attack of some kind. My friend Mabel is a retired nurse. It was not an asthmatic attack that killed Angie Morrison. But if you're sure the police in Edfu won't find any evidence that she was murdered, well, that is, of course, up to you." Violet thought she saw a moment of indecision on the captain's face. She cleared her throat and continued. "I know you are a very important and busy man, but the disappearance of Carrie Larush and the death of Angie Morrison are linked."

The captain sat back in his chair, his arms folded across his chest.

"If you do as she requests, all will be revealed."

"What does this woman request?" Captain Burhan's eyes narrowed, and his caterpillar eyebrows rose.

"First, she requests you and our tour group meet in one-half-hour in the lounge."

"Tell me why this woman wants a meeting. Why does she not meet with my good friend Tarek and me? And why should this group of tourists be included? This is an outrageous request."

Tarek leaned across the table. "This does seem a little unorthodox, but I think we should cooperate with her. Please listen to this woman, Captain Burhan, as a favour to me. I am already in trouble with my superiors. First, the unfortunate death of one of my tour members, and then, Miss Larush disappears." He switched to Arabic.

Violet sat anxiously in her chair, waiting through the long and rapid exchange between the two men. Then, after a long silence, Tarek gave her a hopeful smile.

The captain looked thoughtful, stroking his mustache. "And if I agreed to this woman's foolish demands, then what?" he asked. "If it becomes a farce, I will look a fool." The captain stuck out his chin and re-crossed his arms.

"Oh, no, dear Captain Burhan, you would be an observer." Violet thought it wouldn't go amiss if she used

Ali's flowery language. The captain appeared to have a massive ego. "If the revelations I have promised do not pan out, then we will look the fool, not you." She trusted her friend. Mabel might be a little bull-headed, but her instincts were usually right. Violet swallowed nervously, wishing she hadn't thought of the word *usually*. They would be in big trouble if Mabel was wrong.

"Pan out?" Tarek asked.

"If there is no proof that Angie Morrison met with foul play. Captain Burhan would still have the same results as he has now. But if Angie was murdered and the murderer is revealed. Then Captain Burhan would, of course, take full credit. It's a win, win, for our dear captain, as they say back home."

"Who are they?" the captain demanded.

"It means you cannot lose. It will be my friend and me who will be in the wrong, not you."

The captain looked across at Violet, then at Tarek. "My dear friend, Tarek, is very worried about Miss Larush, and I wish to help my dear friend. So, I will hear you out. If the lady's request is not too outlandish, I will participate. But do not make me look foolish. I warn you."

"My dear captain, I promise you, you will be a hero." Violet took a deep breath. This was a huge gamble. "She would like our entire tour group to meet in the bar lounge. And everyone should bring their passport. You, as captain of the police, can request this."

Tarek regarded the captain. "It is not a lot to ask. If Miss Larush saw something suspicious the night of Miss

Morrison's death, perhaps we should hear her out. That has to be the reason she has been hiding."

They waited in silence while the captain pondered the request. Finally, the captain nodded. "I agree to issue the request for passports." He turned to Tarek and stroked his mustache. "Tell them I must examine their past ports before we dock in Edfu. Please do so now. The sooner we find out from this silly woman what she has seen, the better. I have already determined Miss Angie Morrison's death was natural. But for you, my good friend, I will agree to this foolishness."

"Thank you, Captain Burhan, thank you. Once Miss Larush is back, all will be well," Tarek said, looking very relieved.

Violet's eyes sparkled, and she smiled as she used one of Ali's phrases. "You are a very wise, captain. This will be to your advantage, I assure you." She so wanted to clap her hands in triumph. Mabel would be ecstatic; the captain was buying into their plan.

"One-half hour, gentlemen," Violet said, getting to her feet. She put her hand on the top of her sunhat. The wind was picking up, and sand was drifting across the deck. She nodded regally to the passengers on the deck chairs and walked sedately to the stairs. Then she tore down the steps to Mabel, who was waiting below.

Chapter Twenty-Six

Violet entered the lounge to find Tarek and Captain Burhan already seated on barstools, their backs to the bar. Some German and Japanese tour group members were also in the lounge, occupying chairs and couches with drinks in their hands. Violet bit her lip; how was her friend going to present her case to a room full of bystanders? She wanted to warn Mabel about the audience, but Mabel hadn't made her appearance. Violet was sure Mabel planned a grand entrance. Her excuse to Violet was she wanted to lull the murderer into a false sense of security.

The California sisters arrived next and handed their passports to the captain. He gave them a cursory look and placed them on the bar by his elbow.

"Will this take long?" Lucy asked. "We're missing the scenery."

"No, not long." Tarek looked hopefully at Violet.

"Please, help yourselves to a libation." Rabbie indicated a tray on the bar with long-stem glasses filled with ice-cold cherry punch. "Or perhaps some famous Egyptian beer. Compliments from the captain and crew of The Star."

"It doesn't matter, Lucy, the wind is picking up and blowing sand. This will be a nice break." Janet took two glasses of punch and handed one to her sister. They sat down on the leather couch.

Jean and Marie entered the lounge. They surrendered their passports, accepted a glass of punch, grimacing at the taste, and joined the girls on the couch.

Violet sat on a barstool beside Tarek. She squeezed her hands, gripping them tightly, her knuckles whitened. Would Mabel be able to pull this off? This was a big gamble. It all depended on her friend. She smiled at the three men as they entered the bar. Ronnie, Silvio, and Neville. The men gave Captain Burhan their passports and accepted a bottle of beer.

Neville smiled at Violet. "Would you like to sit with me?" he offered.

"No thanks, I'm fine for now." She self-consciously adjusted her sunhat and smiled back. Neville frowned and followed Ronnie and Silvio to the semicircular couch.

Elizabeth and Marvin entered, looking saddened and tired. "Passports really? At a time like this, I find this very callous." Elizabeth slapped her passport on the bar and snatched a glass of punch off the tray.

"Sorry, Captain, she's upset. Poor Angie's death has hit her hard, I'm sorry." Marvin gave a boyish smile and added his passport to the pile.

Violet watched as Mabel entered the lounge. Mabel was doing her best to look official. But her friend, a short, plump lady with white hair, didn't look all that official. She wore a bright blue top and yellow Capris with an orange scarf draped around her neck. Violet wished she had at least worn sandals. Instead, Mabel was wearing white socks and walking shoes, and one white sock had slipped down, giving Mabel a lopsided look.

Elizabeth smirked. "Send in the clowns." She held up her glass of punch in a toast.

Janet and Lucy grinned, Silvio laughed aloud, and Neville snickered. Ronnie frowned and shook his head. Tarek and the captain both had solemn looks on their faces; they folded their arms.

Mabel smiled and bowed.

Violet looked with admiration at her friend. She had to admit Mabel had a terrible fashion sense, and she was rather colourful, but there was nothing clown-like in her demeanour.

Mabel closed the lounge door and took centre stage. Flipping her long scarf over her shoulder, she began, "Fellow tour members."

The lounge door flew open, and three giggling Japanese girls entered. Pausing in the doorway, they looked around at everyone, giggled again, and went to the bar. Mabel waited while Rabbie took their orders and poured their drinks. Six more Japanese tourists burst through the door. Two more girls and four men skirted around Mabel, who was standing in the middle of the floor. Rabbie opened bottles of beer for the men and poured drinks for the women. There was cheerful chatter and laughter as they joined their friends. Mabel tapped her foot.

"I am sorry, Mrs. Havelock, but the sand is blowing across the sundeck quite strongly. These people have a right to come in here out of the wind," Tarek apologized.

"No problem, I'm fine with everyone being here." Mabel turned and bowed to the Japanese tourists, who, in turn, bowed back. She held her index finger to her lips; they looked at each other and became silent. She turned and made the same shushing motion to the Germans, who miraculously did the same.

Violet was proud of Mabel. Nothing flustered her.

As Mabel turned from quietening the groups, five more German women entered. They went straight to the bar. Each took a glass of punch and joined the group already seated. The women began chatting loudly to their seatmates.

Mabel marched over to the women, looked over her granny glasses, and shook her finger. "Hush, ladies, I am conducting a very important meeting."

"You think you own this lounge? We have rights to this lounge," a tall blond lady rebuked Mabel in slightly accented English.

A big man stood. Violet recognized him as the man in the yellow Speedo and was surprised to see him dressed conservatively in black slacks and a white shirt and tie. Speedo Man addressed the group, and after a longish speech in German, they quieted down, looking curiously at Mabel.

Speedo Man smiled at her. "Will this meeting of yours take long?" he asked.

Mabel looked back across the room at her fellow tour group members, who were becoming restless. "I shouldn't think so."

"*Danka Dir*, thank you," the man said and took a seat.

Mabel strode back to her group, her scarf flaring out behind her like an orange cape. She took a deep breath and began. "We are gathered here today."

Two Japanese girls pulled out their phones and directed the phones at Mabel. Violet wondered what the girls thought they were recording.

"To witness the wedding of this man and this woman." Silvio threw back his head and laughed.

Violet glared at Silvio.

"Perhaps Mabel is going to perform some magic tricks. She's dressed for the part." Elizabeth laughed. The rest of Tarek's tour group joined in. Except for Janet and Ronnie. And Jean and Marie, who looked puzzled.

"Don't be rude, poor Mabel wants to tell us something," Janet rebuked.

Lucy gave her sister a sidelong look, shrugged, but stopped snickering. Ronnie crossed his arms and glowered. Violet scowled at Neville, who stopped laughing and looked down at his hands.

"Ladies and gentlemen, please," Tarek intervened. "Mrs. Havelock has an announcement."

"The circus has come to the Nile," Silvio snickered.

"Don't you want to discover where and why Carrie has disappeared?" Violet asked, jumping off her stool and standing by her friend.

"And Mabel knows?" Marvin scoffed. "Really. My wife and I have only a few more hours to enjoy the beauties of Egypt. Then we have to take our dear cousin home." He set his glass down on the small table and rose to leave.

"Except she wasn't your cousin, was she?" Mabel challenged, striding over to Marvin. He sat back down.

Mabel clasped her hands behind her back and turned to face Elizabeth. "She was your rich niece, wasn't she Elizabeth? Your niece, who has been generously funding your travels."

Violet returned to her barstool and sighed. Mabel was trying to channel Hercule Poirot. But she wished her friend would just get on with it. This was a tough audience.

"I don't know how you know that. But yes, she was my niece, and what difference does that make?" Elizabeth rolled her eyes and chuckled. "Seriously, you should just sit down before you make a laughingstock of yourself. Oh, wait, it's too late. You already have."

Two more Japanese tourists had their phones out recording.

"Hey, that's harsh, do not disparage this little lady," Ronnie drawled.

The German tour group, one by one, left their seats and closed in behind Mabel, watching the procedure. Some took out their phones, pointing them at Mabel and Elizabeth. Violet suspected most of them understood English. If the audience bothered Mabel, she didn't show it.

Mabel continued, "You're right; the relationship between you and Angie is of minor importance. Except to point out that you are good at deceiving people, for instance, you said Angie was an asthmatic. She was not."

"She was, what a stupid thing to say."

"We only have your word for it, and if Captain Burhan has Angie's luggage and cabin searched, they will find no inhaler."

Elizabeth set her glass down and gave Mabel an icy look. "Even if they were so rude to search poor dead Angie's belongings and didn't find her inhaler, it would mean nothing. She used the inhaler up and discarded it."

Mabel turned to address the captain. "I am a retired nurse, and I can assure you, Captain Burhan, no one who has asthma travels with just one inhaler. And if Angie was so foolish to travel with only one. Where is it?"

The captain fingered his mustache. Violet wondered if he believed anything Mabel was saying.

"Elizabeth would have us believe Angie died because of an asthmatic attack. Yet, there was no inhaler in her cabin. That makes no sense. If Angie felt an asthmatic attack coming on, she would have grabbed her inhaler. And even if she used up the medication in her inhaler, we would have found it nearby or in the garbage can. We didn't. Angie was murdered," Mabel said as if addressing a jury. She had the tour group's attention. They looked at Elizabeth for a response.

"You cannot possibly think someone killed Angie," scoffed Elizabeth. "Let alone me. What possible motive would I have to kill poor Angie?"

"Money. One of the oldest motives in the books. I'd lay odds you inherit her money."

"You don't know that. That is a disgusting observation."

"It won't be that hard to find out." Mabel looked over at Captain Burhan. He looked back, puzzled.

"Even if what you say is true. And it might be. I might inherit some of her money. But I didn't kill Angie," Elizabeth huffed. "I was in the bar when Angie died. And it is ridiculous to suggest someone murdered Angie. The door was locked. You were there. You tried the door, and you know the door was locked."

The tour group's heads swivelled from Elizabeth back to Mabel.

"I'll get back to that." Mabel's lips curved into a smile. "But first, let us go to the mystery of Carrie Larush. Where has she gone? And why?"

"She killed Angie," Silvio said, sitting forward on the couch.

Violet saw that many more of the Germans and Japanese had their phones out, aiming them at Mabel and then at Marvin and Elizabeth.

"But how? Remember the locked door?" Mabel smiled knowingly.

"Right, the locked door." Janet sat on the edge of the couch, looking between Mabel and the Tuttles.

"If it was murder," Lucy said, looking doubtful.

Violet wanted to say get on with it. Mabel was enjoying this way too much. She sighed and waited for her signal.

"And who is, or was Carrie?" Mabel asked.

"Ah, yes, yes, the missing lady," the captain exclaimed. Violet thought the captain, at last, looked interested.

Mabel nodded regally to the captain and continued. "Carrie arrived as we came onboard this boat as did Neville. But Neville informed us he did not fly on the same plane as this strange woman. And Carrie did not take the same transport to the boat as he did. The first time you met Carrie was here on this boat, correct Neville?"

"Yes, that's true. The first time I saw that odd woman was in the lobby of this boat." He looked uncomfortable to be singled out.

"And Neville is right; Carrie was an odd woman. I think all of us here can agree to that." Mabel smiled at the tour group. Her jury.

Marvin snickered, and Elizabeth rolled her eyes. The rest of the tour group looked at each other and nodded, then looked back at Mabel in anticipation.

"Carrie never had a meal with us, nor did she take a tour with us. And she always appeared drunk, but she never frequented the bars, either here or on the sundeck. Did she Rabbie?"

Rabbie looked at the captain and Tarek as if looking for permission to speak. The captain nodded. "The lady does not come to my bar," admitted the bartender.

"And I asked the bartender on the sundeck, Fahim, if Carrie was a frequent drinker there. He told me, no, she wasn't," Violet confirmed.

"She's probably a closet drinker and has her own stash," Marvin snickered.

"You would think that wouldn't you? But no. The steward Ali told us he found no bottles of any kind and no dirty glasses in her cabin."

Violet watched as the tour groups swung their heads back between the Tuttles and Mabel as if they were watching a tennis match.

"Maybe she took drugs; she could have been high," Elizabeth asserted. By now, Mabel's audience was enthralled. They turned to see her reply.

"Violet and I inspected Carrie's room, and we didn't find her hand luggage. But we all saw she had one when she arrived. No luggage, but she did have a small black carry-on." Mabel looked at her fellow passengers. "But one black piece of carry-on looks much like the other. Don't you agree?" They did, with much nodding.

"When we arrived dockside, Tarek warned us about peddlers, but you, Elizabeth, paid him no mind. You dashed off and went directly to the street hawkers. And you were quickly surrounded."

"Yes, it was scary. I should have listened to you, Tarek. I'm sorry." Tarek nodded briefly.

"Very foolish. Marie and I travel the world, and we would not do this," Jean voiced.

Mabel nodded to Jean, then clasped her hands behind her back and spun around, confronting Marvin. "You stayed on the bus and sent Angie out to save your wife from the peddlers. I remember you telling Angie to help your wife and that you would bring all the hand luggage."

"Yes, I did. It was probably unwise to send Angie," admitted Marvin

"No kidding, sending a girl to do a man's job," rebuked Neville.

"Seriously? A man's job? What century do you come from?" Mabel confronted Neville.

"Pardon me." Neville sat back on the couch, scowling at Mabel.

"Mabel," Violet cautioned. This was no time for her prejudice toward Neville to surface. Mabel needed to get back on track.

Mabel glanced at Violet, then pasted a smile on her face. "You do have a point, Neville."

"But no harm was done," continued Marvin. "Angie and Elizabeth were unharmed."

"No thanks to you," commented Lucy. "Tarek and the bus driver had to come to their rescue."

"My dear friends. The street vendors meant no harm to anyone," voiced Tarek.

Violet shifted on her barstool; this was getting them nowhere. "Tarek is right; the vendors were just trying to sell their wares," she said. "But I think Mabel has another point to make. Don't you, dear?"

"Thank you, Violet. I do." Mabel turned to Marvin. "You told Angie to help your wife and you would bring all the hand luggage. But you didn't bring all the hand luggage, did you? You left Angie's on the bus."

"An oversight, I was in a rush. There were the goings-on outside the bus with the peddlers. No offence, Tarek." Marvin gave Tarek a boyish smile. "But we're not used to that kind of aggressiveness back home. I was just in a hurry to leave the bus." Marvin took a long drink from his glass of punch. He raised his glass to Mabel. "You're prattling on about nothing."

"Rush or not, you left Angie's bag on the bus." Mabel turned to Elizabeth. "Then, after we had passed through two of those decrepit old boats. You reminded Angie that she didn't have her carry-on, didn't you, Elizabeth?"

"What if I did? She had her meds and jewelry packed in that bag. It was all Marvin's fault, as you just pointed out. This is getting us nowhere. Captain Burhan, may we leave this foolish inquisition?"

"Yes, Mrs. Tuttle is right. This foolish rambling is getting us nowhere. Mrs. Havelock, where is Miss Larush? You promised Miss Larush," the captain said sternly, his bushy eyebrows rising up and down.

"Dear captain, if you would please just bear with Mabel for a few more minutes," Violet flashed the captain a hopeful smile.

The captain smiled back at Violet and stroked his mustache. "I would like to, dear lady, but my time is valuable." He turned to Mabel. "I cannot sit here all afternoon. I demand to see Miss Larush now."

Mabel peered over her glasses at the captain. "All in good time." The captain's eyebrows shot up.

"What Mabel means is she's about to reveal all," Violet interjected. She shook her head at Mabel, giving her a disapproving look. Getting the captain's backup would not help. The meeting in the lounge was first to convince the captain there was a murder and second to expose the killer.

Mabel made a silent 'oh' sign with her mouth and smiled at Captain Burhan. "Yes, dear captain, I will soon reveal all." She twirled on one foot, her scarf flared out as she turned back to Elizabeth. "You carefully set a precedent of mistrust with the bus driver at the Cairo airport. And it didn't surprise any of us when you sent Marvin back for Angie's carry-on because we had also gotten used to you ordering your husband around like a servant."

"I resent that. I do not treat Marvin like a servant. Do I?" She turned to her husband.

"No, dear, you don't. I love doing things for Elizabeth. She is the light of my life." Marvin put his arm around his wife's shoulders.

Elizabeth smiled back at him.

Mabel rolled her eyes and motioned to Violet. Violet got up and left the lounge.

"WHATEVER, AS THE YOUNG ones say." Mabel paced back and forth in front of the couple. "Marvin did go back to the bus for Angie's bag."

"So that settles that little detail," Marvin scorned. "Come on, Elizabeth, we've listened enough to this dippy old broad." He stood, holding out his hand to his wife.

Ronnie put out a big hand and grabbed Marvin's arm. "We will hear the little lady out," he said.

Marvin shrugged and sat back on the couch, looking scornfully at Mabel.

Mabel, grateful for Ronnie's intervention, smiled at him and took a step back. She nearly tripped on a young Japanese girl who was on her knees beside her. The girl's phone was pointed directly at Mabel. She noted that most of the Japanese and German tour groups had their phones out, their phones trained on her, Marvin, and Elizabeth. She straightened her shoulders and her scarf. What the other tourist was doing was not going to distract her. She was on a mission. "As I said, Marvin retrieved Angie's bag, but remember the backpack? Marvin had a backpack on his back. And remember the boats rafted together? This is what happened. After taking Angie's bag off the bus, Marvin ducked behind some furniture, a desk, or even into a corridor on one of the old boats. This is where the transformation took place."

"Ridiculous, what transformation? What are you talking about? You are a stupid old woman making up ludicrous accusations. Accusations that make no sense," Marvin mocked.

Mabel turned and with a sweeping hand motion, said, "Oh, it makes perfect sense. In one of those old boats, a transformation took place. The transformation from mild-mannered Marvin the henpecked husband. Into Carrie Larush." There were snickers and scoffs from her audience.

The captain snorted, and Tarek looked bemused.

Undaunted, Mabel continued, "In your backpack, Marvin, you had a long red kaftan and an even redder wig and huge glasses that magnified your eyes. And ta-da, you became Carrie Larush," Mabel said triumphantly. More murmurs of disbelief came from Mabel's audience.

"You're truly nuts," Marvin mocked. "Me, dressed up as a woman? You are getting more ridiculous by the moment. I think we should all leave." He stood.

"I have decided I will hear what Mrs. Havelock has to say. My friend Tarek and I are concerned with the health of Miss Larush. This woman has promised me Miss Larush. Please sit down," the captain instructed.

"Thank you, Captain Burhan."

Marvin reluctantly sat back on the couch, looking scornfully at Mabel.

"It is kind of entertaining, old man," Neville agreed. Lucy and Janet exchanged a grin.

Jean and Marie set their drinks down untouched, folded their hands, and looked curiously at Marvin.

The door to the lounge swung open, and Violet entered with Ali in tow. Ali hunched his shoulders as if trying to make himself smaller. The little room steward was carrying a cloth bag. He peered nervously at everyone, slinking alongside Violet. Violet ushered him to a barstool farthest from the captain and stood by his side.

Mabel carried on with her summation. "At first, I did wonder how you would know there would be a handy place to change into Carrie. But Ronnie supplied the answer. You've been on a Nile cruise before, haven't you, Marvin? You knew the old riverboats were rafted together. The perfect place to get into your disguise. You were careless when you told Ronnie all about the temples at Edfu. But we haven't been to Edfu. That is our next port of call, and yet, you described it in glowing terms to Ronnie. How would you know about the temples? Could it be because you visited these temples on a previous visit? I think you did."

"I Googled it." Marvin laughed. "You have heard of Google, haven't you?"

"I'm well aware of Google," Mabel said the word Google carefully.

"Anyone who takes you seriously needs their head read," Marvin scorned.

Mabel saw Violet put her hand on Ali's shoulder and give the little man a reassuring smile. A smile that was not reflected in her eyes. Violet was not confident the gamble would pay off.

"Captain, would you look at Mr. Tuttle's passport, please," Mabel requested.

Mabel waited while the captain sorted through the passports. She held her breath as he opened Marvin's passport and flipped through the pages.

Chapter Twenty-Seven

Marvin didn't wait for the captain's pronouncement. "Okay, I've been to Egypt before, big deal. That doesn't mean a thing."

"Then why lie about it? It's because you knew about the rafting. You knew that you could change into being the drunk woman called Carrie."

"And what has dressing up as a woman got to do with Angie's murder? If I dressed as a woman," he snorted and continued, "my wife and Angie would know right away."

"Elizabeth did know. When we came aboard, she signed in for you both. Then she took Angie up to the cabins before you made your grand entrance as Carrie. With your wife's help, you were careful to stay clear of Angie. And it was Angie's hand luggage you brought aboard."

She turned and smiled at the captain. "The Police will find your backpack when they search the old boats at Luxor."

The captain nodded uncertainly.

"So, I like to cross-dress, no biggie. Elizabeth doesn't mind, do you, dear?"

Elizabeth smiled at her husband. "It's Marvin's little vice."

"How many times are you going to change your story, Marvin? First, you deny you dressed up as Carrie. Now you say you're a cross-dresser," Mabel scoffed.

"We had to keep it a secret. Angie wouldn't approve, so we had to be careful not to let her know. Now that Carrie's mystery is solved, may we leave?" Elizabeth directed her question to Captain Burhan. "You may not approve of my husband dressing in women's clothing, but his fetish for women's clothes has nothing to do with the death of Angie."

"Oh, but it does," Mabel answered before the captain could reply. "It was all a ruse. Smoke and mirrors like magicians. The fake arguments and the poor little henpecked husband diverted everyone's attention to what was really going on. Like the disguise and the false story about Angie's asthma, oh yes, and the spilled soup at supper on Marvin's shirt." She addressed her remarks to her jury, then turned back to face Marvin. "This last bit was so you could go back to the cabin and change into the Carrie costume."

Mabel strode to the captain's side and gestured with a flourish to Marvin. "This man, dressed as Carrie, pretended to be a drunk. He spilled two drinks on Angie so she would go back to her cabin to change. Masquerading as Carrie, Marvin went off in a huff. He followed Angie and murdered her in cold blood."

There was an intake of breath from the tour groups.

"That is an unadulterated lie; how dare you accuse me of murder," stormed Marvin. He looked menacingly at Mabel, his boyish façade gone, then it quickly returned, and he heaved a sigh. "I'm insulted. Just because I choose to cross-dress, you accuse me of murder."

Rabbie uttered something in Arabic, eyeing Marvin from across the room. The Japanese tour group gathered closer, as did the Germans. Almost all the tourists were now videoing the proceedings on their phones.

"You are getting more ludicrous by the moment. What about the locked door? You do remember that, don't you? The key was inside. You saw it yourself," Elizabeth scoffed.

"I'll get to that." Mabel smiled, walking back to stand before the accused couple. "I have to admit you were very clever, Elizabeth. You stood in the lounge doorway to discourage anyone else from following Angie. You waited in the doorway until you were sure your husband was safely inside Angie's cabin, suffocating her."

Marvin rolled his eyes. "These are simply wild speculations made by a lunatic woman." He had a confident smile on his face.

Elizabeth curled her lip. "Ridiculous," she sneered.

Lucy and Janet shifted away from Marvin. Marie and Jean made room for the girls. Ronnie and Neville looked suspiciously at the Tuttles. Silvio sat warily, watching Mabel and the Tuttles.

The captain stroked his mustache, looking from Mabel to Marvin, then at Elizabeth.

"Seriously, Captain, you need to put a stop to these outrageous slurs on our good name," Marvin pleaded. He threw his hands into the air. "I did not murder Angie."

"We merrily danced while Angie struggled to breathe," Mabel continued as if Marvin hadn't spoken.

"Captain, how long must we endure this slander? I demand you stop this woman sullying our good name." Elizabeth rose.

"Please sit down, Mrs. Tuttle. I will hear this woman out. I, and I alone, will determine if these accusations are falsehoods."

Elizabeth sunk back on the couch. "You will hear from our ambassador, and you will regret this unjust treatment."

Marvin patted her hand; he looked confidently at Mabel, and his smile turned into a smirk. The captain frowned and shifted uneasily on his barstool.

Before the captain could reply, Mabel barged ahead and said, "Yes, we danced, drank, and laughed while Marvin, dressed as Carrie, killed Angie."

"I repeat, I did not kill Angie someone please put a stop to this woman's ranting." Marvin folded his arms across his chest and shook his head.

Mabel arched one eyebrow and continued, "But you needed time to change back into the mild-mannered husband. That was where your wife came in. She gave you the excuse for your absence by standing in the doorway, hollering down the hallway, and demanding you to go and fetch her scarf from the dining room. But of course, you weren't there, you were back in your cabin, changing into your own clothes."

"Good God, what is the matter with you people? Someone stop this woman and her wild accusations," demanded Elizabeth.

Mabel held up her hand. "Still talking. You gave your husband an alibi just in case someone suspected murder.

We continued to dance; someone ordered drinks, and time passed. Then Marvin came into the lounge waving your scarf. I'm not sure if that was so we would all think he'd fetched your scarf or a signal to you that the job was done. Or both."

Marvin addressed the tour group. "I'm fed up with this. Can't you see she is performing to get attention? This old lady is hoodwinking you all. You can't seriously believe her deranged allegations."

"We are not taking this anymore. This is beyond ridiculous. Captain, we are leaving, we're not sitting here listening to this slander." Elizabeth turned to the tour group. "We should all leave; he has no authority to keep us here. Come on, everyone." She stood.

"I do have the authority, Madam. I request you to sit down." The captain rose from the barstool, his arms folded across his chest. Rabbie joined him, folding his arms as well.

Elizabeth sat, glaring alternately at the captain and Mabel.

The captain puffed out his chest and retook his seat. Rabbie returned to the bar, leaning his elbows on the counter and watching the Tuttles closely.

Marvin squeezed his wife's hand. "Relax, dear, it's okay. The captain will have to let us go soon."

"I'd like to hear what Mabel's got to say," Ronnie drawled. "If it's all malarkey, then you've got nothing to fear."

"We don't fear anything, but we resent this pumped-up harridan spouting all this rubbish," Elizabeth huffed.

"I think you should be afraid, Elizabeth. Because now I'm going to tell the captain here just how you did it."

"How I did what? Murder Angie while I was in the lounge having a drink with you? First, you accuse Marvin, and now me, make up your mind," Elizabeth sneered.

Mabel smiled. "Wouldn't you like to know what gave you away?" She didn't wait for an answer. "You gave it away, Elizabeth. I should have suspected something fishy when you gave Marvin Angie's drink. A drink that was poured for her. Because you knew, Angie would never be coming back for it. She was dead."

"But Mrs. Havelock, the locked cabin door," Tarek said; he was sitting on the edge of the barstool.

"Yes, thank you, Tarek. The locked door. How could anyone, let alone Marvin, kill poor Angie in a room with a locked door?" Elizabeth scoffed.

Marvin smirked.

Elizabeth curled her lip as she glared defiantly at Mabel. "And you were with me when I tried to open the door. You tried the door; you know it was locked. Admit it."

"Yes, you made sure you had a witness to that locked room. That's why you let me come with you. That was easy to figure out. But the sleight of hand, that took me longer to solve the puzzle." Mabel turned to the captain to plead her case. "When Elizabeth asked for their cabin key, Marvin gave her Angie's key or, rather, what he thought was Angie's key."

"Keys? How did this key business work?" Captain Burhan asked.

"Try to keep up. Marvin followed Angie to her cabin; he pushed his way in."

Captain Burhan folded his arms across his chest and scowled at Mabel.

"Mabel means it's hard to keep up," intervened Violet; she tightened her lips and shook her head.

"Yes, yes, that's what I meant." Mabel recognized she had stepped over the mark again. She smiled at the captain and continued, "Marvin followed Angie to her cabin and pushed his way in. Then he smothered her with a plastic bag. He took her key, shut off the light, locked the door, and came back here. Oh, and by the way, Marvin, shutting off the light was a big mistake."

"She is making stuff up," snorted Marvin.

"No one took Angie's key, least of all Marvin. Her key was on the bureau. You saw it," Elizabeth said, smirking at Mabel.

"You gave yourself away again, Elizabeth, but my little grey matter had to work at it." Violet rolled her eyes.

"Grey matter?" the captain asked.

Violet leaned in and whispered, "My friend Mabel is trying to channel Hercule Poirot and his little grey cells."

"Grey cells, grey matter, and channels?" He sat on his barstool, stroking his mustache.

"Captain," interrupted Mabel. "You can ask the purser, Ahmed. He will confirm what I say. When Ahmed and Elizabeth entered the cabin, Elizabeth promptly fainted. She fainted before I had a chance to tell them Angie was dead. She jumped the gun."

Captain Burhan shot out of his chair. "A gun? What gun?"

Mabel held up her hand. "It's an expression. There was no gun. I mean, Elizabeth fainted before she even knew anything was amiss, anything was wrong."

The captain settled back on the barstool. Mabel wasn't sure he knew what she meant. But it looked like he was prepared to listen to her explanation about the key.

She turned to her tour group. "Why, you ask, would Elizabeth do that?" Mabel looked at her jury, and with a satisfied smile on her face, she said, "Well, dear Captain Burhan and friends, I will tell you. During her fainting act, she put her hand on the bureau, depositing the key."

There was an impatient sigh from Violet and a collective shrugging of shoulders and puzzled looks from Mabel's audience.

"Nonsense," Elizabeth exclaimed, her eyes darted to her husband.

He gave a small shake of his head and grinned confidently back at Mabel.

Mabel ignored her outburst and continued, "I should have noticed that then. But as I said, it took me a while to figure out that sleight of hand with the key."

"We will sue you for these inflammatory accusations," shouted Elizabeth. "Captain, you can't take this ridiculous woman seriously. She is spinning falsehoods, darn right lies."

Mabel strode over to the captain. "No, not lies, dear captain. Elizabeth deposited a key on Angie's dresser. She thought it was Angie's key. But it wasn't. It was the key to Carrie's cabin. Marvin had three keys in his pocket."

"Three keys?" the captain asked.

"Yes, the Tuttle cabin key, the key he took from Angie's cabin after he killed her so that he could lock the door behind him. And he had Carrie's key." Mabel stared at Marvin. "Easy to mix them up."

"Ridiculous," Marvin snarled, beads of sweat forming on his forehead.

"Violet and I tried the key left on the dresser in the door of Angie's cabin. The key didn't fit Angie's door, but it did fit Carrie's door. That's when everything fell into place. And as I told you, when we searched Carrie's cabin, we didn't find Carrie's little black carry-on in the room. But we all saw she was pulling a bag when she came into the lounge, did we not?" Mabel tilted her head, waiting.

"Yes, she dumped it right in the middle of the doorway," Lucy agreed.

"I almost fell over the darn thing," Neville piped up.

"Exactly. How could Carrie get back in her/his room without a room key to remove the bag? That's when we became suspicious and asked Ali about the state of the room."

Ali peered sideways at the captain and then down at the bag he held on his lap. Violet patted the little man on his shoulder.

"The only room in that cabin that got used was the bathroom. And the only towel used was a hand towel, the one you used to wash the makeup off your face. And you never used the toilet. The toilet paper still had the little 'V' Ali folds on it. But the wastebasket was full of tissues with makeup. And in the sink, there was long red hair that could only have come from a wig. And I remembered seeing you walk out of the Carrie room. And I asked myself, why was that? The only reason I could come up with was that you were Carrie. And you used the cabin to change into the Carrie disguise."

"Yes, yes, we know Marvin dressed up as Carrie. It doesn't mean he killed anyone. You and your meaningless deductions, you make me sick," Elizabeth stormed. "They make no sense."

"Oh, but it does. It makes perfect sense. Marvin is Carrie, and Carrie killed Angie. Marvin smothered Angie with a plastic bag. The bloodshot eyes, no inhaler, and scraps of plastic under her nails, all the evidence was there to see." Mabel turned to the captain, hoping he wasn't taking offence. He certainly hadn't seen anything. "Your people will find the pieces of plastic under her nails. I have no doubt."

"A plastic bag," Marvin sneered disdainfully. "And just where is your evidence? Where is your evidence indicating that I or anyone else smothered Angie?"

"The evidence is sitting right over there." Mabel walked over to Ali. Ali peeked over at the captain and held up a cloth tote bag. He passed the bag to Mabel and ducked his head, clasping his hands in his lap.

Mabel strode back to center stage with the bag. "You had to get rid of the evidence. You couldn't keep the wig, kaftan, and the murder weapon the plastic bag in your room. Ali might find it when he cleaned your cabin. And you couldn't get back into the Carrie room. You didn't have the key. So, Carrie had to disappear. It was the perfect solution. If the police discovered Angie was murdered, they would blame the murder on the loudmouth drunk who disappeared. The disappearing Carrie would be the ideal suspect. And as you said on the plane, and I quote, '*Egypt is the perfect place to kill her. The Egyptian police are not as smart as we are, our plan is perfect.*' You should have been more careful about what you said and where you said it." Mabel gave Marvin a superior smile.

Marvin and Elizabeth looked disconcerted as they glanced over at Captain Burhan.

Captain Burhan stood, his eyes narrowed. "Please continue, Mrs. Havelock."

Marvin, regaining his composure, scoffed, "Evidence? What evidence? You are bluffing. You have nothing."

"You had to get rid of your costume and the plastic bag. The wig and gown would have your DNA on it, and the plastic bag would have Angie's DNA. So, you waited until we were all in our beds. And you crept up in the dark to the sundeck."

Elizabeth looked with suspicion at the bag Mabel was holding. Marvin patted her hand and shook his head confidently.

"You wrapped your wig and costume in the plastic bag and tossed it overboard into the Nile. But what you didn't know, was that Ali was up on the deck smoking a cigarette." Mabel smiled at Ali, who offered up a weak smile in return.

"Ali is a curious chap. He took the pool skimmer they used to clean the pool and fished out the bag you threw overboard." Mabel opened the cloth bag and reached inside. She held up a clear plastic bag, and crammed inside was a red garment sticking out of the top a hank of long red hair.

"You, stupid moron," Elizabeth screamed. "You told me you got rid of that."

Marvin leapt to his feet and grabbed Mabel, spinning her around and ripping the plastic bag with the dress and hair out of her hands. "Run, toss it in the Nile; that's all the evidence they have." He threw the bag to Elizabeth, who caught it and ran toward the door. Violet jumped to her feet and dashed across the room after her.

Marvin twisted Mabel's orange scarf around her neck, choking her. Mabel stomped her foot down hard on Marvin's sandaled foot. He slumped forward, cursing. She threw her head back, smashing it into Marvin's nose. Blood gushed out, he loosened his grip on the scarf, and Mabel wrenched out of his grasp.

A Japanese girl stuck out her foot and tripped Elizabeth. Violet caught up and tackled Elizabeth, throwing the woman to the floor. Both women gave out a loud grunt as they hit the deck. Violet ripped the bag out of Elizabeth's hand and sat on her. The Japanese and the Germans applauded.

Lucy, Janet, and the Drapeaus watched in astonishment. Rabbie leaped over the bar, and Ronnie jumped to his feet. But Speedo Man was there first. The German man seized Marvin and slammed him to the floor. Marvin's nose now was bleeding profusely. Seconds behind Rabbie, Neville was at Violet's side, helping her to her feet. She held the bag tightly in her hand. Her sun hat had fallen off, leaving her head bare. Tarek also sprang into action, grabbing Elizabeth by the arm. He hauled her up and marched her back into the room.

Mabel's heart was going a million miles an hour. She took a deep breath and strode over to Elizabeth. "Remember all those accidents you had, Elizabeth? Remember almost falling through that hole? And being pushed off the pyramid? Marvin was hedging his bets, if you died, he'd go after Angie. I bet he is your beneficiary." Mabel watched Elizabeth's face go white with anger.

"He did it; he killed Angie. I had no choice. He made me help him. I'm a victim, too," Elizabeth screamed.

Mabel had no doubt that Elizabeth was as guilty as Marvin. But the prosecution would be easier if they turned on each other.

"Marvin Tuttle and Elizabeth Tuttle, I arrest you for the murder of Angie Morrison," Captain Burhan announced. "Rabbie, go and fetch men. We will lock these despicable murderers up until we dock." He leered down into Marvin's face. "Stupid Egyptian Police? Now you will find out what our stupid Egyptian jails are like." He turned to Violet. "May I have the evidence, please?" He held out his hand.

Mabel rubbed the back of her head; her hand came away with blood on it. She grimaced and wiped her hand on her pants. "The evidence is their confession, which everyone heard. And has been recorded by all these phones, and I think everyone here will sign a statement to what they heard."

"Yes, we will take affidavits from everyone." He turned to the Japanese and the German tour groups. "Dear people, we will need your phones."

There was a gasp from the Germans and the Japanese. Mabel suspected the Japanese were as well versed in English as the Germans.

"But only for a short time; we will download your videos and return them in short order."

The Germans and the Japanese reluctantly agreed.

The captain made a slight bow to the tour groups. Then he held out his hand. "Please, dear lady, I would like the evidence you have in the bag, please."

Violet patted her hair and grinned. She handed the plastic bag to Mabel.

Mabel reached into the plastic bag and pulled out a skirt and hunks of long red hair. "This is my reversible skirt." She held it up. "Black on one side and red on the other. And this is dear Violet's hair; she sacrificed it to capture our murderers."

Violet shook her head. "This is probably the worst haircut ever. Mabel is not skilled with scissors. It was Mabel's gamble, and it paid off."

"You mean there is no dress or wig," Captain Burhan gasped, astounded.

Ali grinned, jumped off his stool, and gave a little bow. "Handsome money now, please."

The End

Epilogue

Mabel smiled as she looked across the departure lounge in the Cairo airport. Violet, with her short-bobbed hair, was saying goodbye to Neville. What a trooper her friend was, allowing her to butcher her hair. They had already said goodbye to the rest of their travelling companions, with promises to email.

Neville parted, giving Violet a peck on the cheek and hurried on his way to catch his plane.

Mabel relaxed. "Thank goodness nothing came of that relationship," she muttered. She stretched out her legs, dreading the long flight back to Canada.

Violet waltzed back to Mabel and gave her a small bag. "I brought you a present."

Mabel opened the bag and held up a sleeping mask and a set of little orange earplugs. "Oh. You shouldn't have." She smiled at her friend.

"Oh yes, Mabel, I should."

Mabel grinned.

"Oh, and by the way, Neville is coming to visit me this fall. We have it all arranged." Mabel stared open-mouthed at her friend. Was this a wise idea?

Also by Joan Havelange from Brown Wolf Publishing
Wayward Shot
Death and Denial
Coming Soon
The Trouble with Funerals
The Suspects
Murder Exit Stage Right
Moving is Murder
The Séance Murders

Don't miss out!

Visit the website below and you can sign up to receive emails whenever Joan Havelange publishes a new book. There's no charge and no obligation.

https://books2read.com/r/B-A-CCKUC-VJFMF

BOOKS 2 READ

Connecting independent readers to independent writers.

Did you love *Death and Denial*? Then you should read *Wayward Shot*[1] by Joan Havelange!

When Mabel slices her golf ball into the town cemetery, she and her best friend Violet, think the worst that could happen would be a lost ball. Until they discover a dead body, and it isn't six feet under.

Mabel's ball lies in the middle of his forehead. It can't be murder, can it? The ladies take it upon themselves to solve the mystery of the dead body in the graveyard.

Using the information gleaned from Coffee Row, a collection of eccentric townspeople leads them to investigate

1. https://books2read.com/u/3JqeqK

2. https://books2read.com/u/3JqeqK

golfers and relatives of the deceased. Their investigation frustrates a newly appointed RCMP officer, who does his best to put a stop to their interference. But nothing stops the intrepid detectives. Not the RCMP, a stampede of cattle or even shots fired at them in the dark. They have an uncanny ability to find trouble and dead bodies.

About the Author

Besides being an author, Joan Havelange is an accomplished actor, and director of community theatre, which lends well to her writing. She is a world traveller and an enthusiastic golfer.

She lives in a beautiful little town in the middle of the Canadian prairies. A ski hill, lakes, and rivers are just a short drive away. Joan has been writing fiction since her early twenties, beginning with romance stories. She found that she would rather kill them than kiss them and turned to mysteries and never looked back. She is the author of five whodunit mysteries, one thriller, and her latest, a historical mystery.